Augie's Wine

JOHN H. BROWN

ISBN: 979-8-9911708-4-0

Published by John H Brown
wordsbyjohnbrown.com

Printed in the United States of America
Suggested Retail Price(SRP) $18.95

Cover design by Dick Allowatt

Praise for *Augie's Wine*

"*Augie's War* may be over but his battles have just begun. John H. Brown turns up the heat in this excellent series that sees our hero back from Vietnam into a hornet's nest of intrigue and criminality... that carries us from the soft brown earth of California wine country to the hard black coalfields of West Virginia. Highly recommended."

– Homer Hickam, author of *Rocket Boys/October Sky*

Praise for *Augie's World*

"John Brown ...draws on his culinary expertise and life experience to shape an engaging, complex lead character. ...the plot is wild and involved, but clear and focused."

– *The Pittsburgh Post-Gazette*

"Vietnam veteran's return to the United States sees him facing anti-war protesters and menacing mobsters in this novel. A profound tale of perseverance and family."

– *Kirkus Reviews*

"John Brown's writing is clever, vivacious and gripping. He imparts humorous vignettes, pulse-racing life and death scenes, family dinners and some tasty recipes at the end of the book. Get ready for a riveting story."

– Robert Fanelli Bartus Jr

Praise for *Augie's War*

"One of the most powerful novels I've yet read on the Vietnam War. As a veteran of that awful conflict, I was absolutely riveted by the tale of Augie and his buddies and every word rang true."

– Homer Hickam, author of *Rocket Boys/October Sky.*

"Like Joseph Heller in *Catch 22*, John Brown has given readers a novel that makes clear the insanity of war in all its grim and gritty horror. Brown's novel includes a lineup of zany characters and a sequence of outlandish happenings sure to have readers chuckling, if not laughing out loud."

– James E. Casto, *Charleston Gazette-Mail*

"John H. Brown's storytelling will engage you from beginning to end with amusing, gritty and candid dialogue. Brown's vivid writing allows you to witness gripping scenes you won't forget, and it also conveys how family, friends, and those who have your back can sustain a person through desperate times."

– *Ambassador Magazine*

ACKNOWLEDGEMENTS

My literary journey with Augie Cumpton has reached its final destination with the completion of Augie's Wine. I never anticipated I would create a trilogy when I wrote the first line in what has turned out to be a three-volume series, but I just couldn't seem to create a satisfactory ending for my protagonist until now. And I also wanted wine to play an important role in the novel. After all, I've spent most of my adult life thinking and writing about wine, as well as making it and drinking it daily in my home. I suppose I wanted Augie to have the affection for wine that I have, and to understand how that magic elixir might also influence events, as well as strengthen and cement his personal relationships in the book.

Wine, of course, has always been a part of my life growing up in an Italian American family. There was always a jug of homemade wine on the table at my Grandparents' home. That's where I spent the first six years of my life being cared for during the day by Grandma Iaquinta. Each day she would place a small jelly jar-like glass of watered-down wine on the table right next to my lunch which usually consisted of dishes like chicken soup with pastina, a meatball sandwich or a delicious pepperoni roll made right across the street at Grandpa's bakery. I really didn't like the wine, or even drink it, but that was okay with Grandma. She must have known in her heart of hearts that those daily exposures to wine back then would someday become a major influence in my life.

Once again, I could not have written this novel without the help of my friends and relatives who have provided me with valuable input and editing. I am also especially grateful to Dick Allowatt who has been the cover artist for all three books. I think this front cover is the most dramatic one of them all! You can check out Dick's artwork at www.

allowatt.com. For those of you who have been with me on this literary journey, I hope you approve of the manner in which I have concluded this novel and I hope you're surprised by the ending.

Of course, I am most appreciative to my ever tolerant and long-suffering wife who has patiently reviewed and edited all the words in all of my books for the past eight years.
Grazie Mille, Debbie!

CONTENTS

"In Vino Veritas"
(In Wine there is truth)
Pliny the Elder (AD 23 – 79)

"Make Wine, Not War"
Anonymous

CHAPTER 1
WASHINGTON, D.C.
SPRING 1971

I sat on a metal folding chair in the basement room directly below the main floor of Franken's Spirits, a wine and liquor store in Georgetown. The constant din of shoes shuffling on the ancient wooden floors above me sounded, annoyingly, like customers were dancing to an endless waltz. I stared at the black and white checkerboard-like linoleum floor tiles and tried to concentrate on the words of Jermain Harris who was recounting to our group of Vietnam veterans his recurring nightmare of a search and destroy mission gone terribly wrong.

"I mean, this mama-san was squattin' there in the dirt. You know, jus' sittin'on her heels. An' she's lookin' at the ground. Not payin' no attention to the Chu-Hoi dude who was askin' her about where all the men in the ville was at. She ain't talkin'. Jus' starin' at the dirt."

I remembered seeing Chu-Hoi soldiers at my basecamp in Vietnam. They were former enemy combatants who had been recruited to defect, and then paid by the South Vietnamese Army to accompany American combat troops. They acted as translators and, oftentimes, as cruel interrogators.

Jermain paused to stretch his six-foot-four-inch frame, raising his ebony arms in the air, and then he yawned.

"Now this Chu-Hoi dude is gettin' pissed 'cause mama-san ain't sayin' shit. Me and this cracker from Georgia are watchin' this go down. Seen it a hundred times before in places jus' like this. No men or older boys anywhere. But our guys are gittin' wasted every couple a days by someone. Bouncing Betty's, purji stakes, snipers... Man, they nickel and dime'n us to death. An' we ain't gittin' no payback. An' no one in the ville knows nothin.'"

I looked up and around at the eight other men seated in a circle. We were all veterans of the war, and two of the guys were missing a leg and an arm respectively. These were graphic, physical representations of the effects of the conflict. But all of us in the basement that day carried wounds that were not visible. I had been involved with the group for about six months ever since my old Army buddy, Julius (Jules) Franken, encouraged me to sit in on one of the meetings. I ran into Jules at Blues Alley, a Georgetown jazz club that I occasionally visited when I could afford the cover charge and the drink minimum. One night at the club, I was amazed to see Jules up on the stage playing trumpet in the house band. After the set ended, I went up to the stage to greet my friend. We spent a couple of hours at a nearby bar on M Street catching up. Jules told me he came to D.C. shortly after he got out of the Army to manage his aging uncle's liquor store. He told me he really missed playing trumpet, so he convinced the owner of Blues Alley to let him audition to be an alternate in the house band. He got the job. So, whenever the regular trumpet player needed a night off, Jules sat in for him.

I had first met Jules at Fort Lee, Virginia, during Quartermaster School, right before we both got our orders to the same basecamp in Vietnam. At Fort Lee, we were training to be supply clerks, figuring that if we were ordered to the war zone, we would most likely end up at a basecamp in a rear area, and out of the jungle where most of the real war was being fought. When we arrived in Qui Dong, which is the headquarters of the 123rd Infantry Division, neither one of us was assigned to work in supply. I was posted to the division awards and decorations office as a writer, and Jules, who had played trumpet in a rock 'n' roll group before being drafted, was assigned to the division band. His full-time job was to play trumpet at the infrequent Army ceremonial events – like when politicians or important civilians arrived on base, or for special service-related commemorations such as Veterans Day. And since Reveille and Retreat were recordings blasted through the base PA system, Jules wasn't even required to get up early or stick around till dusk to play. As a result, he spent most of his time reading paperbacks, smoking weed or drinking at the NCO Club.

He was almost able to forget he was in a war zone. Almost. But late one night, Jules' living quarters, his hooch, was on the receiving end of an enemy rocket fired from the mountains five miles away. Four troopers in his hooch were shredded with shards of molten steel, and perished instantly. Five other men, including Jules, were wounded. When I fortuitously ran into Jules at Blues Alley, we immediately reconnected. We also shared the invisible, but emotionally painful, detritus of our mutual experiences in Vietnam.

Meeting Jules was serendipitous for me. I had gotten a job as an elevator operator in one of the House of Representatives' office buildings right after I was compelled to flee my hometown in West Virginia and disappear. I was not dealing well with my Vietnam demons, nor the loss of my girlfriend. I had resumed self-medicating with alcohol and drugs, and I missed work frequently. That was last fall, but I was fired after two months on the job. Then, I was evicted from my small apartment in the Anacostia section of the city. With less than one hundred dollars to my name, I was out on the street. I couldn't go back home to Jeweltown, and I didn't want to call my family again for help after all they had sacrificed to keep me alive. But thanks to the very welcoming and color-blind staff at the 12th Street YMCA, I was able to rent a bed in a dorm room for $5 a night. This YMCA had been constructed in 1912 primarily to provide athletic facilities and shelter for black males living in the Shaw/Cardozo neighborhoods, and as overnight lodging for men of color who were traveling through D.C. I was the only white guy in the place, and the only requirement was that I not drink or use drugs in the building. I had been staying at the Y for about two weeks when I ran into Jules at Blues Alley. Shortly thereafter, my friend convinced me to join his nascent veterans' group. He also offered me a job.

My reverie was interrupted when Jermain's voice rose suddenly. I could sense his story was reaching a climax and I looked over at him. He was struggling to remain composed as he continued.

"We're maybe twenty feet away, me an' cracker boy, leanin' against a tree jus' watchin' this Chu-Hoi dude start to lose it. First, he backhands mama-san an' screams somethin' to her in gook talk. When she don't answer up, he grabs her by the hair an' drags her over to where the Lieutenant and three NCOs was standin' in a circle. They tryin' to figure out what to do next. Call in arty or an air strike on the place? Or jus' burn the ville down?"

Jermain paused. He stood and looked up at the ceiling. Now all we could hear in the room is the soft-shoe shuffling from above while Jermain tried to gather himself and continue with his story. After about ten seconds, he wiped a tear from one of his eyes and sat back down. We all stared intently at the tall, rail of a man who looked down at the floor and began to speak once more.

"Meantime, while the lieutenant an' them NCOs are bullshittin,' Chu-Hoi boy throws mama-san in the middle of the circle, an' she lands on her back. Everybody – the Chu-Hoi an' them four guys are lookin' down at mama-san. The lieutenant starts yellin' at the Chu-Hoi, he say, 'what the fuck you doin man?' But before he can git another word out, mama-san lifts her shirt front up an' pulls the pins on two chicom grenades that's strapped to her body. Me an' cracker boy hit the dirt, but the guys in that circle didn't have no time to git out the way before the grenades blow."

Jermain stopped speaking. He was silently weeping. He covered his face with his hands and mumbled something incoherent before looking up at us in the circle.

"I'm checkin' my clothes for holes an' my body for any missin' parts. Cracker boy looks over at me and says somethin'. But my ears are ringin', so I can't hear nothin' he sayin.' When I look over to where mama-san an' Chu-Hoi boy was at, there's jus' pieces of smokin' rags and lumps of what looks like bloody, raw meat. I jus' can't git that scene outta my mind. The lieutenant an' the other three dudes are face down in the dirt. Well, three of 'em is face down in the dirt, but the other one ain't got no head for a face to be on. Then I jus' jumped up and hauled ass away from there. All these years later, I'm still tryin' to git away from there."

* * *

A few days later, while I was restocking bottles of petite sirah onto a shelf in the store, Jules approached me and motioned for me to follow him. We wound our way along an aisle full of bottles from Bordeaux and Burgundy, and then we entered a large room at the back of the shop. The room was completely full of cases of wine stacked from the floor to the ceiling. Following Jules' circuitous meandering in the room was like traversing vineyard valleys beneath soaring mountains of wine from the greatest appellations on the planet. We arrived at a small desk in the middle of the room. He sat on a metal folding chair and pointed to another one. I took a seat.

"Hey buddy," Jules said, "what are you going to do long-term? I mean, I can't see you working here at this wine shop forever. You're an English Lit major, right?"

I looked over at my friend and shook my head. "Man, I haven't really thought much about anything long-term. Been living day to day and just trying to deal with the demons. You know, the war and other stuff. I haven't thought much beyond just getting through this rough patch. But I guess I need to try and figure out where I'm headed."

When Jules offered me the job at Franken's Spirits, I was just happy to have an income that enabled me to survive. I was able to rent a small, two-room apartment in the Adams Morgan neighborhood of D.C. where I took the bus to and from work. I had sold my '64 Opel Kadett about a month after moving to the city because finding free parking was almost impossible, and because I couldn't afford the exorbitant charge to rent a space.

"You seem to really be into wine," Jules offered, "maybe that's a career to think about."

"Yeah, my old girlfriend. Her name is Lou. Anyway, she really got me interested in the whole wine scene. My Italian family has always made wine, but I never liked the stuff they made when I was a kid. It tasted sour to me back then. Hell, to be honest, I couldn't stand it. But Lou turned me on to some really good wine last year."

"How'd she get interested in wine?" Jules asked.

"Lou actually has a degree in enology and viticulture. She studied about grapes and how to make wine in California. After she graduated, she worked for several California wineries. Then a couple years back, she started her own small winery on a mountaintop over in West Virginia. I could feel her passion for growing grapes and making wine. Guess I caught the wine bug too. So yes, I like everything about wine. And working here has allowed me to learn even more about it. I appreciate the opportunity, Jules. I really do."

"Hey dude, I'm glad you showed up here. Most of the people we hire don't really want to learn anything about wine. Most of them just work for the discount we give them on beer and booze. Never saw any one of them actually buy a bottle of wine, like you do. If you want, I can lend you a couple of books my Uncle Sherman has. They explain the history of wine and where the best vineyards are located around the world. They also describe how wine is made."

"Jules, I'd love to find out more about wine. And I'd really like to go to California sometime and check out the wine scene there. Lou told me that someday soon, California wines will be recognized and appreciated just like the ones made in places like France, Italy and Germany."

"I don't know about that, man. Those countries have been making wine for centuries. They definitely have a jump on us. But hey, if you ever decide to go to California, I'm sure Uncle Sherman can get you in to visit some of the best wineries out there.

"And we have a lot of customers who come in here. They're all wine fanatics. They just love to schmooze about the stuff, especially with my Uncle Sherman. I'd be happy to introduce you to them. There's also a bunch of folks in the wine business who come in here just about every day. They can give you some good information too."

"That would be great Jules. You know, there was always a big jug of homemade wine on the dinner table when I was growing up. Right next to the great food my Italian family cooked for us. And then when Lou showed me how to match wine with food – she calls it pairing – I was hooked. Now, when I can afford it, I try and pair certain wines with certain foods at my apartment. Nothing fancy. Maybe some pasta in marinara with a Chianti Classico. Or a piece of baked white fish with sauvignon blanc."

Jules just smiled at me and said, "Let me know when you're ready to take the next step. I mean, if you're interested in wine as a career, we can help you. Especially out in California."

* * *

When I had saved up enough money, I took Jules up on his offer to help me relocate to California. I bought a ticket that fall to San Francisco, and took a bus up to the Napa Valley. I checked into a small hotel in St. Helena and started visiting the wineries in the area that Jules' Uncle Sherman had recommended. His uncle had also given me a letter of introduction that served as a reference. When I eventually visited Starling Vineyards, the letter – and the fact that the winemaker was also a native West Virginian – got me the job. It was just a gopher-type position, but I was able to learn about wine literally from the ground up. I worked in the vineyards picking grapes in the fall and then pruning the vines in the winter. I also assisted with just about every job that needed to be done in the wine cellar from cleaning barrels and tanks to helping on the bottling lines.

Working at the winery was one of the happiest times of my life and eventually allowed me to combine my two passions: wine and writing. After the winding and rocky road that had brought me to this place,

I finally felt some sense of fulfillment and normalcy. I still missed Lou terribly, but I was healing from the invisible wounds of my Vietnam experience and, right after that, the incident that had forced me to leave home.

Everything worked out just fine for about six years- and then it didn't.

Chapter 2
San Francisco
October 1977

There was a slight, but cold breeze wafting up from the bay that coalesced with the fog and was making my evening stroll uncomfortable. It was after 10 o'clock, and I pulled the lapels from my sport coat up around my neck to ward off the chill. I was in the Marina District, hoping to hail a cab for a ride back to my apartment. Traffic was sparse this time of night and, after standing on the corner for fifteen minutes, I decided to walk along Chestnut Street, hoping to have better luck hailing a cab there.

As I walked along the sidewalk, I suddenly heard the pitter-patter of running feet behind me. When I turned toward the sound, I was immediately struck from behind and lifted off my feet by the blur of what had to be a very large person. I crashed face first onto the sidewalk where the force of the impact left me stunned, shocked and bleeding. I was unable to move. Then, I rolled quickly from under the weight of the person on top of me and got to my knees. I stood and started running as fast as I could down the sidewalk hoping to find some place to escape my attacker. I slowed to turn around, and I caught a glimpse of a man who was climbing into the shotgun seat of what looked like a panel truck. I turned back around and picked up speed again.

I was desperately looking for any business that might be open this time of night. Some place with people who might help me or at least call the police. I spotted the illuminated marquee of a movie theater just up ahead. I could hear the roaring engine of the truck that would surely catch up to me in a few seconds. As I reached the theater marquee, the truck screeched to a halt.

I ran past the attendant at the box office and into the foyer. Then I stopped. Directly to my front were stairs leading to the second-floor balcony. I took them two at a time and stopped at the top where an usher stood staring at me. He asked for my ticket, but I went right past him into the darkened room. I stumbled blindly until the light from the movie screen intermittently lit the theater. It was packed with an audience completely and silently captivated by a film I later learned was "Logan's Run."

I spotted an exit in the balcony and moved quickly down to it, and into a stairway. I almost fell running down the stairs and then stopped at a fire door exit. I held my breath and opened the door, hoping against hope, that my attacker wasn't waiting for me. I found myself in a darkened alley. I couldn't return to Chestnut Street, so I ran in the other direction and wound my way circuitously around a series of buildings until I emerged above onto Lombard.

I found a phone booth and was able to call for a taxi. As I waited for it to arrive, I tried to make myself invisible, crouching on the sidewalk curled up against a concrete wall. I used my handkerchief to wipe the blood from my nose and face. When the taxi arrived, I dashed into the backseat and sat on the floor.

The driver looked back over the front street and stared, open-mouthed at me. "Hey, mister, what the hell happened to you? Your face is bleeding. You didn't rob nobody or nothing, did you?" he asked, with a worried look on his face.

I had to think quickly. I couldn't afford to leave the cab. "No. Nothing like that. It's my wife. Caught me in a bar down the street with a woman. She's chasing me and I tripped and fell. She has a gun so I wouldn't stick around here very long if I was you." I was hoping the driver would believe me. "I'll give you an extra ten bucks if you'll take me to a place in the Mission District."

"I don't want no trouble mister. But I gotta see the money first before I take you anywhere."

I shifted onto my side and reached into my back pocket for my wallet. I got a twenty dollar bill out and thrust it up to the driver. He took it and then he asked, "Where to, bud?"

I gave him the name of a bar about two blocks from my apartment. I wanted to see if there were any strange looking people hanging around the area before I went to my place. I stayed on the floor below the seat back until we arrived at a bar called The Homestead, on Folsom Street. I gave the cabbie another five-dollar bill and then exited the cab.

I walked slowly past the bar and continued until I reached the corner where 18th Street intersected with Folsom. My apartment was about half a block up 18th, and I carefully peered around the corner. At this time of night, there were not many cars parked along the street and traffic was light. However, I spotted what looked like a light-colored panel truck which was parked just up the street. That could be the same truck I saw when I was being attacked. I couldn't take any chances, so I walked back along Folsom and crossed over to Mission Street where I found a cheap, hostel-type hotel called Del Capitan. I paid fifteen dollars to the night clerk and trudged up the worn, carpeted stairs to the second floor. The shock and fear had begun to wear off as I entered my room. I knew I had to think this all through, but I was too exhausted. I took off my ripped and filthy sport coat and threw it on the floor. I kicked off my shoes and immediately fell onto the bed.

Sometime later in the middle of the night, I awoke in a cold sweat. A single shaft of street light pierced the darkness through a small hole in the nightshade. The shade covered a rectangular window that looked like the firing position in a World War II pillbox. The arrow of light caromed off the tile floor and dimly lit the room. I was lying on my back and looking at the ceiling. I tried to sit up and was immediately nauseous. My head throbbed with a thousand pinpricks that felt like someone was using a jackhammer on my cerebellum. I had to lay still. I was also having trouble catching my breath, and I realized I could only breathe through my mouth. I pinched my nose to try and clear at least one nostril and I felt a sticky substance on my fingers. Blood. My nose was clogged and clotted with it. I lay motionless on the bed and tried to remember what had happened.

Slowly, I began to piece together the string of events. Fuzzy and indistinct at first, my memories began to return with an awful clarity as I began to realize the dire implications of what had transpired. They'd found me! After all these years, the fear that had always lurked just below the surface of my consciousness had become a shocking reality. I was immediately enveloped in a dark cloud of panic and despondency. How had they located me?

* * *

It had been more than six years since I had left Washington, D.C. and assumed my new life in California. Last night I had attended an event at the Pierce Street Wine Bar near the Presidio. It was a joyous occasion, and I was thrilled to be there to celebrate with a man who had played such an important role in helping me find purpose and self-worth. A man who had given me a new lease on a life that I thought – under the best of circumstances- would be disjointed and nomadic.

My friend and one-time employer, Alex Starling, was conducting a barrel sample tasting of his eponymous, soon to be released, 1974 Starling Vineyards Private Reserve Cabernet Sauvignon. I was excited to finally taste and evaluate a wine that I had a small role in crafting. After the first sip, I knew the wine was everything that I had hoped it would be. Rich, tannic, and full of dark berry and cola flavors, I'm sure it will be a major success once it's released for sale next year.

I lingered after the event to speak with my friend and to congratulate him. Once he had finished chatting with a procession of well-wishers, I approached him. Alex looked at me, smiled and then loudly exclaimed: "Johnny Harman! What's a good ol' West Virginia hick like you know about wine?" Then he clapped me on the back.

I fired right back at him, "They weren't having any moonshine tastings in town tonight, so I had to settle for something a little less challenging. Anyway, I don't suspect you learned how to make that cabernet back in Marshall County."

"Yeah, you're right about that. I tried to get a real job at the penitentiary in Moundsville, but I wasn't mean enough to be a guard."

Alex Starling is a native West Virginian who had migrated to California to live his dream of making wine. He is also one of the most respected winemakers in the Napa Valley, and he plies his exceptional skills for the winery he owns in St. Helena. I was fortunate to get a job at Starling a few years back as a hired hand and general all-around cellar-rat. I'm sure the fact that I'm from Alex's home state helped me get the job, but I did work hard, and I really loved being in the vineyards and the wine cellar. Later, I published a monthly newsletter on the wines of the Napa Valley and eventually I was hired as a stringer for the San Francisco Chronicle to write about the county's fledgling wine industry. That led to a full-time job at the paper as a columnist and reporter covering California wine.

"What do you think of the wine?" he asked.

"Man, you've really got something here," I said. "It hits all the marks for me, but it's going to need some time in the bottle before it comes around. Don't you think?

Alex nodded, and then added. "You're correct, Johnny. It's going to need to soften a bit in the bottle for a few years before it will be ready to drink. But that's true for pretty much all the '74 c cabernets. Gonna be a great vintage for the Napa Valley, though, I suspect."

I chatted with Alex for a few more minutes and then decided to leave the wine bar around 10 p.m. As usual, the fog, like a damp, gray cloak, was blanketing the Marina District as I walked down Pierce Street toward Chestnut. My intention was to hail a cab there for the ride back to my apartment in the Mission District. That's when things went terribly wrong.

* * *

And now, I lay here wide awake in a flop house with my head throbbing, trying to figure out what I can do to stay alive. I coaxed my legs over the side of the bed and forced myself to sit up. I rose painfully and limped over to the rectangular window, pulled up the shade and looked out into the pre-dawn fog. I had to think. I suppose that the attack could have been a random act of attempted robbery. Maybe I was just in the wrong place at the wrong time and looked like an easy mark to a couple of thugs out cruising for a chump to rob. But no, I couldn't afford to think like that. I had to assume that the attack was an intentional act, and plan accordingly. And anyway, I had spotted a vehicle near my apartment that looked pretty much like the panel truck that my assailant had gotten into. I'll need to go into hiding again because if it's really the same guys, then I'm probably a dead man walking!

Even more alarming and worrisome was the prospect of what my discovery would mean for my family back in West Virginia. They had assisted me in contriving the story that had saved my life. There would be mortal retribution coming their way soon because they had cheated *La Famiglia Vagabonda* (The Wandering Family). My uncle Sal had told me that *La Famiglia Vagabonda* was an affiliate of the Mafia or Cosa Nostra. They were also known as the Black Hand, and they controlled organized crime activities in western Pennsylvania and northern West Virginia that included illegal gambling, prostitution, and drug trafficking.

I had to come up with a solution to this problem for me and my family. I had faced tough times before – both in the war and when I returned from Vietnam. I was able to survive those perilous challenges, and I would do everything in my power to overcome this new threat. I would certainly need assistance, but I had made some good friends out here in California, and I knew I could depend on them to help me. I thought of that Beatles' song 'A Little Help from My Friends.' I had to conclude that, in this desperate situation, I would probably need a LOT of help from my friends.

However, none of my California friends really knew about my past, or even my real name.

Chapter 3
Johnny Harman... AKA...

Johnny Harman is not my given name. I changed my name seven years ago to protect myself and my family. I've been living a lie since 1970 when I was forced to leave my hometown to maintain the fiction that I had disappeared. By now, those friends I left back in West Virginia must think that I am dead. Only my family knows that I'm alive, but not one of them knows where I live, nor do they even know my assumed name. It must be that way, or their lives would be in jeopardy too.

I had lived a pretty normal life up until the events immediately following my return from Vietnam in the spring of 1970. Well, I don't suppose that war could be considered normal in any sense of the word, but at least I knew who the enemy was in Vietnam. However, when I got home, I was completely blind-sided by the indelible memories and emotional trauma that my wartime experiences left on me. I was a mess, and I tried to obliterate my war memories with drugs and alcohol. And then, as if that burden was not enough to bear, a series of disquieting incidents at home completely upended my life.

My real name is Augustino Lee Cumpton, but everyone back home calls me Augie. Through a wild series of events, I was forced to leave my old world behind and establish a new identity. To be honest, I've grown to like my new life, my job and my coterie of new friends. But it certainly was not a conscious choice on my part, and I really do miss my family. I guess that's a good place to begin this tale.

I grew up in Jeweltown – a small city in northern West Virginia. I'm an only child and my parents, Harry and Gina, are working class folks who raised me with the help of my large Italian American family in the Riverview neighborhood of Jeweltown. My Father was born in Cork, a small, isolated village tucked away in the Allegheny mountains. His parents were second generation Irish Americans who had moved to Cork in the early 1900s from the farmlands of the Shenandoah Valley in Virginia. Grandfather Cumpton sold his farm to take a foreman's job at a clothespin factory in Cork. I'm sure Dad would never have left Cork after high school were it not for World War II. But I'm glad he did. He enlisted in the service and eventually was stationed stateside in Jeweltown as an Army recruiter. That's where he met and later married my mom.

My mother is one of eight children born to Italian immigrants – Salvatore and Luisa Costanza. My Grandparents followed other immigrants from Calabria in southern Italy to settle in northern West Virginia, and to work in the coal mines, glass factories and steel mills. Mom was born in a one-story company house near the mine where Grandpa Salvatore was employed. He worked miles underground, digging coal by hand, for the West Fork Coal Company. Grandpa toiled for sixteen long years and saved most of his earnings. When he quit his mining job in 1916, he moved the family to Jeweltown where, with the help of several friends, he constructed a building and started his business – The Chestnut Bakery.

Grandpa baked Italian hard crust bread, pepperoni rolls, and hoagie buns for more than fifty years. That bakery is where I spent afternoons in the early 1960s selling bread after school. Later, in high school, I worked overnight on most weekends sacking Chestnut Bakery bread, buns and pepperoni rolls. By then, Grandpa Salvatore had retired, and my uncles Dante and Giorgio ran the business. That's where I met a whole host of unforgettable characters who frequented the place: like Frankie "Tapper Two" Secondo who had a strange habit of whistling tunes between words and phrases while tap dancing; and Rosie Infantano who ran an illegal bar that Grandpa Salvatore called a speakeasy where she sold home brew and bootleg liquor, and sometimes provided other more exclusive services to her late night male guests; and Jimmie Ponza, the owner of the Ruff Avenue Pool Room, who is a dear friend of our family, especially my Uncle Sal.

Uncle Sal is the oldest of my mother's siblings and he is like a second father to me. He's also a disabled World War II veteran who knows what war can do to you – even if you escape with no physical wounds. He understood the invisible trauma that those serving in a combat zone would experience, and he was the one family member who understood what I was going through when I returned from Vietnam. Uncle Sal did everything in his power to ease my transition from soldier to citizen, and when events after my return from the war added a mortal complication to my life, he is the person who came up with the plan that saved me.

Outside of my immediate family, the one other person that made my life worth living after I came home from Vietnam is a young woman who became the love of my life. I had never had any serious relationships until I met Louise Erickson. Lou was born and raised in Washington D.C. and had transferred from Georgetown University to the University of California at Davis to major in enology and viticulture – the study of grape growing and winemaking. I met Lou in Canaan Valley at a bar called the Duck In. Canaan – which the locals colloquially pronounce "Ka-naane" – is a remote mountain valley located in the Potomac Highlands of northeastern West Virginia.

I was hiding out there at the home of my friend – the real Johnny "Hambone" Harman. Hambone was an old friend from college, and he was a construction worker living in Canaan Valley. He also played guitar in a rock 'n' roll band that happened to be entertaining us the night I met Lou at the Duck In. I must admit that when I saw her that evening at the bar, I don't remember much about our encounter except that I was immediately transfixed by her amazing green eyes. I had been smoking hashish with Hambone before I got to the Duck In, and I had continued my trip to oblivion by drinking shots of tequila at the bar. I vaguely remember introducing myself to Lou and then, later, dancing with her. But that's about it. Fortunately for me, Lou came by Hambone's place the next day to make sure I had made it home safely. From that day on, our relationship blossomed into something special. She tolerated my erratic and self-destructive behavior with patience and love, and she gave me a reason to try and overcome my daily struggles with the horrific nightmares, survivor's guilt and my growing dependence on drugs and alcohol to dull my memories. But then, tragically, Lou became a victim of the trouble that had followed me after the war, and which forced me into hiding from the Black Hand. Lou had been kidnapped by the mob and held bound and gagged for three days. Later, when the issues affecting Lou and my troubles with the mob had been resolved, the damage to our relationship – at least from Lou's perspective – was fatal. I've never given up hope that I can reestablish what we once had, but Lou has shut me out of her life.

I still struggle with issues related to my service in Vietnam, but I have moderated my drinking and I no longer use drugs. I've also been helped by other Vietnam veterans who I meet with occasionally to talk through our mutual wartime experiences. I find the meetings are helping me slowly learn how to live with my awful memories. All of us in this veterans' group have lost friends or have had to deal with the trauma of that war. But it has been especially difficult for me because I lost three close friends, one of whom sacrificed his own life to save mine in Vietnam. The guilt I feel for surviving when they did not has been compounded by tragic events after I left the war. Two good friends were murdered because they helped me during my time in hiding from the Black Hand. One of those men, Johnny Harman, gave his life so that I could live. The least I could do to honor him is to take his name.

CHAPTER 4
NAPA FRIENDS

Gabriel "Topo" Rojas was one of the first friends I made when I began work at Starling Vineyards in the fall of 1971. In fact, he was my immediate supervisor. Alex Starling introduced me to Topo my first day on the job. I remember Alex taking me down into a cavernous wine cellar to meet the man I would be working with. The cellar smelled of spilled wine, damp wood and a pleasant kind of forest floor, earthy aroma. As we walked down the metal spiral staircase, I heard a hiss and then felt a slight mist gently caress the skin on my arms. I looked up to the high wooden ceiling and noticed a series of pipes with what appeared to be sprinkler heads on them. I glanced quizzically over at Alex.

"Hey Johnny, that mist you feel is what we use to limit Angel's Share. It's really a light spray of water to keep the cellar humid. It's standard practice now in a lot of wineries. With all that expensive wine aging in oak barrels, we can lose about fifteen percent to evaporation if we don't keep the cellar at just the right humidity level. That way, we can keep the Angel's Share to a minimum," Alex said, smiling.

We walked over to a tall, upright stainless-steel tank where a small man was checking the glass dials on the front of the large, twenty-five-foot tall container, and then writing on a clipboard. Alex tapped the man on the shoulder and then looked at me.

"Johnny, meet your boss," Alex said. "You two guys have something in common, but I don't know if it's anything you'll want to reminisce about. You're both Vietnam vets."

I reached out and down and took the man's extended hand. The letters on his nametag read: 'Topo Rojas.' "Pleased to meet you Topo," I said, pronouncing his name "Top-oh. "I'm Johnny Harman."

Alex quickly corrected me. "Johnny, it's 'Toe-poe'."

"Sorry Topo," I said, pronouncing it correctly on the second try. "I didn't mean to offend you. Hell, I'm a hillbilly from West Virginia. I can hardly speak English let alone Spanish."

"No problem, Johnny," Topo said, smiling up at me. "Topo is the nickname my family hung on me when I was a child. Topo means mole in Spanish. I guess I was small – even for a Mexican kid. I hoped I would grow taller, but I'm thirty now so I think I'm stuck at this altitude."

I chuckled. Then I asked, "Where did you spend your all-expense paid tour of Southeast Asia?"

"I was with the First Infantry Division – The Big Red One. That was back in '67 and '68. I spent most of my time crawling around under the Ho Bo Woods. North of Saigon. I was a "tunnel rat," Topo added.

I was impressed. I had met a few tunnel rats during my time in Vietnam. They were all small men – usually less than five feet tall – and they crawled down into enemy tunnels equipped with only a flashlight and a small caliber pistol. They were fearless grunts whose job was to find, engage and kill any VC or North Vietnamese soldiers they encountered. The elaborate tunnel systems in Vietnam were originally hand-dug all over the country during World War II by the communist Viet Minh. The Viet Minh were the predecessors to the Viet Cong, and they used the tunnels in their war against the Japanese invaders. These subterranean sanctuaries accommodated everything from sleeping quarters to armories, and some even housed field hospitals.

Because of Topo's introductions, I was able to make several new acquaintances when I started work at Starling Vineyards, and the closest of these friends were veterans like me. In fact, our group of Vietnam veterans continues to meet regularly at a bar in Yountville called the Railcar. The Railcar is actually an old boxcar that had been converted into a bar, and we gather there to discuss the troubling emotional and psychological remnants of the war we all had experienced. I remember one of the first group sessions I participated in at The Railcar. We were all seated around a large table in the far corner of the establishment. The windows of the bar look out toward terraced vineyards that rise up a small hill and surround The Veterans Home of California. That's where a few of my new friends live. I was happy to be invited to join the group since I had benefited from participating in a similar veterans' gathering back in D.C. before coming out here. On this particular occasion, Topo was telling us a story about his day job as a tunnel rat in Vietnam.

"Man, that hole was about as wide as this," Topo said and stretched his short arms out in front of him in a circle so that the fingers of both his hands touched. Topo's arms are short because Topo is short. Jockey short. So short that someone five feet tall towers three inches above the thick, jet-black hair growing on his head. Topo put his arms down and continued with his story.

"I take my fatigue shirt off, put my pistol in my pocket, turn my little flashlight on and put it between my front teeth. Then I crawl down into that hole headfirst. About three feet in, I see what looks like a wooden ladder and I grab the first rung and continue down headfirst. There ain't enough room for me to turn around. That's good because it means I can't flip over. I just creep down to where the ladder stops. And then I crawl forward on the dirt for a couple of feet to where I can stand up.

"I pull the pistol out of my pocket and point it straight ahead. I take the flashlight from my mouth and aim it in that same direction. I see what looks like another ladder sticking up out of another hole. It's about twenty feet ahead of me so I move toward it. I turn the flashlight off and move slowly toward the next ladder. I need to be really quiet now. That way, I can sneak up on any dinks down there before they know I'm around."

Topo paused. He raised his glass and took a long pull on a copper-colored draft beer. He belched loudly and then took another sip from the frosty mug of Anchor Steam, a beer that's been produced in San Francisco since the late 1800s. Then he continued.

"There I am in total darkness now. Remember, I'd turned the flashlight off, but I still have my gun in one hand and the flashlight in the other. I held them out in front of me as I crept to where the next ladder was. I'm about to put the flashlight and gun in my pockets so I can use both hands to climb down.

"But then, I hear something hissing directly in front of me. I quickly turn on the flashlight and see two snakes coiled on a ledge and looking straight at me. I know what they are right away. They're cobras, you know, those deadly snakes with a flat head. Suddenly, one of them strikes at me just missing my left ear. I didn't wait for the other one to strike. I just pointed the gun at the slimy bastards and squeezed the trigger until the pistol stopped firing. Then, I turned and hauled ass out of there. When I got back up on level ground, the first thing I did was change my pants," Topo added.

The table exploded with laughter. I was impressed at Topo's non-chalant attitude and his ability to make light of a very harrowing incident. I looked around at my new friends and noticed that one person was not laughing at Topo's tale. Retired Army captain Genevieve "Looks" Loveleigh was not even smiling. I found out later that Captain Loveleigh was given her nickname, Looks, by a colonel she served with in the medical corps. She described the man as a self-congratulatory, misogynist buffoon who thought the nickname demonstrated his facile dexterity with the English language. The nickname stuck, though, because everyone thought it was a clever moniker, and because Looks was, indeed, a very good-looking woman. She was also a highly trained surgical nurse, and a practicing Catholic nun, at the time, who volunteered to serve in Vietnam. When she arrived in-country, she was granted the temporary rank of captain and was quickly promoted to head of surgical nursing at the 6th Convalescent Hospital in Cam Ranh Bay.

"I don't think Gabriel's near-death experience is anything to laugh at," she said, looking directly at the diminutive man. "He could have been killed. Or worse, died a slow death from being bitten by a cobra. I've had to try and save more than one snake bite victim in Vietnam. And I'm batting zero."

Everyone doing time in Vietnam was envious of anyone who was stationed at Cam Ranh Bay. It was considered "country club" duty. The place had paved streets, air-conditioned buildings, real bathrooms, pizza parlors, bowling alleys, tennis courts and well-stocked service clubs and PX's. It was the safest American basecamp in Vietnam, and there had never been a successful enemy ground attack at Cam Ranh Bay. That is, until the early morning hours of August 8, 1969, when a small unit of Viet Cong sappers breached the defensive perimeter and proceeded to the 6th Convalescent Hospital. They tossed high explosive satchel charges into several buildings there, including one where Captain Loveleigh was billeted. Disregarding her own shrapnel injuries, she began treating the wounded while the enemy attack was still in progress. When it was all over, two G.I.s were killed in the attack and more than ninety were wounded.

When Looks returned home from Vietnam, she left the convent and was recruited to continue her health care career as a surgical nurse at St. Helena Hospital. In her spare time, she enjoyed visiting Napa Valley winery tasting rooms and sampling the local wines. In fact, that's where she met Topo one afternoon at the Starling Vineyards' tasting room. When Topo learned that Looks had served in Vietnam, he invited her to join the veterans' discussion group that met regularly at The Railcar in Yountville. And later, because of her keen wine palate, Topo asked her to manage the Starling Vineyards tasting room on weekends. Alex Starling was also very impressed with Looks' wine tasting acumen, and he asked her to join his small team that regularly monitored and evaluated Starling wines.

Topo shook his head and smiled at the tall, statuesque woman who sat slouched back in her chair. Her long, shapely and tanned legs were extended under the table. Looks was a striking woman with a milky white complexion, brown eyes and chestnut brown hair cut short and worn pixie style. This day she was attired in baby blue short-shorts and a pink peasant blouse that was unbuttoned to just above her ample cleavage. She was alternately swirling and sniffing a glass of Chardonnay and trying to keep a straight face.

"Hey Looks," Topo said, "I get it. But you gotta laugh at this stuff or you'll fucking implode. Anyway, it's pretty funny thinking about it now. But I have to admit, it literally scared the shit out of me at the time."

Looks is an amazing woman. She served with great skill and dedication during her time in Vietnam. For her courageous actions during the VC sapper attack at Cam Ranh Bay, she was awarded a purple heart as well as a bronze star for valor. When her one-year commitment ended and she was released from the Army, Looks returned home to her convent. However, after several months of serious contemplation, she decided to leave her religious order – The Sisters of Penance – who lived and prayed in a monastery in the hills above the Napa Valley. All nuns are bound by the vows of poverty, chastity and obedience. Looks had not forsaken the vows of poverty and chastity, but she did have a problem with obedience. She simply felt she could not, in good conscience, continue to serve as a faithful acolyte for Catholicism.

As a fellow Catholic, I was curious about her decision, particularly since I had been educated throughout grade school and high school by nuns – all of whom seemed to be fanatically dedicated to the church. But first I had to call upon decades of accumulated Catholic guilt to suppress my prurient interest in the woman I called Ginny – which is short for her given name of Genevieve. It seemed disrespectful to refer to her as Looks, even though she didn't seem to mind or, to take offense, to others using the nickname.

I remember a conversation I had with Ginny right after we first met. I wanted to know why she had left the church. So, I asked her: "Then what – to mix a metaphor – was the straw that broke the camel's habit? I mean, what happened to make you leave the convent?"

"Nice try, Johnny. But as a mixed metaphor, that's a non sequitur," Ginny said and smiled. Then she stopped smiling and asked me: "What do you know about Vatican II?"

"Not much. I know what I've read about the most visible changes that came about as a result of Vatican II. Like doing away with the Latin Mass. But I really don't know anything much about changes in doctrine."

I had read that Vatican II was convened so the Catholic Church could be brought into the 20th Century. It was the brainchild of Pope John XXIII who assembled an ecumenical convocation that began work in 1962 and finished in 1965. It dealt with things like opening dialogues with different religions, providing for more input from lay people, and making the Catholic Mass more understandable. However, it took years for Catholics to recognize and understand the far-reaching implications of Vatican II. For me personally, I really didn't notice any major differences until after I returned from Vietnam. Then, I realized Vatican II had upended and changed just about everything I was taught in catechism class: Mass was now in English; musicians were playing guitars during the service; the altar was turned toward the congregation; and confession was optional.

I added, "What was really shocking to me, though, was that all the weird and scary stuff they taught us in grade school – like indulgences, purgatory and sins – have been revised. I wonder what happened to all those pagan babies I prayed for? You know, to get their sentences to purgatory reduced?"

Ginny just shook her head. "I can see why you might wonder about that. But for me, I had real hope that the church was going to change because of Vatican II. I mean, really come into the 20th Century. I was optimistic at first. We were told that we would be able to live outside the convent if we chose to. And that we could even think of ourselves as individuals. When I joined the Army to serve as a nurse in Vietnam, I was feeling good about the future of the Catholic Church. And I was looking forward to doing the Lord's work in Vietnam. You know, caring for the injured and comforting the dying. But after a few months, I began to feel depressed and sad. About the futility of the war. The senselessness of the constant maiming and killing. On both sides.

"And then I became an emotional, physical and psychological victim of the conflict myself. I tried to justify and rationalize my role in the war – a war I was against. And I couldn't. When I got back to the States and went back up to my convent, things had changed radically. Some of the girls in my order were tethered to the traditions of the church. They became antagonistic to those of us who were welcoming the changes promised in Vatican II. So now, there was a serious split among the sisters in my order. Some, like me, embraced the changes, and others fought against them – and us. Anyway, it must have been the perfect storm of circumstances – my disillusionment with the war; and then the controversy over implementing the changes in Vatican II. I guess that's why I left."

I was impressed with, and attracted to, this complex woman. We were kindred spirits borne out of our gut-wrenching and heart-breaking experiences in Vietnam, along with our mutual disenchantment with Catholicism when we returned from the war. And years later, our friendship would become so much more.

Topo and Ginny are now two of my best friends in California. They're folks I can count on – just like the friends I've relied on to help me in the past. Unfortunately, many of my friends from the war and from back home suffered because of their friendship with me. When I first met Topo and Ginny, I felt pretty confident that my new friends would not suffer the same fate.

At least, I thought so at the time.

CHAPTER 5
THE BAD GUYS

Gennaro "Cheech" Aresti and Marco "Tubby" Pacifico were frustrated. They had bungled the initial attempt to grab the jamoke they had been sent to find. They should have gotten him. They had a good plan, Cheech thought. They knew this guy worked at *The San Francisco Chronicle*, so they rented a truck at the airport and drove to town and found the newspaper building around 3 p.m. They parked their truck along the street right in front of the Chronicle and waited for their guy to leave work so they could grab him. They had a picture of him, but he didn't show until around 6.30 p.m. When he left the building, he immediately hailed a cab. The two mob guys followed the cab across town to where their man got out along a busy street and went into a place called The Pierce Street Wine Bar. They waited down the street until he left and started walking along the street. That's where things went sideways.

Carmine Amato, the aging capo of La Famiglia Vagabonda back in Pittsburgh, was not happy. Cheech and Tubby had gotten the order from Carmine yesterday to fly out to San Francisco and find this guy who calls himself Johnny Harman. Carmine told them his real name is Augie Cumpton. They were told to grab him, tie him up and drive him all the way across the country back to Pittsburgh. They were ordered not to kill the man. Carmine didn't tell them why they had to bring him back alive, but Cheech heard it had something to do with a botched job several years back. He figured the boss wanted to sweat this guy, before they whacked him, and find out how he managed to be alive and well in California when he was supposed to be dead. But when he and Tubby messed up the snatch and grab, the boss changed his mind. He decides that Cumpton needed to die now.

"Yinz guys fucked this up real good," Carmine screamed at Cheech, who had lost a coin flip with Tubby to determine who would have to call the boss with the bad news. "Next time you see this guy, don't worry none about grabbing him. Just waste his ass. But you gotta make it look like an accident. Don't come back here unless you get this done," he warned, and then he hung up on Cheech.

The two Mob members looked like Mutt and Jeff. Cheech was tall and stout with a pock marked face, dark bags under his eyes and sagging jowls. He was only marginally more handsome than Frankenstein's monster. He was the brains of the duo with an IQ just slightly above 90. Tubby, who was attired in a white suit and tie, was short and squat and sported handlebar mustache. He had the physique of the Pillsbury Dough Boy. He waddled when he walked and his cherubic, baby face exuded innocence. He was the embodiment of the phrase, "looks can be deceiving," because Tubby had the strength of a powerlifter with the agility and quickness of a professional football defensive back.

Both men were stone cold killers, but Cheech viewed murder as just an occasional, if sometimes messy, occupational requirement. Tubby, on the other hand, was a brutish psychopath and a killing machine who took great pleasure in inflicting excruciatingly long and agonizing pain on his victims. When La Famiglia Vagabonda needed someone in their crew to conduct an interrogation, particularly of a rival thug who was headstrong and unwilling to spill the beans, they could always count on Tubby to get the job done. However, if Carmine needed the information quickly, he never assigned Tubby because the deranged little man insisted on dragging out the interrogation as long as possible. Tubby was not interested in getting the required information expeditiously. On the contrary, he would ask the abductee totally irrelevant and incongruous questions just to extend the time he had to torture that person.

Cheech looked over at his roly-poly partner. "Holy shit, Tubby. We gotta find this guy and then put him down. And Carmine says we gotta make sure it don't look like a hit. I don't get it. I heard a couple of our guys picked up Cumpton in West Virginia a long time ago. And one of 'em shot the guy. Then they threw him in the river. Supposed to even have pictures of his body after they whacked him. It don't make no sense."

"What'd he do?" Tubby asked almost gleefully.

"I don't have no fuckin' clue. They send us all the way out here to snatch the guy and bring him back to the Burg. Now, all of a sudden, Carmine puts a hit on him. It ain't like we're on our own turf out here.

And now we can't just whack the guy. We gotta make it look like an accident," Cheech said, shaking his head.

"Okay, Cheech. I already have a couple of ideas on how to get rid of this asshole," the rotund little man added, smiling evilly through tiny yellow teeth "But once we get him, it'll probably take at least a day to do it right," he said, and wiped the saliva from his lips as he grinned like a Cheshire cat.

Cheech just stared at his partner and shook his head. "Look you Jagoff, I ain't interested in grabbin' the guy and holdin' him all day so's you can get your rocks off before we waste him. We gotta figure a way to do it right when we find him. And it can't look like he was murdered. You capeesh?"

Tubby just smiled and nodded.

The two mob guys were tired. They had spent the night in their panel truck parked near Cumpton's apartment. They watched in shifts, alternating every two hours, waiting for the man to appear. By 9 a.m., it was clear he wasn't coming back to the apartment. Now the pressure was on to locate the guy quickly and get the job done. If they screwed things up again, they would be in big trouble.

After a few moments of reflection, Cheech said, "Okay. Here's what we're gonna do, Tubby. I don't think this guy is dumb enough to come back here. He knows we're after him. But he works at the local newspaper, and he probably don't think we know that. We'll go there and stake out the place. I think that's our best bet now."

So, Cheech drove the short distance from the Mission District to the San Francisco Chronicle building in SOMA, the neighborhood South of Market Street. Cheech found a parking spot three blocks from the newspaper building's entrance. Then, he and Tubby separated and positioned themselves where they could signal each other if either one saw Cumpton walking toward the building. They could not afford to mess this up, Cheech knew.

CHAPTER 6
WARNINGS

I stood inside a phone booth down the street from the Del Capitan Hotel, and I put a dime in the coin slot. It was 6 a.m. and the sky was just beginning to brighten with the first rays of dawn when I dialed zero. When the operator answered, I placed a collect call to my Uncle Sal back in Jeweltown. He accepted the call without hesitation.

"Augie, it's great to hear your voice. It's been... what... a couple of years since you checked in?" I could tell my uncle was excited, but I could also detect anxiety in his voice.

"Uncle Sal, how's Mom and Dad? And the family? I sure do miss you guys," I said, trying to figure out how to break the news about the troubling events of the past twelve hours.

"Everyone's fine, Augie. Your parents' health is good. Your Dad actually retired last year from the glass factory, and your Mom is trying to keep him busy. You know, with projects around the apartment. How you doing?"

I continued to struggle with how to express my concerns. Was I being paranoid? Was the attack just a bad experience and nothing more? No, I needed to let my uncle know what I believed in my gut. Even if this turned out to be a random assault, I had to let Uncle Sal know just in case this was the real thing – and I felt it was.

"Well... I'm... I'm afraid I have some bad news," I said, but before I could get another word out, my uncle interrupted me.

"What Augie? What's wrong?"

"I think the mob guys found me. Don't know for sure, but I was attacked right along the street last night. A guy knocked me down from behind and tried to get me into some type of van or truck. But I got away and ran. I was able to escape, but I was afraid to go to my apartment. Good thing, though, because I spotted a vehicle down the street from my place that looked like the van or truck those guys were in."

"Augie, where are you? And how could those guys find you? I mean, after… what… seven years? Uncle Sal sounded incredulous.

"I've been living in California for six years.In San Francisco now. Right before I left home, you had Snaps Feldman make me a whole set of identification documents like a driver's license. Even a new Social Security number." Snaps is a friend of Uncle Sal's and a professional photographer with a few other sideline businesses that aren't exactly on the up and up.

"I asked Snaps to change my name to Johnny "Hambone" Harman. Hambone was the friend who let me hide out at his place in Canaan Valley when I was on the run. He's also the guy those mob assholes tortured and killed because he wouldn't tell them where to find me… I…"

I had to pause and take a deep breath. I needed to compose myself.

"Augie, you still there?" Uncle Sal asked.

"Yeah, I'm here. Anyway, I have no idea how they discovered me, but I'm sure it's them. Hey uncle, I called to warn you.You need to tell the family to be careful."

"Augie, don't worry about us. Remember, I was the contact person – through Jimmie Ponza – that dealt with those dirtbags when they came down to pick you up back then. And I was the one who turned you over to them. If those guys contact me, I'll tell 'em to check with their own crew. If they have any questions about your whereabouts, they need to ask the guys they sent to pick you up. As far as we're concerned, you've been dead for seven years."

Uncle Sal did turn me over to the mob guys, but that was a ruse he cooked up. He had gotten the drop on them when they came down from Pittsburgh to get me. He drugged them and had Snaps Feldman take what appeared to be compromising photos of them engaging in homosexual activities. Uncle Sal then used the pictures to blackmail them into agreeing to go along with the deception. If they didn't, then my uncle would see that the photos got sent to their mob buddies in Pittsburgh. Uncle Sal even provided them with a plausible cover story. The mob guys were to tell their boss that I had tried to escape during a pit stop on the trip to Pittsburgh. That when I tried to run away, they had been forced to shoot me. The two thugs were even provided pictures of my "dead" body that Snaps had staged. Those pictures saved my life and eventually allowed me to establish a new identity in California.

"Augie, we'll be okay here. But you need to find a place to hide out.

Right now. Do you need any money? I can send you a money order."

"I'm okay. I have a very close friend in the Bay Area who will let me hide out for a while. You might remember me talking about Della Mae Smith. She's from Jeweltown and now she's a lawyer out here.

"But you're going to need money if you have to go on the run again," Uncle Sal insisted.

"I have a getaway stash at Della's place too. You know, things like clothes, cash and even a passport with my new identity. I can stay there until I figure out what to do next. But my first concern is you guys back in Riverview."

"I understand and appreciate your concern, but we'll be fine. Let me talk to Jimmie Ponza about this. He's about to retire, but he still has contacts with the mob guys in Pittsburgh. He can quietly check on this. In the meantime, I'll try and come up with a plan to help. And Augie, I'm so sorry this has come up again. I thought we had finally gotten past all this. And that we might be able to get you back home sometime."

"I know, I really do miss everyone, especially Mom and Dad. Please let them know that I think about them every day. That I'm fine and in good health. But you can't tell them about this latest problem. I don't want them to worry even more about me."

"Of course, Augie. I'll keep this under my hat. Hopefully, it wasn't the mob guys. Anyway, let me check around. You can give me a call tomorrow about this same time, and I might have something for you. Take care and stay safe," he added, and he then hung up the phone.

Once again, my trouble, like some virulent disease, was being transmitted to the people closest to me. Unfortunately, this disease can be fatal. Five people had died – three of my fellow Army buddies in Vietnam, and two other friends who tried to help me when I was hiding from the mob seven years ago. I hope my warning call to Uncle Sal would prove to be a false alarm, but sadly I don't think that's the case. He needs to be prepared, God forbid, for what might be coming.

CHAPTER 7
LOU

I left the telephone booth and walked quickly back to the Del Capitan and to my dingy room. I lay on my bed and tried to think of my options. I had warned Uncle Sal and now he would alert the family back in Jeweltown about this worrisome development. But there was one more individual who needed to know what had happened overnight. Because that person, Louise Erickson, who I thought had left my life forever had returned. Lou and I had reconnected!

It happened just a couple of weeks ago, and it was true serendipity that we met; a one-in-a million coincidence that brought us back together. And for the past two weeks, I had been the happiest man on earth. But now I would need to call Lou with the bad news that I had been discovered. I would have to warn her that her life was likely in danger once more.

While I always cherished memories of our brief time together, I had come to the sad conclusion that I had lost Lou after our short time together in 1970. I had always hoped that we would be able to reunite after the events that caused Lou to end our relationship. I thought time would heal the emotional and psychological wounds she suffered because of me. I called her several times in the months after our breakup, but she refused to speak with me. I also wrote her a letter apologizing for the awful experiences she endured, and I begged her to give me a chance to make things right. To no avail. Then, when I moved out to California, I lost all hope that we would ever get back together. For the last several years, I had moved on from thoughts of ever reconciling with Lou. Then just two weeks ago, I walked into the ballroom of the Fairmont Hotel in San Francisco and there she was!

I was at the Fairmont to cover an awards ceremony honoring a group of young winemakers whose wines had achieved national acclaim. One of the honorees was Louise Erickson who was there to receive an award for her 1973 Rattlesnake Ridge Sangiovese. Lou was looking as lovely and radiant as ever, and I could not take my eyes off her. I remembered watching Lou plant the vines that produced her award-winning wine. That was years ago on a mountain plateau in northeastern West Virginia.

And now, almost miraculously, she appeared. I stood to the side and rear of the stage and watched while Lou was handed a gold medal for her wine. I waited there until the ceremony was concluded and the group had finished posing for photos. When she began to walk down the steps from the stage, I stepped in front of her. I could feel my heart beating in my chest.

"Hello Lou. Remember me?"

Lou, who was always quick on the uptake and about as composed a human as I've ever known, was momentarily speechless. Then she recovered and immediately flashed me her slightly crooked smile, and looked up at me with her mesmerizing green eyes.

"Augie, my goodness, what in the world are you doing out here?" Then her smile faded, and her countenance changed. She seemed almost sad.

"I'm so sorry, Augie. I know I treated you terribly all those years ago. I wanted to talk to you about why I couldn't see you anymore. Honestly, it's haunted me all these years. I should have contacted you, but I just couldn't get past what we all went through back in 1970…"

I interrupted her. "Lou, I didn't mean to startle you. I really didn't know you would be here. And, by the way, congratulations on the award for your wine. I remember watching you plant those vines. I'm here officially, really. I report on wine for the Chronicle now and I was assigned to cover this event."

Lou seemed momentarily speechless so I continued. "And, Lou, you don't owe me an apology for what happened. I'm the one to blame. I should never have let them take you. After all that happened, and after you went home to D.C., I tried to call and apologize. I even wrote you a long letter. I hoped that we could resolve our issues and get back together. But don't worry, I know you've moved on. And I have too," I said, knowing now that I really hadn't.

"No Augie. I should have had the courage to face you. To tell you why I felt the way I did after I was kidnapped. I just couldn't get past the memories of what happened to me." Lou's voice was breaking and she struggled to remain composed.

"I think part of the reason I didn't want to see you was because I was afraid. Afraid that I would want us to get back together. I'll always cherish the times we had together. But I thought – even though I still cared for you deeply – that my ordeal would eventually drive a wedge between us. And Augie, please believe me when I say that I don't blame you for what happened. I'm just sorry things ended the way they did."

I needed to change the subject. I didn't ever want to relive those awful moments when I thought Lou would be killed by the mob, or later, after she had been rescued, when she abandoned me. I was just happy that she was able to survive. At least, I would always be grateful for that small consolation. But I was convinced that, after her abduction, we would never be able to repair the damage to our relationship.

"Tell me about this sangiovese." I pulled out my reporter's notebook and pen from my coat jacket.

I interviewed Lou for about ten minutes, and then I handed her my business card. She stared at it for several seconds, and then she looked up at me. There were tears in her eyes. "Johnny Harman. You've taken Hambone's name, Augie," she said. Her voice was now husky with emotion. "I can't imagine the pain you've had to endure. You've lost so many friends... in the war... and after. I feel really selfish for..."

I held up both my hands to get her to stop speaking. "Please Lou, you don't have anything to feel selfish about. I put you in that terrible situation. When those mob guys had you, I was completely out of my mind with fear that I would never see you again. And I was so thankful and relieved when we got you back that I didn't even consider how your experience might affect us. I was the one who was being selfish. It took me a while, but I finally realized that our relationship could not survive after what you went through. How could it?" I asked.

Lou did not respond right away. I couldn't judge the expression on her face, but she looked serious, and she was staring intensely at me. When she spoke, it was softly in a tentative, almost apologetic, tone.

"Augie, I really don't have any right to ask this question, but I wonder if you are in a relationship right now?"

I was shocked by her question and momentarily unable to respond. Then I said, "Lou, I've dated around over the years, but I've never been involved with anyone for any length of time."

She seemed relieved. "I have one more question. Would you be willing to meet again? I mean, later this afternoon here in the hotel. There's a seating area in the foyer right off the bar, and we could meet there. But I need some time alone to sort out a couple of things first."

"Sure. I'll come by later. After I file my story. Will 3 o'clock work for you?" I wasn't sure what Lou wanted to talk about, and I hoped she didn't feel the need to apologize further for what happened to us.

"I'll see you then," she said and quickly walked away.

I went back to the office and began to write my story, but I had difficulty concentrating. I couldn't help but wonder what Lou needed to speak with me about. It was painful to be in her presence and know I could never really be with her again. I couldn't imagine how anything positive might result from continuing to engage in this hurtful – at least for me – postmortem of our relationship. I finally finished my story, filed it with the copy editor and then left for the Fairmont Hotel.

I got to the hotel a little after three and spotted Lou sitting in a mission-style armchair in an alcove of the foyer. I sat in a chair directly across from her and waited anxiously for her to explain why she wanted to see me again.

Lou is a very attractive woman with dark, almost raven black hair. She has an oval face, a milky white complexion with full lips and a slightly crooked, almost aquiline, nose. She also has long legs and an athletic body, but it's her incredibly deep, liquid green eyes that have always dazzled me. It's hard for me to look at her and pretend that I'm not affected by her appearance, and by memories of our passionate times together. I was trying my best to look unaffected.

She smiled at me and said, "Thanks for coming, Augie. I know I seemed mysterious about wanting to speak with you again, but I really needed a couple of hours to sort through a few things."

"Lou, you're certainly not imposing on my time. But I am curious about why you wanted to meet."

"Okay here goes," she said and leaned forward toward me. "Seeing you again after all these years has been quite a shock – a pleasant one, but disconcerting too. I've been trying to forget you now for seven years. I've even dated other men to see if that might help me to forget about our time together. But that didn't work. Still, I've pretty much succeeded in putting you out of my life. And now, after all these years, and... well... as soon as I saw you this morning, I haven't been able to stop thinking about us," Lou paused and took a deep breath.

I was startled. I couldn't believe my ears. Was this a dream?

Lou continued, "I thought about those few, sweet, short months. Especially those happy times we spent together in Canaan Valley. I guess this might sound silly, but it's almost like we were fated to meet again sometime, somewhere. I've been repressing thoughts of reconnecting with you for the reasons I mentioned earlier. But seeing you today has made me realize that I'm not being honest with myself. That I really do miss you and want to try again. And I hope I'm not presuming here, but I feel you may still have feelings for me too," Lou said.

It was as if I had been struck by lightning! I just looked at Lou and then I stood up. I took her hand as she stood, and we embraced for several seconds. When we parted, I finally found my voice.

"I had given up all hope of ever having you back in my life. I tried to pretend that I was over you. But that was a lie. Because deep down, I never stopped thinking about you. Of course, I still have feelings for you."

Lou looked at me with that crooked, half smile. "Now, don't get all mushy on me. That would be totally out of character."

"Mushy, not me," I replied. "Heck, I wrote the playbook on hardcore, no nonsense-type affection. I am a John Wayne kind of guy," I said and chuckled.

Lou immediately fired right back, "No Augie, you're no John Wayne. You're more like Moe, Larry or Curly." We both laughed at that and embraced again.

Lou and I had not spoken or seen each other for nearly seven years, yet it was like we had never been apart. We spent the rest of the afternoon at the Fairmont catching up. After about two hours, we had exhausted all the peripheral details regarding our lives over the past seven years. I felt like it was time for us to discuss some practical issues – like how we could successfully reboot what would now be a bi-coastal relationship.

"It's hard to believe that after all these years we've found each other again," I said. "But things are going to be a little complicated. You know, with me being out here on the west coast and you back east. We probably ought to talk about that,"

She nodded. "I agree, but I'm not concerned about the distance between us, or even the amount of time we can spend together. It seems obvious that our feelings for each other are as strong as ever. You're right, though, we'll need to work on the logistics, but I'm sure we can make this work." Lou then reached over and squeezed my hand.

I've always been amazed at Lou's ability to cut through the clutter and get to the heart of the matter. "I agree. We'll figure a way to work things out. In the meantime, we're in one of the greatest cities on earth with some of the best restaurants and wine lists anywhere. What do you say we continue this discussion over dinner?"

We got a cab to one of my favorite spots. Tadich Grill is the oldest restaurant in San Francisco and one that specializes in fresh seafood. It also has an extensive international wine list. We got to the restaurant and sat at the bar while we waited for a table to open. It was wonderful having dinner again with Lou. She's the most knowledgeable person I know when it comes to selecting the right wine to pair with just about anything on a menu. While we waited, we ordered a dozen local Tomales Bay oysters on the half shell, and Lou selected a Muscadet to pair with them. As the bartender poured our wine, Lou explained that Muscadet is made from Melon de Bourgogne, an obscure grape grown in the Loire Valley of France. The wine was the perfect match for the oysters. Later for dinner, Lou selected steamed Dungeness crab and I chose sauteed abalone. Since both our entrées were drizzled with drawn butter, Lou suggested we pair them with a rich, full-bodied white wine. One of my favorite wineries is Chateau Montelena near Calistoga in the Napa Valley. I selected the 1973 Montelena Chardonnay, which had recently earned international acclaim. It was a delicious accompaniment to our seafood dishes, and I was delighted that Lou approved of my selection. Later, we concluded dinner with cups of strong, black coffee and glasses of Dow 20-year-old Tawny Port.

We left the restaurant, and I hailed a cab for the short ride to Nob Hill and the Fairmont where Lou would be staying for the night. When we arrived at the hotel, I wasn't sure what would happen next. We stood for a moment in the foyer, then, without a word, Lou extended her hand to me, and we started walking to the elevator. We exited the lift on the seventh floor and walked to Lou's room. When we entered, Lou turned to me, and we kissed long and passionately. Then silently, but hurriedly, we began to undress each other as we moved toward the bed. Lou lightly nudged me and I fell gently back onto the coverlet and we made love. It was the first time we had been together for more than seven years. So, we spent the rest of the night making love.

When I drove Lou to the airport the next day, we made plans to get together sometime in the next few weeks back at her cabin in Canaan Valley. On the ride back from the airport, I smiled to myself and thought that, aside from the moment we were able to secure Lou's release from her kidnappers back in 1970, this was the happiest day of my life.

CHAPTER 8
FATE IS A FICKLE MISTRESS

Just two weeks ago in San Francisco my world seemed full of possibilities, but things had changed drastically. I had just gotten off the phone with Uncle Sal, and I was dreading the call to Lou. It was 6:30 a.m. on the West Coast, and I hoped to catch Lou before she left her apartment. After the third ring, she answered.

I tried to think of a way to break the news softly. I couldn't.

"Lou, I hate to tell you this, but I'm pretty sure those mob guys have found me here in San Francisco. I don't know how. But I'm almost positive it's them. And I don't know if they have any idea where you live, but you really need to leave town for a few days. Away from D.C. I'm sorry to lay this on you so suddenly, but I'm worried," I said, and expected an emotional response from her.

Lou didn't immediately reply. When she did, her voice sounded sad. "Are you sure it's them, Augie? I mean, after all these years how could they have found you?"

I quickly explained the events of the evening before to Lou, and I hoped she would take my warning seriously. "Again, I don't have any idea how they found me, but I'm almost certain it's the thugs from the same mob who were after me back in 1970. Even though I can't identify the guy who attacked me, I'm positive I recognized their truck. The one they tried to put me in. I spotted the same type of vehicle parked near my apartment last night. They were most likely waiting for me there. Lou, you need to take this seriously and get away for a while," I said, trying to keep my voice steady without audibly expressing the panic and fear I felt.

"Okay. I don't think they would know about my place in Canaan Valley. I can go there for a while, but I can't just disappear. I've got to work in my winery and deal with this year's vintage now," she said, sounding more frustrated than fearful. "And how will I know when it's safe to go back to my apartment?"

The truth is I didn't have any hard and fast answers. "Look, I'll know more about the situation tomorrow. Uncle Sal is checking with Jimmie Ponza. He's the guy who dealt with the mob for my family before, and we trust him. He's going to find out what's going on. If you give me the phone number at the cabin, I'll call you sometime tomorrow. But in the meantime, please Lou, you have to leave for Canaan now."

Lou gave me the phone number. "Alright Augie. I'll drive over to the cabin this morning. I do need to stop at my apartment near the vineyard and get a few work things to take with me to Canaan. But be sure and call me as soon as you have an update."

Then Lou quietly added, "I can't believe this is happening again, Augie. It's like a déjà vu nightmare."

"Lou, let's not let this issue sidetrack us again. Let's stick together and work our way through it," I pleaded with her.

"Augie, I hope we can. I really do," she said and then hung up.

I returned to the Del Capitan and tried to plan my day. I would have to stay in hiding, but I would also need to get on the move very soon. At around 8 a.m., I phoned my boss – the Lifestyles Editor at the Chronicle – and asked him to let me to use my accrued vacation time immediately. I explained there was a family emergency, and I had to get back to West Virginia right away. I also asked him if I could come by and pick up my paycheck.

It was three days until payday, but I told my boss I needed the money now for the trip. I had hidden about two thousand dollars in cash at my friend Della Mae's place in Oakland, but I would need every extra dollar I could come up with if I had to go into hiding. My editor wasn't happy, but he agreed to both requests.But he told me that I would need to wait until tomorrow to pick up my paycheck. I was forced to extend my stay at the Del Capitan for another day. The only time I left the room was to sneak out after dark and get take-out at a Mexican restaurant. Now I sit in this dingy and depressing room eating luke-warm tacos and refried beans. I can't help but contrast this low-rent meal with the excellent dinner Lou and I shared a couple of weeks ago just a few miles from where I'm sitting right now. I wonder if I'll ever live long enough to enjoy another meal with her.

Lou, though, is so much more than just my lover. She opened my mind to another part of my life that I didn't realize was important to me: the world of wine. I had grown up in an Italian American family where wine was an important part of everyday life. Like bread, it was on the table daily at lunch and dinner. I was encouraged to sip it during our large family dinners and at holiday celebrations, but I didn't like it at all. Then I met Lou, and she opened my eyes – and palate – to the wonders of wine, and she exposed me to the incredible variety of wines produced around the world.

After we parted, my interest in, and fondness for wine grew and eventually led to my job at Starling Vineyards. There, I combined my winery work experience with my educational training as a writer which eventually led to my job with the Chronicle.

And working in the vineyards and the cellars at Starling also helped resurrect vivid memories of my Grandpa Salvatore and my uncles making wine back in Riverview. It was a tradition as strong as fealty to the church and loyalty to our family that drew my male relatives together each fall to crush, ferment, and press California grapes into dark and powerful red wine.

Some people in our neighborhood referred to the product of our labor as "Dago Red."

CHAPTER 9
DAGO RED

As a child, I was terrified by one wine-related chore that the children in the Costanza clan were required to perform at our frequent and large family dinners. Grandpa Salvatore would randomly call upon one of the twenty or so first cousins in our family – which included me – to go to the cellar and fill a jug with red wine from one of his barrels. Back in those days, people whose names contained more consonants than vowels referred, pejoratively, to wine made by Italian immigrants as "Dago Red." I vividly remember one time when it was my turn to fetch the dinner wine at my grandparents' home. At these dinner gatherings, my parents, aunts and uncles would be seated around a large dinner table in the kitchen while the kids were seated at small card tables set up in the next room.

On this particular day, Grandpa appeared in the doorway of the room where we sat noisily chatting. He was carrying an empty gallon jug. Suddenly, the room became so quiet that, as my Uncle Dante would say, "you could hear a fly fart." Grandpa then pointed to me, and in his booming voice declared: "Augustino, it's your turn to get the vino."

I just about slid under the card table, and I'm sure my face was as white as the flour Grandpa used to make bread at his bakery. I got up slowly and, when I got to Grandpa, he handed me the jug and kissed me lightly on the top of my head. I walked through the kitchen where the adults in my family were happily chattering, and I glanced over to my mother who nodded and smiled at me. When I reached the door to the cellar, I paused for a moment, took a deep breath, opened the door and descended into the dungeon-like chamber. As I walked down the tile steps into the dark, dank and musty basement, I imagined the place full of creepy, crawling spiders, giant, yellow-fanged rodents, and slithering snakes. It was easy to have these disquieting thoughts because the basement was always dimly lit, and because I had witnessed my grandpa and uncles butcher a panoply of mammals there. On those days, the cellar served as the family abattoir where a menagerie of pigs, goats and rabbits met their fate, and became the sausages, chops and roasts that graced the Costanza dinner table. So, these were the nightmare-like thoughts that raced through my pre-adolescent mind as I opened the heavy wooden door to Grandpa's wine cellar.

As I entered the dark, earthen-walled chamber where Grandpa kept his barrels of wine, I waited for several seconds until my eyes adjusted to the darkness. Then I began to creep slowly toward where I knew a strand of string hung that was attached to a single light bulb. I put the gallon jug on the floor and moved a small wooden stool under the hanging string. To reach the bulb, I carefully climbed onto the stool, reached up and pulled the string. Immediately, the swinging bulb cast ghostly apparitions onto the dirt walls. I quickly jumped off the stool, grabbed the container from the floor, positioned it directly under the spigot on the barrel and filled the glass jug to the top. Not bothering to turn off the light, I left the wine cellar and rushed as fast as I could through the basement and up the stairs into the kitchen where Grandpa sat at the head of the dinner table. He stood up, smiled and took the jug from me. He poured the liquid into his small jelly jar-like glass, and passed the jug to one of my uncles who then filled his, and handed it on to the next person. When the jug had been passed to everyone at the table, Grandpa raised his glass to the family, and loudly proclaimed, "Salute." He took a big sip, and then immediately turned his head and spit a steam of crimson liquid across the room that splashed, amazingly, right into the center of the kitchen sink.

Grandpa looked menacingly down at me and grumbled, "Augustino, coglione! This is no vino. You bring me aceto."

The dinner table exploded in laughter, but I didn't understand what had just happened. Then my Uncle Giorgio translated Grandpa's words for me so the whole table could hear. "Augie, Grandpa said, 'you dickhead, you brought vinegar not wine.'"

That embarrassing experience only deepened my distaste for the fruit of the vine. It wasn't until a full decade later that my opinion changed, and that was when Lou introduced my mind and palate to the incredible world of wine. She exposed me to wines that not only pleased my amateur taste buds, but also opened my eyes to the pleasure of pairing wine with complementary food. Now I understand why my family insisted on having a jug of wine on the table at lunch and dinner. It always sat next to a loaf of bread that had been baked right across the street at Grandpa's Chestnut Bakery. And that big jug of Dago Red, like the bread it accompanied on the table, was made for more than just daily sustenance. It was part of my family's culture and tradition. For generations before arriving in America, the Costanza family had made wine at home every year and, when Grandpa came to this country in the late nineteenth century, he brought that winemaking tradition with him.

Like so many of his neighbors in the Calabrian hill town of San Giovanni in Fiore, Grandpa made his way to northern West Virginia to work in the coal mines. He and Grandma lived in a tiny house the mining company rented to them in the coal camp along with other laborers. Most of their neighbors were southern or eastern European immigrants, or were US citizens who were indigent minorities. Grandpa toiled for a pittance digging coal by hand in those dangerous and dirty mines, and he saved most of his meager earnings; however, each year he put aside enough of his wages to join with others of Italian descent to purchase California grapes and make homemade wine. In that way, he was able to preserve one of the most important and cherished Italian traditions, and also ensure that there would always be wine on the table to accompany the humble meals they consumed in the squalor of the coal camp. When Grandpa left the mines to build his bakery and start a new life in Riverview, he continued making wine, and he was joined in that labor of love by his sons and his grandchildren, including me. I had almost forgotten about my participation in our family's winemaking endeavors until Lou piqued my interest in wine. Then I thought back to those times decades ago in Riverview.

I recall my uncles and my older cousins gathering every fall in the side yard of Grandpa's home where they would help him crush more than a ton of grapes. The grapes came from vineyards in the vast Central Valley of California where they had been picked by Mexican day laborers and then transported by train across the country. I remember climbing into the cargo bed of an old Chevrolet pickup truck with a few of my cousins for the trip to the train depot in Jeweltown. Other members of the Costanza clan drove their own trucks and met us at the train station where we all helped unload a boxcar full of grapes into the family vehicles. The grapes were packed in thirty-six-pound wooden boxes called lugs, which we carried to the trucks. When the trucks were loaded with grape lugs, the process was reversed once we got to Grandpa's house. There, we moved the precious cargo to the side yard where the winemaking process would begin.

It was a joyous occasion for Grandpa and my uncles, and, indeed, the whole family. I remember there were two picnic tables in the yard next to the ancient wooden grape crusher. On the table were platters loaded with bowls of fried peppers in tomato sauce; loaves of hard crust bread; hunks of parmesan, provolone and dried ricotta salata cheese; rings of Italian sausage; and sliced soppressata, pepperoni, capocollo, salame piccante, prosciutto and mortadella. All this was washed down with jugs of homemade wine, along with cold bottles of beer and soft drinks. The drinks were snatched from steel wash tubs filled with ice. This culinary bounty was waiting for us when we unloaded and stacked the lugs of grapes next to Grandpa's ancient hand-crank crusher. But before the first lug was poured into the crusher, there were two other traditions that had to be observed.

First, Father Rocco Speralunga, the parish priest at Holy Trinity Catholic Church, would appear in the yard, and the family members gathered there would become silent. Attired in his black cassock, he would raise his right hand and bless the grapes. Then he would pick up a small vial of holy water and sprinkle the first lug of grapes about to be crushed. Next, Grandpa would point to a certain person among us who was not a member of the family and beckon to her: "Rosalina, vieni qui, you come now."

Rosalina Carmaletti, like the women hired to be mourners at funerals, provided a service deemed necessary before winemaking in our family could commence. Rosalina, who was thought to be a gypsy, was hired to perform the ritual *pigiatura* or stomping of the grapes. While the women chosen to do the initial stomping were traditionally required to be maidens, adjustments had to be made in order to begin the winemaking process when the ripe grapes arrived from California. And anyway, as my Uncle Dante often exclaimed, "the grapes can't wait for maidens, or they would turn to raisins before they ever got crushed." Rosalina was neither young nor a maiden, but she was always ready, willing and able to assume the role of Vestal Virgin if called upon, and if she was compensated for her time.

On this particular occasion, Rosalina walked up to where Grandpa stood next to a large, square wooden box filled with grapes. She was attired in an ankle length, colorful, flower-patterned dress, and wore a purple headscarf, silver necklaces and copper bracelets on each wrist. She smiled seductively at Grandpa, flashing two gold-capped front teeth, and then she said with unbridled enthusiasm, "*Salvatore, che muscoli, bell'uomo!*"

All the adults howled in laughter, but Grandpa's face turned beet red, and he looked sheepishly at Grandma. She was not smiling. I looked up at Uncle Giorgio who was standing next to me and asked. "What did she say to Grandpa?"

My uncle looked down at me and explained. "Augie, Rosalina said, 'Salvatore, what muscles! You handsome man.'"

Rosalina ignored the laughter, removed her leather peasant sandals and stepped into the box. She put her hands on her hips and began dancing the tarantella, and delicately stomping the grapes with her bare feet. Rosalina did her grape stomping tarantella for a couple of minutes and then, as was the tradition, she invited the kids in the family to join her. I was too shy to participate, but my cousin Benito – who most of my aunts and uncles referred to as the family 'juvenile delinquent' – was the first to jump right in without taking his shoes off. He began frenetically stomping and splashing grapes and purple juice up onto Rosalina's dress. Without hesitation, the gypsy woman grabbed Benito by both ears and tossed him out of the box and into the yard. Everyone howled again, and even Grandpa smiled.

Then it was time for my uncles and Grandpa to get to work. Using a hand crank, they would grind the grapes which fell from the crusher into one of Grandpa's old wine barrels, the top of which had been sawed off. Once the barrel was full, my uncles would use buckets to carry the grapes and juice into the basement where it would be dumped into other large, open topped barrels for fermentation. This activity continued until all the grapes were crushed and placed in fermenting barrels. The fermentation would usually last for about ten days, and then the crushed grapes and new wine would be taken from the fermenters in buckets, and out into the yard where a large basket press had been set up. The new wine and grapes would be poured into the basket press where the 'free run' new wine would again be carried in buckets back into the cellar, where it was poured into Grandpa's barrels for aging. When the basket press was full of grape skins, that solid matter would be pressed to get even more wine. All that newly pressed wine would rest in Grandpa's cellar for a year, and then it would be bottled right before it was time to start the winemaking process all over again.

When I got the job at Starling Vineyards a few years back, I worked with folks who applied the latest viticultural practices to grow the grapes in the vineyard, and then they used state-of-the-art equipment to make the wine in their cellars; but the basic process by which grapes become wine hasn't changed for millennia, and the times I spent helping Grandpa and my uncles make Dago Red are precious memories that hold a lot more meaning to me now than I could ever have imagined.

CHAPTER 10
DELLA MAE

Lou was not the first woman to command my attention and affection. That girl (and now woman) is Della Mae Smith, and she was my first love. I had fallen for her in high school, but unfortunately that romantic relationship, like the one I had with Lou, ended abruptly too. I eventually attributed my break-up with Della Mae to teenage immaturity and a kind of coming-of-age life lesson. However, both experiences left me feeling jilted and depressed, and wondering what defect in my emotional or psychological makeup caused the only two women I had ever been in love with to suddenly reject me. The old saying 'time heals all wounds' certainly seems to apply to my present situation with both women – which is as good as I could ever have expected. My romantic reconnection with Lou is nothing short of a miracle and my renewed relationship with Della Mae, though strictly platonic, is one of great warmth and deep affection.

Della Mae and I both grew up in Jeweltown. Since many public schools south of the Mason-Dixon Line were segregated back then, Della Mae, who is Black, attendedBooker T. Washington High School. I attended a Catholic school across town, St. Alphonse's. While we were dating, few of our friends and none of our relatives knew that we were seeing each other. However, the decision to keep our romance secret rested solely with Della Mae. Conversely, I was completely, and naively, unconcerned with what other people might think of our relationship.

I fell hard for Della Mae. However, when our interpersonal communications began to turn more physical, and eventually led to our making love, Della Mae quickly ended it. Later, she went off to Marshall College in Huntington, West Virginia on a full academic scholarship, and she got involved in the Civil Rights Movement there. She was even arrested once when she joined some folks who staged a sit-in at a cafeteria in Huntington that refused to serve colored people.

When she earned her B.S. Degree from Marshall, she accepted a scholarship to Harvard where she attended and graduated from law school. With her law degree, she moved out to Oakland, California, and for several years worked as an attorney for the Legal Aid Society. Later, she opened a small law office and represented mostly indigent and under-served clients who were mainly Black, Hispanic or poor white working-class folks. Also among her clients were people who existed on the fringes of society, and sometimes outside the law, such as gang members and drug offenders.

When I came out to California, I made it a point to look up my old high school flame. It was early 1972 when we finally got together. I felt I needed to tell Della Mae about why I was really out in California, including why I was now calling myself Johnny Harman. She needed to know the whole story and then decide if establishing any type of relationship with me was prudent. I never expected her to have any feelings for me after our ill-fated high school romance. I just assumed she would characterize our short time together as puppy love. The last thing I ever wanted was to put Della Mae in harm's way, and so she had to know about my past problems, and the potential jeopardy that might put her in. After I told her about all this, she looked at me for several seconds before responding.

"Augie… I mean I guess I'll need to call you Johnny… I appreciate your concern for my well-being. And I'm so sorry for what you've been through. But yes, I still want to be friends. Even if I have to call you by a different name," she said and smiled.

I was relieved, and so we renewed our relationship, but this time as friends. Since that time, we've spent many hours together catching up on our hometown and on our mutual friends. We saw each other regularly, attending concerts or dining together. We also spoke by phone once or twice a month. One evening, a few months later, after we had returned from a Carlos Santana concert at the Berkeley Community Theater, Della took my hand and looked into my eyes.

"Augie," she said quietly, "we need to talk."

I could tell by her tone that this was going to be a difficult conversation. "Sure. What's up?"

"Augie, do you remember back when we were seeing each other? I mean, the circumstances of how we would meet and how we kept things under wraps?"

"Of course, I do. I wasn't the one who wanted to keep things quiet, though. Hell, I would have let the whole world know we were dating. But I could tell that's not something you wanted anyone to know. And when you broke up with me, I figured you were afraid things were getting out of hand. You know, with the physical relationship we had moved to," I said.

"Well, you're right about that. But as much as I hoped we could continue dating, and even let the relationship grow, I didn't really think we had much of a future together. I mean, long-term. Particularly, given the times we were living in, and the obvious fact that you're white and I'm Black. As much as I hoped that we could navigate those waters, I didn't have the courage to go public with things. I was terrified, not only with how your folks might react, but also how my own family would feel. And we were living south of the Mason-Dixon line where the worst of the racial animus was taking place. I'll admit it now – I was a coward. I was afraid to let our family and friends know about us. I didn't think we could survive the scrutiny. Anyway, that's why I stopped seeing you. And when we made love that time… well… that moved things to a whole different level. Sure, I was concerned about getting pregnant, but I was also afraid we were approaching the point of no return. But the lovemaking? I had never experienced anything as wonderful, and I was in love with you then."

I was floored! I suspected that Della Mae was fearful of the consequences of our relationship going public, but I thought it was all on me. That she didn't care for me. That maybe when we made love that one and only time, I didn't please her. That I was awkward and clumsy and that she was disgusted with me. I never suspected that she really cared that deeply for me.

"Della, I didn't know what to think when you broke things off. I was hurt and I was embarrassed. And I was convinced that I had violated you. That you felt I had gone too far. I tried to call and apologize, but you wouldn't let me. I thought I would never see you again. And now I can sense that you're about to cut me loose again."

"Oh Augie. No, I don't want to end our friendship. But I need to tell you something. I've been secretly dating a client. I know… I know. That's at least an ethical violation. But it happened. I represent people who are on the margins of society. Like Black activists and homosexuals. You know, people who are different and who believe that some laws in this country discriminate against them. I suppose you've heard of the Black Panthers. And I suspect you probably believe their version of Civil Rights activism is extreme and violent. Sometimes they can be, and that's unfortunate, but many times people in their organization are judged guilty by association."

I interrupted her. "Della, you don't need to tell me all this. And I'm not here to judge you. I…"

Della Mae interrupted me. "Augie, please. Let me finish. I need to tell you what's going on. We're friends and I want you to know about this. Please, hear me out."

I nodded and she continued.

"Anyway, this guy – I'll just call him Larry – he's a member of a gang. He was referred to me by a friend of mine. It turns out, Larry was involved in a bank hold-up. He was driving the getaway car for the guy robbing the bank. A bank security guard was shot after he pulled a gun on the robber – my client's partner – and wounded him. The robber returned fire and killed the guard. This robber was seriously injured and arrested at the scene. Larry got away, but his partner, in a plea deal, identified Larry as the driver. Larry is on the run. I met him secretly about a year ago to try and give him legal advice. Since that time, our relationship turned personal. I never wanted this to happen, but it did. Larry is still on the run, and I see him very rarely, but we've become intimate."

I just shook my head. "Della, you really need to be careful. You're risking your law license. And if you're discovered, you might be arrested."

"Believe me I know. But the reason I'm telling you this is that when you showed up a couple of months ago, you seemed troubled. And from what little you've told me about your Vietnam experience… and then what happened to you and your family when you got home… I realized that I still have feelings for you. But it's not fair to you – or to Larry – to allow our friendship to become anything more. That's why I'm telling you this. And I hope you'll understand that we can only be friends."

I'll admit, I was disappointed when Della Mae told me all this a few years back, but I understand and I respect her point of view. We continue to get together several times each year, and we speak on the phone regularly. I've never asked about Larry, and she hasn't indicated that there is any change in their relationship. So, I go with the flow. I really do cherish our friendship and, now that Lou is back in my life, the lines separating us are even more clearly defined. I could have easily fallen back in love with Della Mae when I first arrived in California, but she, wisely, wouldn't let me.

Della Mae Smith and I have remained close friends. She has allowed me to store my getaway stash at her place in Oakland. Since the mob guys have found me, I'll need to get up to Della Mae's place soon, get my stuff and then figure out what to do next. Maybe Uncle Sal will have some ideas. I sure don't.

CHAPTER 11
MURDER AT THE BART

I had spent a long, boring day, and a restless night at my fleabag hotel, but now I would need to move. I knew I would be taking a chance by going to the newspaper office today, but I really needed that paycheck. I checked out of the Del Capitan around 10 a.m. I would have to be careful, and I would try to disguise my appearance. I went to a Salvation Army clothing store in the neighborhood and paid five dollars for an old gray raincoat, and a floppy green Boonie hat like the ones we wore in Vietnam. Then I walked to my bank, and withdrew all the cash from my checking and savings accounts, which totaled just about $1800. I took a cab to about a quarter mile from the Chronicle building. My plan was to get my check and then take the Bay Area Rapid Transit (BART) train to Oakland and Della Mae's apartment where I would retrieve my get-away stash.

I got out of the cab, buttoned up my raincoat and pulled my Boonie hat down over my face. Fortunately, the day was overcast and cool so my attire was appropriate and would not attract any undue attention. Even though I would not be able to identify my attackers from the night before, I spent the next thirty minutes walking all around the Chronicle building observing passing vehicles and those parked near the place. I was on the lookout for a light-colored van or panel truck parked somewhere in the general vicinity. As I made my way circuitously toward the entrance of the building, I stopped frequently along the way, peering into businesses as if I was shopping, but using the reflections in the windows to search for any sign of someone following me. When I finally reached the Chronicle, I pushed through the double glass entry doors and quickly walked into the building. So far, so good, I thought.

* * *

Cheech and Tubby were exhausted. They had spent the last day trying to locate Cumpton, but he hadn't shown up at either his job location or his apartment. This morning, they returned to the area near the San Francisco Chronicle building hoping to spot the man. They had old black and white photos of him. Cheech and Tubby each held a photo while they watched the area for their target. Cheech was on one corner of the newspaper building and Tubby was situated on the other. They watched the entrance for more than an hour, but Cumpton never showed up. They were prepared to wait all day if necessary because this was their only real hope of locating the guy.

Cheech knew they would be in deep trouble with Carmine if they went back home without getting the job done. On the other hand, there were only two of them and this was a very large city that neither of them had visited before. Just then, Cheech looked over to where Tubby was standing and saw his partner waving one of his arms wildly. Tubby was pointing with the other arm to a man who was quickly walking down the sidewalk in front of the newspaper building. The man was wearing a trench coat and had a wide brimmed, green hat pulled way down, partially obscuring his face. Tubby immediately started following him until the man entered the building.

Cheech joined Tubby and spoke quietly, "You sure that's him?

"Yeah. That's the guy. He walked right past me. I didn't try to do nothin' either, Cheech. Just like you said. What are we gonna do now?"

"Okay listen up. I didn't see no back way out of this building. That means he's gotta come out the same door he went in. When he does, we'll follow him. He don't know what we look like and if we're real careful he won't make us. I'll look for a spot where there's not a lot of people around. That's where I'll walk up to him from behind and put a gun in his ribs. Then you'll go back, get the truck and pick us up. Once we get this asshole in the truck and tied up, I'll figure a way to waste him. And make it look like he had an accident."

* * *

I spent a few minutes in my boss' office when I picked up my check. I thanked him for being understanding and told him the reason I needed to take time off was that my grandmother was ill. My boss didn't seem to suspect anything out of the ordinary. He asked me to call him in a few days to let him know when I would be coming back. But I suspected that I would not be returning – ever.

Before I left the building, I paused at the double glass doors for a few seconds before going out onto Mission Street. It was late morning, and the sidewalks were full of shoppers and office workers. I pulled my hat a little lower and walked around the corner to 5th Street. My plan was to make my way up 5th to the Powell Street BART station where I would take the train to Oakland and Della Mae's apartment. Then I would call Uncle Sal to see if he had been able to find out anything. I'm certain he will confirm my worst fear – that I had been discovered by La Famiglia Vagabonda. I didn't know what I would do with that information or where I might go, but I hoped my uncle might have some ideas. As Lou had said earlier, this is like a 'déjà vu nightmare.'

* * *

Cheech and Tubby allowed Cumpton to get about a half block ahead of them before they began to follow him. Cheech suspected right away that it would be nearly impossible to find a spot along the sidewalk where they could confront Cumpton without attracting attention. There were just too many people. Where was this guy going in such a hurry, Cheech wondered? Then he saw a sign indicating in big letters that the Powell Street BART station was a quarter mile up ahead. That had to be where the guy was going, he thought.

"Hey Tubby. I think Cumpton is headed to the subway station up there," Cheech said, and pointed up 5th Street. "I got an idea. Let's move a little faster. Once he goes down the steps to the subway, it's going to get really crowded. That'll make it easy for us to work our way up to him... without him noticing. When we see the train coming, we can shove the guy on the tracks right before it gets to where he is. People will think it was an accident."

Tubby was not usually a critical thinker, but he did ask his partner a practical question. "What if he ain't standing next to the tracks? Can we just shove the folks behind him? You know, so they push him and anyone in front of him on the tracks too?" Tubby was smiling gleefully at the prospect of causing maximum pain and suffering.

Cheech shook his head. "No, goddammit! Here's what we'll do. If there's folks ahead of him, I'll get 'em out of the way and make sure he gets to the front of the line. Then I'll clear a spot for you right next to him. That way, you can give him a shove when the time comes. But it can't look like you pushed him. It has to seem like Cumpton tripped or something. Maybe you can kind of turn sideways and look up the track. You know, like you was lookin' at the train that's comin.' Then just give him a big nudge right before it gets there. You understand?"

"Yeah. I got it."

"Okay. But we gotta get closer to him now. We can't let him get on that train," Cheech said, as he picked up the pace.

* * *

As I approached the station kiosk, there was a line of people making their way onto the escalator leading down to the trains. I got in the line and took the opportunity to turn completely around. I was trying to determine if anyone seemed to be looking in my direction or exhibiting any suspicious behavior that might indicate I was being followed. I was unable to detect anything out of the ordinary as I got on the escalator. At the concourse level, I went to one of the vending machines, bought a ticket and followed the signs directing me to the subway train to Oakland on Platform 1. The Oakland train would be arriving in three minutes, and the platform was crowded with commuters, three deep, waiting in line. I took my place behind an elderly lady. In front of her was a young Black woman sporting a large and fluffy Afro. The person at the head of the line, and right next to the subway tracks, was a man wearing a gray trench coat. He was carrying an unopened umbrella in one hand and a briefcase in the other.

As I waited in line, I thought of my years in California. I had left Washington in 1971 with a very uncertain future, but over the years I had made real progress. My new life in the Napa Valley and later in the Bay Area had been a very productive and healing time for me. And now that I had reunited with Lou, my life was definitely on an upward trajectory. That is until two nights ago.

Just then, I heard sounds of the approaching subway train. I looked back toward where the tracks disappeared around a bend in the tunnel, and to where the subway cars would soon appear. I felt as if I was being gently nudged forward which forced the elderly lady and the woman with the Afro in front of me to move sideways – one to the left and the other to the right. Suddenly, I found myself at the front of the line standing next to the businessman with the umbrella who was now situated to my left. I looked down to the tracks in front of me and peered once again toward the bend where the train would soon emerge. The crowd behind me seemed to compress even more, and I felt a moment of panic, fearing that I might be pushed onto the tracks.

* * *

Cheech squeezed himself into the group of commuters waiting to board the Oakland train. He ignored the angry looks of the people he roughly moved out of the way as he cleared a path to the front of the line. When one person began to complain indignantly, Cheech simply stared at the offended commuter with a look so chilling that the man became suddenly mute. Cheech was now directly behind Cumpton who he pushed forward to the front of the line, forcing the businessman to move laterally. Then Cheech moved aside, allowing Tubby to squeeze his way to the front of the line with the businessman to his left and Cumpton to his right. Just then, the sound of the approaching train could be heard. Tubby carefully positioned his right arm very softly around Cumpton's waist. The train was now visible and began to slow down. Tubby grasped Cumpton by the waist and shoved.

* * *

I felt the person to my left squeeze even closer to me. I turned and looked at the man. He was small and overweight, and he was staring intently at the approaching train. Then he looked up and smiled at me with little yellow teeth. Suddenly, I felt his arm around my waist. He was going to push me onto the tracks! I reacted immediately and turned forcefully to my right and away from him, hoping to escape the grasp of this madman who was trying to murder me. I felt him losing his grip on my waist as I moved into the crowd behind me. I heard screeching brakes, and I turned, momentarily, and watched in horror as the little cretin shoved the businessman with the umbrella and briefcase onto the tracks. There were loud shouts and screams and, in the ensuing mayhem, I quickly wove my way through the panicking and horrified crowd. I ran up to the concourse level and, avoiding the escalator, I took the stairs two at a time until I emerged, breathless, back on 5th Street. I looked back behind me and down the escalator, but there was no sign of my assailant. I immediately flagged down a taxi. I got in and told the cabbie to take me to Oakland, and I gave him Della

Mae's address.

I was shaking and out of breath. That deranged little thug had nearly murdered me. Once again, I would need to seek the assistance of a friend, but now I needed to calm down and think rationally.

I forced myself to concentrate on positive thoughts like my resurrected relationship with Lou, my new life in California and to the many good friends I had made out here. Friends like my boss and fellow Mountaineer – Alex Starling. Alex not only gave me a job at his winery, but he was also instrumental in helping me launch a Napa Valley wine newsletter called The Grapeline. That monthly periodical eventually led to my job with the San Francisco Chronicle.

CHAPTER 12
THE GRAPELINE

Ever since Lou opened my eyes to the wonders of wine and later, when Alex hired me at his winery in the fall of 1971, I have been intrigued and seduced by the ancient process of growing grapes and making wine. As a kid growing up in an Italian American family, I saw a bottle of Dago red on the dinner table every day. As I got older, I recognized that wine was part of our culture, and that winemaking was an important family ritual and an annual tradition.

In college, my go-to wines were usually inexpensive, sweet, high-octane products that were consumed only when I tired of chugging beer, or when I could not afford cheap bourbon or hundred proof, rotgut vodka. I actually learned (unintentionally I'm sure) some things during my years at the university, but an appreciation of wine was not among them. Ditto for when I was drafted into the Army in the late 1960s. There were no wine by the glass offerings at the base Enlisted Men's Club at Fort Knox. Back then, I thought of wine as something only wealthy, culturally elite folks drank regularly. I specifically remember one magazine ad for a sophisticated looking bottle of wine called Mateus Rosé. Later, during my all-expense paid trip to Vietnam, I recall thinking that I had hit the jackpot when I spotted Mateus on a shelf at the base PX – and for only two dollars a bottle. Mateus, a Portuguese sparkling rosé, looked expensive in its fancy curved bottle and I thought of it as the quintessential luxury wine. Anxious to sample the stuff, I bought three bottles of the wine, and jogged a mile back through hundred-degree heat to my hooch. Once there, I discovered that I would need a corkscrew to open the bottles. Since none of my hooch mates had one, and since I was desperate for a taste of the good life, I jammed the muzzle of my M-16 rifle into the cork until it was forced down into the bottle. The cork was hammered into the space wine had previously occupied, and now my fatigue shirt and living area were decorated with splashes of pink. Undeterred, my friends and I swilled the tepid wine in short order and with gusto. Then we spent the rest of the afternoon and evening hours visiting the latrine.

That may have been the last time I had a sip of wine until I met Lou. On that occasion, I was hiding from the mob at the real Johnny Hambone Harman's home in Canaan Valley. It was only the second time I had ever been in the presence of that lovely, green-eyed woman, and I watched as she uncorked a bottle of Napa Valley Cabernet Sauvignon. I remember that she would not allow me to taste the wine until we sat down to dinner at a rickety old picnic table on Hambone's deck. Then, she demanded that I take a bite of the ribeye steak I had grilled for us before putting the wine to my lips. It was an epiphany! That was the first time in my life that I had truly experienced the pleasure of sipping good wine. The food and wine combination was exquisite, and it demonstrated to me that pairing the cabernet with the steak improved both the wine and the food. From that day forward, I was on a quest to learn more about wine, and to sample as many different types as time, and my meager budget, would permit.

When my Vietnam buddy Jules and his uncle provided me with the introductory letter that led to my job at Starling Vineyards, my love for all things associated with wine took a professional and vocational leap, and eventually led to wine becoming the central focus of my profession. I had been employed at Starling for two years by then, and I had worked in just about every facet of grape growing and winemaking. Over the course of my time there, I was often invited by Alex to his home for meals where we discussed issues at the winery, and often ended the evening with conversations on what the future might portend for me. Alex seemed to want to help me find my path to some other, longer-term, vocational goal. I remember one seminal conversation, in particular, that resulted in a career course correction for me.

"Hey Johnny, I know you like the wine business, but what about long term? I mean, I certainly am pleased with your work here. And you know, you're welcome to stay at the winery as long as you want. But you've also told me about your goal of being a writer. Have you thought about how you might move in that direction?"

I couldn't explain to Alex the reasons I hadn't pursued my dream of using my English Lit degree to find a job where I could use the skills I had acquired. Or why, for the last few years, I had only been in survival mode. That I just needed a place to earn a living and exist anonymously. And I certainly couldn't tell him of my trouble with the Black Hand. But Alex was right. I did want to eventually find some occupation that would allow me to use my writing skills. Maybe work in advertising, public relations or even at a newspaper. I suppose I needed to think more strategically about this. Maybe I could apply for a teaching job somewhere. I wasn't sure what California requires as far as credentials, but I would probably – at a minimum – need to produce a college degree. But I didn't have one. Not as Johnny Harman, anyway. So, the teaching idea probably wouldn't fly.

"You're right, Alex. I really do need to think about the future. You know, look for something that would give me the chance to use my degree. I probably do need to see what jobs are out there for someone with my educational background. You have any ideas?"

Alex smiled slyly and there was a twinkle in his eye when he responded. "I have an idea for a job here in Napa that needs to get done, and you just might be the one to make it happen."

"Hey Alex. I'm all ears," I said and wondered what he had in mind.

"And this could be a way for you to hone your writing skills too."

Alex explained that for the past decade, he and a few other winemakers had been trying to get the Napa Valley Winery Association to do some self-promoting. To find a way let the wider world know more about the people that grow the grapes and make the wine in Napa Valley. And also to get the word out that Napa wines are among the best produced anywhere.

"I'm not talking about a big advertising campaign, Johnny. We don't have the money for that. Something on a much smaller scale that would communicate the good things we're doing out here. Hell, most people in California don't even know about us. It would be great if we had some way to get the word out. So that people around the state, and even outside California, could learn about Napa Valley wineries. And, of course, our wines."

"Hey Alex, have you guys ever considered doing a newsletter? A monthly or even quarterly publication that would let folks know what's going on up here. It's a pretty simple and inexpensive way to get the word out."

Alex smiled broadly. "That's a great idea, Johnny. Would you be willing to think about how we might get something like that started? What would it have in it? Who would we send it to and how much would it cost? Things like that. Maybe you could put together a proposal and present it to the next meeting of the Association."

I was excited. "Sure. I'd be happy to put something together. When's the next meeting of the association?

"It's next month. You can use the office at the winery to work on the proposal. And I'll pay your regular salary for doing this."

For the next month, I split my workday at Starling Vineyards. I spent mornings in the wine cellar or out in the vineyard, and afternoons in the winery office putting together a proposal for the newsletter. I suggested naming it, "The Grapeline." I actually did a rough mockup, to size, of what the newsletter would look like with a layout showing where pictures and artwork could be placed. I even wrote a sample story on the work of the Napa Valley Winery Association, and I fit it into the newsletter mockup. Then I worked with a local photographer to put the presentation on slides. A week before the Napa Valley Winery Association meeting, I presented my ideas to Alex.

"Johnny, this is just what I was looking for. I hope you don't mind, but I'm going to have your presentation added to the agenda at the meeting next week. You'll have about ten minutes to explain it to the association. Most of our members are really nothing more than glorified farmers. They're a conservative group, and I can't predict how they'll respond. But this will give them something to chew on."

A week later I stood in front of about seventy-five members of the Napa Valley Winery Association at the fire hall in St. Helena. I had a Kodak Carousel slide projector fired up and ready to go. I was last on the agenda that had now extended beyond two hours. I stared into the stern and impatient faces of the association members who had just sat through a meeting featuring such exciting topics as eradicating powdery mildew from south-facing vineyards; and inhibiting malolactic fermentation in low PH wines. After Alex introduced me to the group, I quickly explained the value of using a newsletter to get the word out about the association. Just as I was about to turn on the slide projector, an elderly gentleman – whose eyes were closed and whose chin was firmly planted on his chest – snored loudly. The group chuckled, and I later thought that gentleman's snore was the only overt show of emotion before, during or at the conclusion of my whole presentation. When the lights were turned back on, and before I could utter my concluding remarks, someone in the first row of seats loudly asked: "How much?"

It turns out that question and my answer(s) dominated the abbreviated Q&A session as most of the audience raced for the back of the room where I could hear bottles of wine being uncorked. It was obvious to me that the leadership of the Napa Valley Winery Association knew the key to keeping members in their seats until the very end of the agenda depended on this age-old tactic. As I walked dejectedly toward the back of the room, Alex met me and handed me a glass of white wine.

"You look like you could use this," he said and smiled. There was a tall, sandy-haired man standing next to Alex. "Johnny, I want you to meet Caspar Dinwiddy. Caspar is the county animal control officer, and he is a big supporter of our wine industry here in Napa."

I took the glass from Alex and shook Caspar Dinwiddy's hand. "Pleased to meet you Caspar."

"Likewise. I really enjoyed your presentation," he said with a slight New England accent. "I've been advocating for just such a newsletter. For years. Alex, and a few others in our association, like Warren Winarski at Stags Leap, Jim Barrett who owns Chateau Montelena and Robert Mondavi, are all of a like mind. Unfortunately, most of the members here just attend the meetings for the excellent beverages served at the end."

I had to laugh. "Well, that's a great membership benefit. But I have to ask: What's an animal control officer's interest in the wine association?"

Before the man could answer, Alex chimed in, "Caspar is also involved in the wine industry. He is the owner of Zodiac Winery. It's a relatively new operation. Caspar hired an Italian winemaker who believes in using astrological charting and signs of the Zodiac in planting his grapes and vinifying his wine."

Caspar quickly added, "My winemaker, Santino Lupini, is from Puglia along the Adriatic Coast. He firmly believes that using astrology as a guide is the purest form of winemaking since it allows the stars in the universe to direct his operation. While I might not share his unorthodox views, I will say that Zodiac has a pretty loyal following. We decided early on to introduce our product to people who are firmly committed to astrology."

Caspar added, "They probably don't care about what the wine tastes like, they buy it by the case because of its association with astrology. I gave Santino broad authority to make the wine, and he has done a good job. But I handle all the marketing. I hired an advertising agency to place ads in astrology magazines, and a direct mail company to target the subscribers. And our sales are off the charts."

"And Johnny," Alex added enthusiastically, "Caspar wants to underwrite the cost of the first few issues of the newsletter. By himself."

"I was impressed with your slideshow," Caspar said. "And thank you, Alex, for allowing Johnny to do this. Finally, someone has taken the initiative. I'm willing to provide the seed money to get the project started. Hopefully, the membership will see the value of The Grapeline and understand it's an investment worth making."

I was surprised and happy, but I was also skeptical. "Thanks so much Caspar. And you too, Alex. But it will take a good bit of time to produce the newsletter. I don't know how I'll be able to split my time…"

Alex interrupted me. "Johnny, I know this is a full-time commitment. Don't worry about your job at Starling. It will still be there if this doesn't work out. And I'll pay your salary until the newsletter is accepted as an association expense. If it isn't, then you can continue to work at the winery. Okay? Will you be our editor?"

Of course I accepted the offer. After the first three issues of The Grapeline, the Napa Valley Winery Association agreed to take over the expense of putting out the newsletter. Eventually, the ads we sold for placement in The Grapeline covered all the expenses, including my salary as its editor. My writing career was launched then and would eventually lead to my first job with the San Francisco Chronicle as a stringer covering wine news from the Napa Valley.

I became good friends with Caspar Dinwiddy who is heir to a centuries-old family trust. Caspar would never be required to earn a living, but his love for wine brought him to the Napa Valley where he established Zodiac Winery. Caspar's desire to perform some sort of public service, and his love of animals, led him to apply for, and get appointed as, the St. Helena animal control officer. He's also intrigued by the potential for the Napa Valley to be recognized by the rest of the world as a great wine appellation. Alex told me that Caspar is a bit of an eccentric, and that often makes him the target of ridicule and derision by some in the winemaking community. Most of the criticism is directed at his unorthodox winemaker/ astrologist Santino Lupini. Others scoff at Caspar's day job, snidely referring to him as "Caspar the friendly dog catcher." But I like the guy. I also share his view about the potential for Napa Valley wines to someday be considered among the best in the world.

Caspar is also very connected to an international cadre of wine lovers, many of whom he met during his years of study at Oxford. It was there, as a member of the Oxford University Wine Circle, that he met and became friends with Steven Spurrier. Spurrier, an Englishman, would later own and operate a wine shop and wine school in Paris.

A few years later, I would accept an offer from Caspar to travel with him to Paris to attend an international wine tasting that had been organized by his English friend. Steven Spurrier asked Caspar to recommend a few Napa Valley wines that he (Spurrier) might select to place in the competition. That tasting, which came to be known as the "Judgement of Paris," proved to be the most meaningful wine event of my life. It would also play a role in helping elevate my position from stringer to wine columnist for the Chronicle. The raucous party before the tasting, which I'll explain in detail later, proved to be almost as memorable (from what I can remember) as the wine event itself.

None of this would have happened had it not been for my employer, friend and advisor Alex Starling. His wise counsel led me on the path to my career. He's just one more great friend who went the extra mile for me. Just about the time I start to wallow in self-pity because of my current predicament, I think of all the friends and family who have supported me through the years, and I count my blessings.

CHAPTER 13
SAL COSTANZA

It was mid-morning when Sal Costanza received the troubling call from his nephew. Sal hoped Augie was wrong about being discovered. After all, it had been years since Sal had concocted the wild plan – with the assistance of the Costanza family and several good friends – to make it look like Augie had been killed trying to escape from the mob. There had never been any doubt expressed by the mob about what had transpired, Sal thought, or they would have known immediately. The mob would have reacted swiftly and violently had they suspected the Costanza family had duped them. But Augie was adamant. He was convinced that the mob had found him, and had sent a crew out to California to kill him. Sal needed to find out so he went to see his old pal Jimmie Ponza.

Jimmie is the septuagenarian owner of the Ruff Avenue Poolroom. The Ruff is the local hangout for working class men who reside in the Riverview neighborhood of Jeweltown where the Costanza family lives, and where Augie had grown up. Jimmie Ponza is also a bookie, and he allows patrons of the Ruff to bet on sports, gamble in card games and at the pool tables, and even collect cash for skillfully playing the pinball machines.

All these activities are illegal, but local law enforcement agencies look the other way if the games are peaceful, and as long as the police get their "commission." Jimmie also has "business" connections with La Famiglia Vagabonda in Pittsburgh. For a substantial monthly stipend, the mob allows him to operate his business without interference or competition in Jeweltown. It was Jimmie Ponza who had brokered the negotiation between the Costanza family and the mob. The deal resulted in an agreed upon transaction that would send Augie to the mob in exchange for the release of his girlfriend, Lou, who had been kidnapped and held by the Black Hand guys.

On the agreed upon day, Lou was released to the Costanza family and Augie was handed off to a couple of mob guys for the trip to Pittsburgh and certain death. Sal had kept Jimmie in the dark about how the family had deceived the mob in order to protect the owner of the Ruff from retribution if the ruse had failed. But the mob had never suspected that they had been conned.

Until this day, Jimmie Ponza thought Augie was dead, and he had often expressed his anguish to Sal that his negotiation with the Black Hand had not been able to save Augie. Sal had wanted to tell Jimmie the truth many times over the years, but he felt his friend still needed plausible deniability with his mob associates just in case they ever found out the truth about Augie.

However, if Augie's presumption that he had been discovered proved true, then Jimmie needed to be told the truth once and for all. Even if Augie was wrong, Sal felt compelled to finally come clean with his friend about what had actually occurred years ago, particularly since he was going to ask for Jimmie's help once again.

Sal walked the short distance from his home to the Ruff Avenue Poolroom. When he entered the establishment, he went to the bar and ordered a draft beer.

"Hey Sal, how you doing?" the bartender, Mickey O'Shay, said and handed Sal a frosty mug of Budweiser.

"Hi Mick. Is Jimmie around? I need to speak with him."

"Sure. I'll let him know you're here. He's upstairs in his office."

Within a few minutes, Sal watched as Jimmie walked toward him. He noticed that his friend was not smiling. In fact, Jimmie looked concerned.

"Sal, you must have been reading my mind because I was about to give you a call. I just got off the phone with Carmine up in Pittsburgh. You remember him, right? He's the old guy, the capo of their crew that I dealt with a few years back. When we were trying to save your nephew. Well, Carmine called, and he was really pissed off. Said I lied to him. That Augie ain't dead. That he's alive and living in San Francisco. I didn't believe him at first. Then he says they got proof. What the hell does that mean, Sal?"

Sal couldn't respond right away. He was shocked and incredulous. Augie was right about his suspicions. "Jimmie, that's why I'm here. To tell you I got a call from my nephew just this morning…"

"What the hell! You mean he's really alive? I don't know whether

I'm happier about that or more pissed off that I wasn't told about this. How could it be? I heard the mob guys had pictures of Augie. Said he was shot dead. Now you're telling me he's alive in California! This is unbelievable. What the hell's going on, Sal?"

Sal spent the next ten minutes bringing Jimmie up to speed on what had happened back in 1970, including how he and the family and a few friends pulled off the deception. When he was finished telling the story, Jimmie was silent for a moment before responding.

"Sal, you didn't trust me enough to tell me about this back then? And you let me believe all these years that Augie was dead? Do you know how many sleepless nights I've had since that time? How guilty I always felt that I failed you and the Costanza family?" Jimmie said with emotion, his voice unsteady.

"Jimmie, I wanted to tell you a thousand times what really happened. I know you've felt guilty, but I wanted you to be able to be truthful with those mob assholes. That way if they found out about what really happened, you could truthfully say you didn't know anything about our scam. That if anyone was to blame it had to be their guys. That's why I didn't tell you. And now, they call you to see if you knew about this all along. What can we do?"

Jimmie didn't respond for several seconds and then he said, "You know what? If they knew what really happened... you know... if the guys who you blackmailed spilled the beans and told Carmine everything, then you and me and a few other people would already be dead. They would have just come down here and wasted our asses. That means Carmine don't know the whole story. All he knows is Augie's alive. That's gotta be it. Because when I asked Carmine what the two guys who picked up your nephew told him when he confronted them. With the news that Augie is alive. The old man didn't say anything for a while. Then he told me that one of those guys is dead, and the other one's out of town. I got the impression the guy out of town is really on the run. I didn't say it out loud to Carmine, but I wanted to tell him that if anyone screwed up, it's gotta be his guys."

Sal quickly added, "That's a lucky break for us then. I told Augie the same thing when he called me this morning. That we can claim the same thing with Carmine too. That we assumed that Augie was executed. Until they get their guy – the one who's on the run – to tell them what really happened, we have some time. But they're definitely after Augie. They tried to grab him in San Francisco, but he got away.

I'm sure they were sent out there to kill him. He's on the run again, and I'm not sure what we can do to help him. But I'm also worried about you too, Jimmie."

"Sal, don't worry about me. I don't think they'll do anything to me. At least not for a while. I'm a good customer. I send them a lot of dough each month. And besides, I really didn't know anything about what you and the family did to keep Augie alive. But I'm glad you did. You can't imagine what a relief it is for me to know that. And Sal, I know the two guys Carmine sent down to pick Augie up. They're scumbags, especially the one they call "Vito The Scar."I think the other one's last name is Mancini. But Carmine told me that one of 'em is dead. I'll try and find out if it's Vito or the Mancini guy. From now on, though, you gotta level with me, okay? We can't keep anything from each other. I'll let you know if I hear anything more, and you let me know what else I can do to help Augie."

"Jimmie, I'm sorry to drag you into all of this again. You've been a great friend for decades, and my Pop, Salvatore, thought the world of you. I promise to keep you up to speed on this."

"Hey Sal, I told you that I owe your father a debt I can never repay. He saved my life when I was a little kid. Kept me from going to work the day that mine exploded back in 1906. In Monongah. So, I'm forever indebted to the Costanza family."

CHAPTER 14
CALIFORNIA DREAMIN'

It was a twenty-minute cab ride to Della Mae's apartment in the Elmhurst neighborhood of Oakland. Elmhurst had once been the industrial hub of town; full of canneries, glass factories and die-casting businesses. However, after World War II, most of those businesses had shut down, and the area is now composed of predominantly working-class minorities, including Blacks, Hispanics and Asian-Americans.

When I exited the cab, I quickly did a three-hundred-sixty degree turn to make sure I hadn't been followed. Then I made my way up the stairs to Della Mae's Craftsman-style duplex apartment. I located the hidden key under a cement planter on the porch and entered. Since Della wouldn't be home for several hours, I went into the small office she kept just off the kitchen, and I plopped down on an old leather couch. I was exhausted and stressed out from the events of the past couple of days, especially the attempt on my life at the BART station just an hour ago. I kept replaying that terrifying moment when I was sure I would be thrown onto the tracks in front of the subway train, and the evil smile of the deranged little man who had tried to murder me. He couldn't have been the one who had assaulted me in the Marina District. That guy was much taller and heavier. That meant there were at least two thugs after me. How could they have found me?

I was slipping back into the trough of depression that I had fought to crawl out of right after I was forced to leave my home and family. I couldn't allow this to happen again. I tried to focus on the positive things I had experienced the last several years, and particularly in the past two weeks when I was able to reconnect with Lou. Now, however, my biggest fear is that Lou will be put in harm's way again. I really wouldn't be surprised if she decides that enough is enough, and then gives up on our star-crossed relationship. I can't really blame her if she abandons me once again, but I can't dwell on things I can't control.

Those were the last thoughts I had as I fell into a coma-like sleep.

* * *

I'm third in a scattered column of grunts humping through a rice paddy in Quang Ngai province. We're slogging through waist-high water that smells of wet earth, mold and human feces. Tall elephant grass on either side of the paddy acts as a barrier and stifles any possibility of a breeze. Debilitating heat and humidity hang over us like a malodorous and oppressive cloak. My rucksack is carving deep ruts into my shoulders, and the weight of my steel helmet, flak jacket and bandolier of ammo add to my mounting misery. All the while, with each painful step, vampire-like mosquitos and leeches feed on my blood and sweat. We're on a search and destroy mission, and I'm hoping we won't find who we're searching for because I'm convinced we will be the ones destroyed. We're just chum bait. The Army lifers running things are using us to draw out the enemy. Then they'll send jets to drop napalm on them – and us. It's all about body counts even if we're the ones getting counted.
Suddenly, there's a flash and the trooper a few feet in front of me is propelled into the air. He hangs there momentarily suspended – a grotesque silhouette juxtaposed against the azure sky. Jagged, bloody stumps dangle from his torso. As the explosion and concussion envelop me, I'm flung into the murky water and swallow a huge gulp of the vile liquid. I rise choking, vomiting rice paddy water, and trying to catch my breath. I can't see anyone in front of me now except the bobbing and disfigured bodies of my fallen comrades who are floating face down in the rice paddy. I raise my M-16, pull the charging handle back and squeeze the trigger, but nothing happens. The place is eerily quiet, and I can't understand why I'm not receiving enemy fire. It seems as if I am now alone in the rice paddy. Then in the distance, maybe twenty yards ahead, I see a short, squat figure moving toward me through the water carrying a large K-bar knife extended out in front of him. As the man gets closer, I can see that he doesn't appear to be an enemy soldier. He is dressed in civilian clothes as he moves quickly toward me. I squeeze the trigger again and again. Nothing. The short, roly-poly man is now smiling at me through small yellow teeth. As he gets to within a foot, he lunges at me with the huge knife... No, no, no I scream...

* * *

"Augie. Augie, wake up! You're okay. You're just dreaming. Wake up."
I hear a voice and then I feel someone shaking me. Della Mae is standing over me. My upper body is drenched in sweat, but I'm relieved to realize I'm alive and that I was just dreaming.

"Della. I'm sorry. I was having a strange dream… I guess it was a nightmare," I said and then I struggled up into a sitting position on the couch. Della left the room briefly and returned with a towel and a large glass of water. I took the towel and dried myself and then drank the whole glass of water. Della Mae sat next to me on the couch. I looked at her and suddenly realized that I should probably explain why I was in her apartment unannounced, and in such a discombobulated condition.

"Thanks Della. Sorry. I've been on the run – literally – for the last couple of days. I don't want to get you involved in my problems, and I promise I'll leave here soon. I just stopped by to pick up my things, but I needed to rest for a while. Then I fell asleep. I…

Della Mae interrupted me. "Hold on Augie. Slow down. What's going on? And you certainly don't have to leave. You're always welcome here. You know that. Now, what happened?" she asked again, and looked at me with real concern.

"Okay. Here's the quick and dirty version. You remember the story I told you when I first got here? About the mob guys who had been chasing me back in West Virginia until we devised a scheme to make them think I was dead? Well, it looks like they somehow found out I'm alive and living out here. They've sent a couple of hit men to the Bay Area to get me."

"Good lord, Augie. Are you sure?"

"Yes. They tried to grab me two nights ago down in the Marina District, but I got away. And then earlier today, they somehow spotted me, and they followed me to the Powell Street BART station. One of them actually tried to push me onto the tracks in front of a train. To murder me. I was able to get away from them again. And I don't think they know where I was exactly headed. But they do know I was trying to board the Oakland train. Della, I don't want to put you in any danger, but I need to get my getaway stash you let me keep here." I stopped to catch my breath.

"Augie, I really thought you were paranoid when you told me that story way back in 1972. About that Black Hand organization and how they were after you. I'm ashamed to tell you this now, but after you told me what happened, I called my brother Lionel back in Jeweltown. I was catching up on old friends and I asked him 'whatever happened to Augie Cumpton?' I remember that he kind of sighed. Like he was sad. Or maybe frustrated. "

"Your brother was a good friend. I didn't really know him when you and I were in High school, and I never told him about our relationship once we became friends later."

Della sighed. "You're right, Augie. I could tell he considered you a good friend. He told me the rumor was that you had gotten in some kind of trouble, and that you had just disappeared."

"Yeah. That's kind of a cover story my family used to keep folks from asking too many questions."

"And I'm sorry, Augie. I know you were upset when you first came here and told me about all this. It seemed like you were troubled. That the war might have something to do with the way you were talking. But please don't worry. I kept my promise to you and never, ever told a soul about who you really are. As far as speaking about you to anyone I know, I always call you Johnny. Johnny Harman."

"I believe you. And I can understand how you might have thought I was paranoid. Particularly when I told you about the problems I was having adjusting to civilian life after Vietnam. When I left D.C. to come out here, I was doing a lot better handling all that war stuff. I really am lucky to have run into my old Vietnam buddy Jules. He not only gave me a job when I was really down and out, he also introduced me to a group of Vietnam vets who met regularly at his uncle's liquor store. To talk about their war experiences. And when I started work at Starling, I found another group of veterans out here. I still meet with them about once a month up in the Napa Valley at Yountville. I'm not sure I'll ever get completely over the bad war experiences, but the meetings allow me to talk about things. And that really seems to help."

Della just stared at me for a few moments, then she said, "Augie, I hate that you've had to deal with all that. Like everyone else, I watched the war on TV. Walter Cronkite on CBS and Huntley and Brinkley on NBC. From 1968 to about 1975, Vietnam was always the lead story. It seemed surreal. And most of my friends were anti-war demonstrators. We treated you guys like you were the enemy. None of us had any empathy for what you were going through. Then a couple of years ago, our country left Vietnam. And now the war is just an afterthought. It's terrible about all the lives wasted over there, but we never think about the guys who came home. Like you. And for that, I am ashamed," Della said and wiped tears from her eyes.

"Hey there," I said smiling at my friend, "I didn't tell you all this to start a pity party. I'm not mad at anyone for being against that war. It was awful. But all wars are awful. My uncle Sal and his buddies from World War II dealt with the same issues that we faced. I don't guess anyone who fights in a war should ever come home unaffected. You would have to be a robot not to be changed by the experience.

"Right now, though, I've got to deal with a more pressing problem. So, if you agree, I'd like to spend the night here. In the morning, I'll leave. I promise. And Della, I'm open to any ideas you might have about where I might go to hide out for a while."

Della didn't immediately respond. Then she said, "I know some people who might be able to help."

CHAPTER 15
WORD FROM HOME

"Mister Costanza." the nasal-toned voice of the operator said. "You have a collect call from Augie. Will you accept the call?"

"Yes, I'll accept the call." Sal Costanza waited for the operator to connect them.

"Hey kid, how you doing? Any problems overnight?"

"No, everything is okay so far," I lied. "What did you find out from Jimmie Ponza?

I didn't tell my uncle about the incident at the BART Station. I didn't want to add to his worries. And I really hadn't been able to get much sleep at Della Mae's apartment. The few minutes I slipped into unconsciousness were riddled with troublesome visions of the rotund little man with the yellow-toothed smile just before he attempted to murder me.

"Augie, Jimmie actually got a call from the capo of the gang up in Pittsburgh. This guy, Carmine, tried to accuse Jimmie and our family of hiding you. But Jimmie told Carmine that if you're alive, we don't know anything about it. That we turned you over to the two guys he sent down here to get you. Jimmie said he wanted to tell Carmine, 'if Augie's still alive, it's because you guys botched the job.' What he did tell Carmine is that as far as we're concerned you were dead. And Augie, I never told you this, but Jimmie never knew anything about how we conned those assholes. We kept him in the dark. Jimmie was pissed that I hadn't told him about what we did. But he's relieved you're still around."

"But Uncle Sal, where do we go from here? I can't just wait around for these murderers to come after me again. And what about the two Black Hand guys you made the deal with a long time ago? They're going to tell Carmine the truth. That it was a big scam. And then you and the family are going to be in their gunsights." I was frustrated and angry, but I was even more concerned about what the mob might do to my parents and the family.

"Augie, I know this isn't what you want to hear, but you gotta stay hidden somewhere until we can get Carmine to call off his attack dogs. Jimmie's working on that. It's probably going to take a while. He has to convince Carmine that the Costanza family honored the deal. That we sent you to them in exchange for your girlfriend. Jimmie will tell them they need to clean up their own act. And he will plead with Carmine to leave you alone. "

"I'm confused, Uncle Sal. How can Jimmie hope to keep this ruse alive once the two guys who came to get me fess up? Then we're all in deep shit. I can't believe that Carmine hasn't gotten his guys to tell the truth by now."

"That's really our ace in the hole, Augie. Carmine told Jimmie that one of the guys he sent to Jeweltown to get you died a couple of years ago. And the other guy can't be found. He must have skipped town once he learned that you were spotted alive and well in California. Jimmie's going to try and find this guy and deal with him. Maybe offer him some cash to stay hidden. Remember, we still have the pictures, and he won't want them to ever to see the light of day. We can't let the Black Hand find this guy before we do. Otherwise, he'll tell them what really happened. And then who knows how Carmine might react."

"Holy shit! If Jimmie does find the guy that's on the run, how much is it going to cost to keep him under wraps? You and the family have already spent thousands of dollars to keep me alive. I can't keep letting you foot the bill for my screw-ups, Uncle Sal."

"Look, you can contribute to whatever this might cost if you want. But you've already paid a price greater than anyone in our family. You had to leave everything and everyone you cared about behind. And then pretend you're someone else for almost a decade now. And Augie, it isn't just about saving you. This is a family matter, and we all have a stake in the outcome. Remember, those Black Hand guys tried to blow up the bakery. The bakery that your Grandpa Salvatore built with his own hands more than fifty years ago. And they would have killed your Uncle Giorgio if you hadn't jumped in and saved his life. So, we owe you big time."

"I don't know about that, Uncle Sal. But we really do need to find out who this guy is and if he's willing to deal with us."

"Let's just see how this plays out, Augie. Jimmie still has some pretty good contacts with the mob. And one guy in particular, Frankie Silver, actually grew up in Riverview and was a regular at Jimmie's poolroom. His real last name is Argento, but his mother changed it to Silver. It turns out she was a local lady of the night, and Frankie never knew who his father was. The Ruff Avenue Poolroom was like a second home to the kid when he was a teenager, and Jimmie always took care of him. He treated Frankie like the son Jimmie never had. He made sure the kid got a meal anytime he was in the poolroom, and he gave him odd jobs around the place. Jimmie said he lost track of him for a long time until Frankie showed up a few years ago at the Ruff. Turns out Frankie had spent some time in prison. Spent about five years in the pen up at Moundsville for stealing a car. When he got out, he moved to Pittsburgh where he became a member of La Famiglia Vagabonda. And since he's from Jeweltown, Carmine made Frankie Jimmie's new contact with them. He comes into the poolroom at least once a month to collect money for the mob. Jimmie hopes he'll be able to get some inside information from Frankie. About which one of those guys is on the run. Right now, though, you just need to stay out of sight."

"Okay. But I'm going to call you every day to see if you have any updates. I'm not sure how those guys found me in the first place. And I'm worried they'll be able to track me down again. But I'll do my best to go underground. I have some friends out here I can trust, and they'll help me. Seems like I'm always depending on other folks to keep on this side of the ground."

"Take care Augie. We'll get through this, I promise. Bye now," he said and hung up.

I really missed my family. They had sacrificed so much for me. All of them, especially Mom, Dad and Uncle Sal. My parents were getting up there in age too, and I wondered if I would ever get the chance to see them again before they passed away. I grew up in a large Italian American family and we're all very close. Most of the family lives on one block in Riverview. Just about every Sunday, we would meet at my grandparents' home for an Italian food feast where the creation, preparation and consumption of an incredible array of Calabrian-inspired dishes took center stage.

Food was always the glue that bound us together as a family. It was also the most common topic of conversation, and even contentious debate in a family where just about every adult was known for perfecting at least one special dish. I suppose that's not surprising since our family patriarch, Grandpa Salvatore, was a baker. Unfortunately, Grandpa died right before I was forced to leave town, but my Grandma Luisa is still alive. She's in her late 80s.

As far as the rest of the family, Uncle Sal said most of them only knew that I had left town and that I was alive and well. Only a few members of the family were aware of the plan Uncle Sal put together to scam the Black Hand guys. However, no one, not even Mom, Dad or Uncle Sal, knew where I was living, nor did they know of my new identity. It had to be that way to protect them – and me. From time to time, particularly on holidays or on my parents' birthdays, I would call Uncle Sal for updates on the family. Friends and neighbors were simply told that I had left town without telling anyone where I was going, and that no one knew what happened to me. I was like the prodigal son: only I would never be able to come back home like the guy in the bible.

Of course, there were rumors too. Uncle Sal told me that one of them was that I had gotten into serious trouble with underworld types over gambling debts, and that I had to leave town for my own safety. That one was almost accurate. But whenever Uncle Sal was asked about my whereabouts by anyone outside the family, he would simply say that no one had any idea where I was or what had become of me.

Next, I needed to call Lou and make sure she was safe, and that she had gone to hide at her family's cabin in Canaan Valley. Della Mae had left for work first thing this morning and she told me to use the phone to make whatever calls I needed to make. She also said she would try and get home early today and hoped, by then, to have arranged a place for me to hide out. It was 11 a.m. in Oakland when I dialed Lou's phone number at the cabin in Canaan Valley. She answered after the first ring.

"Augie. I'm glad you called." Lou sounded stressed.

"What's the matter, Lou? You sound worried." I was starting to panic.

"No. I'm okay. It's just that… Oh Augie, I think those mob guys are looking for me again," she blurted out, her voice unsteady.

"What happened? Did they follow you? How do you know they're looking for you?"

"Augie, I know you told me to go straight to Canaan yesterday morning when we spoke. But I needed to make a stop at my apartment in Romney to pick up a few work things. And I was very careful. I drove past my apartment several times and then I parked about a half mile from my place. I waited there for a half hour before I went to the apartment. I didn't see any strangers in the area, but when I got to my apartment the front door was slightly open. I turned and started to run, but then I stopped and just listened for about ten minutes. The apartment is small. You remember. There was absolutely no sound coming from inside. I quietly walked into the place, but whoever had been there was gone. The place was a mess, though. All the drawers were opened and upended, and the closets had been ransacked. There were papers and utensils all over the floor. I don't know if they found anything useful. I don't think there was anything there that would let them know about this place in Canaan... but I'm not sure and I don't know what to do now. I'm..." she couldn't finish the sentence.

"Lou. Calm down. If they knew where you were going, they would have found you by now. I assume you checked the cabin out before you entered it. Right?"

"Yes. Of course. I waited over at the bar. You know – the Duck In – where we first met. Anyway, I spent two hours there and then came over here. No one's been around here. But I didn't sleep a wink last night. What should I do, Augie?"

"Okay. The first thing is just stay in the cabin. If you need to go to the store, you can do that. But make it quick and then come right back. I'm going to meet with a friend out here later today who's helping me find a good place to hide. A place way off the beaten path. In the meantime, Uncle Sal and a friend of his are trying to get the mob to back off. Uncle Sal thinks they have a pretty good plan to do that. But it's going to take some time. The first thing they're trying to find out is how the mob guys found me. After all these years. I mean..."

Lou interrupted me. "Augie. I know how that happened. I know how they were able to track you down. And it's really my fault."

I was incredulous. "How did you find out? And why is it your fault?"

"Okay. Remember a couple of weeks ago when I was up on that stage at the Fairmont Hotel with the other winemakers? You know, to receive the award for my sangiovese?"

"Of course. I was there to cover the award ceremony for the Chronicle. That's when I first saw you. Right before we reconnected."

"Well, it turns out that a photographer – probably from your paper – took several photos of us up on the stage. Then he must have shopped the picture to one of the wire services. Augie, you were in the photo. You were standing just to the side and back of us and you were in the shot."

Lou explained that before she left D.C., she was sorting through her mail, and she came across a letter from the California Wine Institute. It was postmarked two days after the wine award ceremony. In the letter was a clipping from the San Francisco Chronicle – a photo of all the awardees standing with their ribbons. And there I was clearly pictured behind them in the clipping for all the world to see. Lou's theory is that the clipping was sent to all the major newspapers in the country. She surmised that one of the papers where the photo appeared was the Pittsburgh Press.

"That's how those thugs knew you were alive and living somewhere in the Bay Area. They must have checked and found out you worked for the Chronicle too," she added.

"Damn, Lou. That must be it. But when those scumbags saw the photo and read the caption with your name and winery printed underneath it, they had to assume that we're still together. That's why they came down to Romney looking for you. They wanted to get you to tell them where I'm living so they could find me and finish the job. Lou, you can't stay there. You need to come out here with me until this blows over. You're at serious risk if you stay there. They'll start looking for you everywhere. And eventually they'll come to Canaan and nose around. I think you would be safer with me until this issue gets resolved. You need to get away from there right now."

"Oh Augie, I don't know how I can just pick up and leave. What's going to happen to the vineyard? I need to get it ready for winter. And I've got to move the new wine around in the winery. There's a lot to do in the next couple of months. I need to be here for that..." her voice trailed off.

"Look Lou. We'll work something out. The vineyard and the winery are issues we can fix. We'll get some people to take care of things until you can get back. But you have to leave now. Call and make an airline reservation and call me right back with the details. Then drive to the airport right away. By the time you get here, I'll know where we're going to be hiding out and I'll take you there."

Lou was quiet. She didn't respond for almost a minute. Then she said, "Okay Augie. I'll come out there. But it seems like we just can't catch a break."

Sadly, I thought Lou was right. I wondered if we were just not meant to be.

CHAPTER 16
VITO THE SCAR

Vito Scaramungi was born in New Kensington, Pennsylvania in 1935, the son of Sicilian parents who had immigrated to America ten years earlier. Vito's parents came from Siracusa, an ancient city perched on Sicily's southeastern coastline abutting the Ionian Sea. Vito's father, Lorenzo, was a laborer in a New Kensington steel mill. After a few years on the job, Lorenzo was recruited by the local mafia affiliate, La Famiglia Vagabonda, to help organize a union at the steel plant. La Famiglia Vagabonda controlled gambling, prostitution and bootlegging in western Pennsylvania and northern West Virginia. This organized crime group wanted to establish a presence in a legitimate business where they could legally collect union dues as well as expand the market for their illegal endeavors. Through threats, violence, intimidation, and the assistance of labor organizers like Lorenzo, the mob succeeded in establishing a union at the steel mill. Lorenzo Scaramungi was rewarded for his participation in the effort by being appointed president of the union. He was also offered the opportunity to become a made man and a member of La Famiglia Vagabonda.

When Vito dropped out of high school, he followed in his father's footsteps working at the mill. As a fifteen-year-old, Vito should not have been permitted to work in the steel plant, but since his father was an official of the union, the child labor laws were ignored, and Vito was given the job. After a few years, he was also invited to become a member of the mob. Membership in the Black Hand was a natural fit for Vito who, within a very short time, became proficient in the skills that were highly valued by his bosses: extortion, loan sharking, kidnapping and murder. A few years later, his colleagues in the mob gave him a nickname: The Scar. The new moniker was both a shortened version of his last name, as well as an accurate description of the serpentine mark that snaked across his face. The ugly scar began just below his left ear, slithered across the bridge of his nose and across his face to his right ear. That mark was the result of a failed attempt on the part of a rival underworld thug to slit Vito's throat from ear to ear. In this case, the assailant's desire to murder Vito was thwarted when the Scar ducked, and the straight razor slashed his face instead of his throat. Vito fell to the floor bleeding, rolled over and fired a pistol shot into the would-be assassin's face. From that day forward he was known as "Vito The Scar."

By the time the Scar was thirty-five, he had become one of the top earners and cruelest enforcers for Carmine Amato, the boss of the Black Hand. It was late summer in 1970 when Carmine ordered the Scar to go down to West Virginia and pick up this young guy – Augie Cumpton. Supposedly, Cumpton had been involved in the killing of one of Carmine's soldiers. So, Cumpton went into hiding. The mob had searched high and low, but they were unable to find him. Later, when the mob kidnapped Cumpton's girlfriend, a deal was struck between Cumpton's family and Carmine. The family agreed to turn the young man over to the mob in exchange for the release of the girlfriend. It should have been an easy job for the Scar and his partner, Guido Mancini, who accompanied him to pick up Cumpton. The Scar drove while Guido was in the back seat of the car guarding the girl who sat, trembling, with her hands tied and a hood over her head. Unfortunately, for the two mob guys, the Costanza family got the drop on the Scar and his partner. They drugged them and took compromising pictures of the thugs who they dressed as women. There were also photos of the Scar and his partner appearing to show them engaging in homosexual acts. The Costanzas' ruse further involved photos of a presumably dead Cumpton that the Scar and his partner were given and instructed to provide to Carmine. They were to tell the boss that they had been forced to kill the kid when he tried to escape. If the Scar and his colleague refused to go along with the hoax, the Costanzas threatened to send copies of the embarrassing photos to Carmine. Further, they were warned that those same lewd pictures would be sent to Pittsburgh if anything bad happened to Augie Cumpton, anyone in his family or his girlfriend.

The Scar and his partner did not have any option: they were forced to go along with the hoax. Fortunately, Carmine believed their story, and everyone in the Black Hand organization thought that Cumpton was dead. That is, until one of the mob guys saw the picture in the paper of Cumpton alive, and presumably well, in San Francisco.

Vito knew that he had literally dodged a bullet when one of his colleagues phoned to tell him of Cumpton's sighting. Obviously, Vito needed to get out of town and go into hiding. He was sure that if Carmine found him, he would be tortured and forced to reveal the ruse concocted by the Costanzas. Then he would face a long, slow and painful death. Since his partner in the hoax, Guido Mancini, had died a few years earlier, Carmine would now focus all his energy on finding Vito. Consequently, the Scar immediately left Pittsburgh and drove to a hunting cabin he owned at a very remote location in the central Pennsylvania mountains. That's where he came up with a plan to resolve his problem with the boss.

Almost everyone in La Famiglia Vagabonda agreed that Carmine should have retired a decade ago, but he had hung onto his position with threats and intimidation. He was the last of the old-timers, and most of the guys in the mob family hated him. There just wasn't anyone with enough balls to challenge the old man. That is, until the Cumpton sighting forced Vito to consider the only option that would guarantee his own survival: the elimination of Carmine. He knew that unless the capo was out of the way, he could never go back to La Famiglia Vagabonda. He also believed that if he got rid of Carmine, and his equally old and loyal right-hand man Nunzio, the other guys would fall in line. He spent his waking hours plotting, planning and then refining his scheme to eliminate the old boss.

For his plot to succeed, Vito Scaramungi would need to convince the three most ambitious, influential and ruthless members of the Black Hand crew to support him, and to back his play. But he also knew that he had to provide a logical and believable explanation to these men for why and how Cumpton had survived. He had an idea that he thought was plausible, and he ran it by each of the three men individually. He admitted to them his explanation to Carmine was not accurate as to how they had disposed of Cumpton's body. It was true that Vito had presented pictures to the boss of a seemingly dead Cumpton who had been shot in the back of the head trying to escape. However, he explained to the three men whose backing he would need, that instead of throwing Cumpton's body into the river, they had just left him there next to the highway. Vito explained that it was broad daylight, and he and his partner were afraid that someone in a passing car might see them disposing of Cumpton's body. So, they had quickly taken two pictures of the dead man, and then they left the area.

Obviously, though, Cumpton did not die. The Scar said the only explanation must be that he had only been grazed by the bullet, and then he had somehow made it home where his family helped him disappear. For the past seven years, everyone thought Cumpton was dead until he was discovered alive with a new identity in California. Vito suggested to his mob colleagues that it was time to put this old issue behind them. Going after the Costanza family to seek revenge for something that happened seven years ago was unnecessary and a waste of time. Vito explained how the trouble with the Costanzas began.

"Look, the Cumpton kid pulled one of our guys off his uncle. Our guy was there to try and shake down the uncle to pay us for protection. For their bakery business. The uncle refused and our guy starts beatin' on him. He was about to kill the guy. So, Cumpton grabs one of them wooden paddles they use to take bread out of the oven, and he hits our guy. Knocks him out then and puts him in his car. Our guy wakes up and drives back to the Burg, and then a week later he dies. We send a crew down there, and they can't find Cumpton. So, we kidnap a guy that worked with him. We beat on this guy real hard for a couple of weeks and then, when he don't tell us where Cumpton is, we whack him. Then, we grab another one of Cumpton's friends. A tough little son of a bitch who let Cumpton hide out at his house. When he won't tell us nothin', our guy blows him away. Finally, we kidnap Cumpton's girlfriend. That does the trick. We trade her to Cumpton's family, and they give him to us in return. When you think about it, the score's three to one in our favor. We lose one guy, and we kill three – if you count Cumpton. The only one we lose is the guy Cumpton accidentally kills.

"We need to put this behind us now and move on. And we have a real good earner for us in Jeweltown who's helping us work things out. This guy, Ponza, has a poolroom there, and he's been sendin' us a ton of money each month for almost forty years. From his small-time parlay and numbers business. If we don't get this thing settled, he'll bail on us. And we'll lose a nice chunk of cash. So, once I get rid of Carmine and Nunzio, I say we move on from this Cumpton shit."

Eventually, the three soldiers in La Famiglia Vagabonda that Vito approached agreed to back him. However, his associates had two demands before they would approve his plan: first, that they would not be required to participate in the murder; and second, that each of them would reap a substantial financial reward by being given control over a larger geographic territory in the mob's area of operations. The Scar happily agreed to their demands.

What Vito didn't tell his mob buddies was that once he got rid of Carmine, he also had a score to settle with a guy in Cumpton's family named Sal. Sal was behind the scam he and his partner were forced to agree to. Sal is the jamok who has the fake pictures and has been blackmailing him. Once he gets those embarrassing photos back, Vito vowed that he would go down to West Virginia and take care of Sal, Augie Cumpton and anyone else he could find in the kid's family. That would be the icing on the cake. But first things first.

Vito The Scar spent his time in the mountain cabin formulating his plan. It was not without risk, but it was the only way he could see to resolve his problem. Anyway, he knew it involved something he was good at – murder.

Chapter 17
Della Mae, Meet Lou

I was worried about Lou, and anxious to get her to California and away from the mob guys who were looking for her. Right after I spoke with her this morning, Lou was able to reserve a ticket on a flight out of Dulles Airport. Her United flight arrived at Oakland International Airport around 7 p.m. Della Mae had let me use her car to pick Lou up. I spotted Lou at the baggage counter carousel. We hugged briefly and then I helped retrieve her luggage. I was startled by how I felt just being in her presence. And when I glanced into those emerald-green eyes, and she flashed me that slightly crooked smile, my troubles seemed to vanish. It was still difficult for me to believe that after all the years of thinking I had lost her forever, we had been able to reunite. But it's equally worrisome and disconcerting for me to accept that the accident of fate that had brought us together is also the reason we're both running for our lives now. I could not help but wonder if our relationship, like Shakespeare's ill-fated lovers, Romeo and Juliet, was star-crossed.

"Any problems getting to the airport, or any issues along the way," I asked.

"No Augie. So far, so good. I hope. Where are we going now? And how long do you think I'll have to be out here?" Lou was calm, but I could hear the tension in her voice.

"Honestly, I really don't know. Hopefully not more than a couple of weeks. But first, we're going to my friend's place here in Oakland to spend the night. She's going to help us. You remember Della Mae Smith?

"I remember that you told me she was the only other girl you've ever been in love with," Lou said in mock anger. Then she smiled. "Sure, I've always wanted to meet the competition."

I knew Lou was joking, but I needed to make sure she didn't have any lingering doubts about the nature of my relationship with Della

Mae. Once we had secured her bags in Della's car and I pulled out of the parking lot, I tried to reassure her.

"You know, Lou, I came out here in the fall of 1971 to find a job. I didn't know a soul, and I was lonely. I had no friends, and I didn't have any link to my past life. Then I remembered that Della Mae was living in California. I took a chance and looked her up, and I discovered she had a law practice in Oakland. When I called her, she seemed pleasantly surprised to hear from me. She said her brother Lionel had told her that I had survived Vietnam. But Lionel didn't have any idea about what had happened to me after I left Jeweltown. So, I filled her in about why I had to leave home, change my name and start a new existence. And Lou, I told Della Mae about you and the way things ended with us," I paused for a moment to catch my breath.

"Augie, she must have thought that I was some kind of monster. I mean, just abandoning you without an explanation," Lou said, her voice almost a whisper.

"She didn't say anything like that about you. She was just shocked and horrified about what we had gone through. Both you and me. Anyway, then she filled me in on her life since we had last seen each other a decade earlier. We both agreed that our brief time together was just a puppy love kind of thing. She said she was happy I looked her up, and that she missed home too. Della also said that she was in a relationship, but she didn't tell me much about the guy. Since that first meeting, we've stayed in touch over the years. We talk on the phone maybe once a month. And every now and then, we get together for dinner or to go to a concert. But that's the extent of our relationship. I consider her a good friend and I trust her. She also lets me keep what I call my "getaway stash" at her apartment. It's a suitcase with clothes, a passport, and some cash I keep there in the event that the mob finds out I'm still alive. After it became clear that they're after me again, I went to Della Mae's place to grab my stash. When I told her that we needed a place to hide out, she offered to help."

When I was finished with my story, Lou just said "I understand."

Lou was quiet for the remainder of the ride from the airport. She had to be exhausted from the long day as well as the way in which her life, like mine, had been upended in the past couple of days. It was 8:30 when we got to Della Mae's apartment. I carried Lou's bags up the stairs and knocked on the door. Della Mae opened the door and smiled at us. She was dressed in a white terry-cloth robe.

"Hi Lou. I'm Della. Welcome to my humble abode," she said and moved aside allowing us to enter the apartment.

"It's a pleasure to meet you, Della. Even under these crazy circumstances. And thanks for helping Augie. He speaks very highly of you. And he said you're going to help us find a safe place to stay."

We moved into the apartment and Della Mae led us to a couch.

"Have a seat. And, there's no need to thank me. Augie would do the same for me. Anyway, this is serious business. And I've found someone who is willing to help you two. I don't know if Augie told you, but I've spent my entire law practice defending people who exist on the margins of society. Some have broken the law and are unrepentant criminals, and I try not to prejudge them. Everyone deserves legal representation under our system of justice. But a lot of the folks I represent are good people who've had bad things happen to them. Most are poor and many of them are minorities. I try and help them navigate through a system that's stacked against them." Della Mae paused and then smiled before continuing.

"Look, I know that sounds self-righteous. And I don't mean to preach. It's just that in my business I see the good, the bad and the ugly. And sometimes, the difference between good and bad is subject to interpretation. And sometimes that's the ugly. Anyway, I immediately thought of one person who might help. He's someone I trust, and I contacted him. Jack is his name, and he lives a few hours north of here in Mendocino County."

I looked at Della Mae and then I asked, "did you tell Jack that the folks looking for me... I mean us... are killers? That they 're members of organized crime, like the mafia?"

"Yes, I told Jack what you told me. Of course, I didn't tell him your name or give him any details or specifics... in case you decide not to go up there. I just made sure he knew that helping you might be very dangerous. That it might put him and the people around him at risk. Jack was a former client of mine. He's a Vietnam vet like you Augie. Jack got in some serious trouble up in Mendocino after he got back from the service. But he was framed. Set up by some corrupt local county cops. They planted marijuana in his cabin in the mountains and threatened to prosecute him unless he agreed to work for them. When he refused, they put him in jail. They charged him with dealing drugs. One of my former clients recommended me to Jack and I agreed to take his case. Over the next several months, I was able to get him out on bail and eventually, we were successful in getting the charges dropped."

"How'd you get the charges dropped?" I asked.

"Turns out, Jack wasn't the first person set up by those same cops. I called a friend of mine at the statehouse over in Sacramento. That person knows someone in the hierarchy of the California Highway Patrol, and they agreed to investigate."

I had to smile. "Sounds like the way we do business back home," I said.

"Yeah, well that's for sure. But the Highway Patrol hit the jackpot. The local cops were actually using guys they had framed, like Jack, to sell dope. They were using them to sell marijuana and other substances those cops had confiscated during legitimate drug busts. The cops were dealers themselves. They never thought they'd get caught because that part of Mendocino County is pretty remote. It's also an area where people from all over the state would come to buy their pot."

"What's Jack doing now? I assume he's still up there in the mountains?"

"Yes. He's still there. And Lou... and you too Augie... Jack owns a small vineyard and winery. It's in a very isolated part of the county. The vineyard is close to the Pacific Ocean, and it's up in the mountains. Jack says that the site allows him to grow wine grapes especially suited to his vineyard."

Lou had been quietly listening, but she jumped right in. "That's pretty cool. I mean literally cool, like in temperature. And that means he can grow white wines like riesling and chardonnay or reds like pinot noir. Those grapes thrive in cooler climates."

"I didn't know that, but I do know the wines I've tasted from his vineyard are really good. Anyway, Jack's agreed to let you guys stay with him for as long as you need to."

Della Mae gave me the directions to Jack's place in the Mendocino County mountains. We would make the trip tomorrow – Thursday morning – and it would be a three-hour drive from Oakland to the secluded vineyard. I looked at my watch. It was after 10 o'clock.

"Hey Della. If you don't mind, I'd like to hit the sack. I'm sure Lou's exhausted too."

"Sure Augie. I've put sheets on the sofa bed in the other room. And Lou, please feel free to use my bathroom and the shower. I'm a night owl and I won't be going to bed for a couple more hours. I have a lot of work to catch up on," she said.

Lou and I took turns using Della's shower and then we got into the sofa bed. Lou gently, but firmly, resisted my amorous advances. "Augie, she'll hear us. Go to sleep" she said.

But I couldn't fall asleep. Too many things were all happening so fast. I was grateful, though, for Della Mae's help because I didn't know where else to go or what to do. However, I really didn't want to put her or her winery friends in danger. Hopefully, Uncle Sal and Jimmie Ponza were working on some ideas that would help resolve the problem soon. In the meantime, we would take Jack up on his offer and hide out at his place in Mendocino. At a winery! What a strange coincidence.

It seems like just about every facet of my new life in California involves something to do with wine. I tried to concentrate on the happy times and special experiences I've had working in, and writing about, the wine industry. So, I thought back a couple of years ago to a seminal event to which I was privileged to be invited. That day stands out as one of the most interesting, illuminating and exciting wine-related experiences of my life.

CHAPTER 18
DECEMBER 1975
OPUS ONE

Caspar's offer to fund my job as editor of the Napa Valley Winery Association newsletter – The Grapeline – in 1973 launched my newspaper career at the San Francisco Chronicle. He and Alex Starling have both played important roles in my vocational ascendancy from winery cellar rat at Starling Vineyards to my job as a writer for the Chronicle. Both Caspar and Alex have also provided me with introductions to some of the most respected winemakers in the Napa Valley. But Caspar's circle of friends in the wine world extends well beyond the borders of the United States.

From his days as an undergraduate at Oxford, Caspar's love of wine has only grown, and his cellar in Napa is full of bottles from some of the greatest wineries in the world. He has developed a special fondness for the red wines of Bordeaux. Over the years, his good friend, fellow Oxford Classmate and Paris wine shop owner, Steven Spurrier, has introduced Caspar to the supple and addictive flavors of Bordeaux red wine, colloquially called Claret. In French, Claret means "clear or pale, and it is the word British wine importers centuries ago used to describe the red wines of Bordeaux. Now, those "pale" wines are much darker and fuller flavored, but the moniker Claret has stuck, especially among the British who seem to have a special affinity for the wine. Steven Spurrier also introduced Caspar to many of the most famous owners and winemakers in Bordeaux, including Baron Philippe de Rothschild, the owner of Chateau Mouton Rothschild. Mouton is considered one of the greatest of all Bordeaux red wines, and its lineage goes back centuries.

It was early December – a few weeks before Christmas – when I got a call from Alex Starling

"Hey Johnny, what are you doing this Saturday afternoon?"

"I don't have any plans. I was thinking of doing some Christmas shopping."

"Well, you might want to go with me and Caspar to a private tasting. It's going to be held at Domaine Chandon. You know, the new sparkling wine operation in Yountville. The folks at Chandon are going to host us for lunch and then a tasting too. I've also asked Ginny and Topo to join us. What do you say?"

Domaine Chandon was the first sparkling wine facility owned by Champagne producer Moet et Chandon built outside of France. The Napa winery opened its doors in 1973, and I had written a story on Chandon for the Chronicle soon after. Domaine Chandon is an architecturally unique winery with a blend of stone and glass on the upper-level public spaces that provide stunning views of the surrounding vineyards and mountains. The walkways to and around the exterior buildings are surrounded by lush gardens, fountains and native flowers. Chandon would also be opening a restaurant on the premises a little later. Until they construct what is expected to be a state-of-the-art wine cellar, they're producing their first sparkling wines off-site at Trefethen Winery near the town of Napa.

"I would love to go. I've always wanted to sample their sparklers. What will we be tasting?"

"Well, I don't think we'll be tasting Chandon's sparkling wine. From what I understand, it will be at least two or three more years until they release their first official wine. This tasting should be interesting though. Caspar's friend from Paris – Steven Spurrier – has put this shindig together. He's invited a few winemakers from here in Napa as well as a special guest from France. A guy named Phillipe de Rothschild. He has a fancy title. He's a baron and he owns Chateau Mouton Rothschild."

"Holy shit, Alex. That guy just got his winery upgraded by the French and declared a First Growth in Bordeaux. I think it just happened a couple of years ago. Wow. I can't wait to see what we'll be tasting."

I had read quite a bit about the world-famous wines made in four communes near the city of Bordeaux. These wine appellations are in the southwest of France not far from the Atlantic Ocean. In the Bordeaux commune of Médoc, the French government established a rating system for the sixty wineries domiciled there. That was in in 1855, and the ratings were based on the prices the wines were able to command in the export market which was – and still is – dominated by the British. Of the sixty wineries classified in 1855, there were only four Premier Cru or "First Growth" wines. Wines in the Médoc are principally made from cabernet sauvignon with lesser amounts of grapes such as merlot, malbec, cabernet franc and petite verdot in the blend. In 1973, Chateau Mouton Rothschild was upgraded from Second Growth to First Growth. I had never tasted Mouton, but I had sipped several less expensive wines from Bordeaux, and I really loved the complexity of flavors and aromas they exhibited. I was thrilled to be invited to the tasting and hoped – against hope – the Baron would open a bottle of Mouton for us.

Alex chuckled over the phone. "I gotta say, I'm pretty excited too. Caspar told me Steven Spurrier asked him to recommend a few Napa cabernets for the tasting, including one of our wines along with bottles from Mondavi and Heitz Cellars. This blind tasting will include a few bottles of Bordeaux too. I'm not sure how our wines will do in a head-to-head competition with them, but I'm intrigued. By the way, Spurrier told Caspar that Bob Mondavi and this guy Rothschild are considering a joint venture to produce a Napa Valley wine. I don't know the details, but they've been meeting quietly for years trying to work things out. Apparently, that's why the baron has come to Napa. And the tasting and luncheon are being held at Chandon so he can visit with some of his French friends who operate the winery here."

It was a cold and rainy Saturday in Yountville when I met Topo and Ginny in the parking lot of Domaine Chandon for the tasting. Fortunately, we had brought umbrellas and we deployed them as we walked quickly through a light drizzle and entered the reception area. We spotted Caspar, Alex and Steven Spurrier engaged in an animated conversation. Alex saw us and waved to us to join them. There were about twenty other people milling around in the reception area.

"Gentlemen, let me introduce to you the Starling Vineyard brain trust," Alex said and made the introductions. "Well, let me clarify. Johnny, here, abandoned us a while back to cast his lot with the Fourth Estate. He's now a wine writer for the San Francisco Chronicle."

"Well then, I suppose we should all be watching our Ps and Qs," Steven Spurrier added in his clipped, British accent.

"You can all breathe easy," I said. "Alex was crystal clear. I had to give him my word that everything I see, hear or taste today stays buttoned up and secret."

Steven chimed in, "Thank you, my dear man. I promise to give you a little advance notice about what I'm hoping to put together later. If it is actually accomplished, I think it will be newsworthy."

Then Caspar added, "Johnny, Steven asked me to do a little leg work, on the QT, for him here in Napa. He's trying to organize a special event next spring that will involve French and American wines. That's all I can say right now, except that today's tasting plays into what he's planning. I assured him that you would honor his wishes today."

"Of course," I said and wondered if I had agreed to something I would regret later.

I followed our group and the other guests into what looked like a conference room that was set up for lunch. The room had a very large window that looked out onto a vineyard that rose gently up a hill and filled our viewscape. The rows of perfectly manicured, but now dormant grape vines, wrapped serpent-like around the wire trellises to which they were trained. I walked behind Alex as he led our group to our seats at a long table. On the table behind each place setting was a name tag indicating where we were to sit. We all sat down, and I watched Spurrier walk to the head of the table. He paused for a few seconds and then he spoke to the assembled group.

"Good afternoon, ladies and gentlemen. My name is Steven Spurrier, and I was asked to arrange a luncheon and a wine tasting for some very good friends of mine in France, and here in Napa. Before our lunch is served, let me introduce some special guests we've invited. First, I want to welcome my great friend from Bordeaux, the Baron Phillipe de Rothschild, who is taking time from some business meetings he has in Napa to join us. He will also be with us for the tasting to follow."

I looked at the elderly gentleman who rose slightly, nodded and sat back down. The baron was attired in a brown leather sport coat under which he wore a tan wool V-neck sweater. Around his neck, he sported a rainbow-colored ascot. He was a handsome man, but bald to mid-scalp where a forest of long, white, straggly hair sprung out in all directions like it was being powered by some intracranial electric current.

Spurrier continued with his introductions. "I'm also happy to welcome Francis Ford Coppola to our event today. You may know Francis for some cinematic things he's done, but he's here as a member of the Napa Valley Winery Association, and the new owner of the Inglenook Winery."

I was stunned. I couldn't believe my star-struck eyes! Coppola was one of my heroes, and I loved his *Godfather* movies. I could also identify with his depiction of Italian American life, especially, and unfortunately, the graphic and violent ways of the Cosa Nostra. Most of the people in this room today probably thought Coppola's *Godfather* movies were pure fiction, but I knew better.

Spurrier also introduced other winemakers in attendance, including Robert Mondavi; Mike Robbins of Spring Mountain Winery; Jim Barrett of Chateau Montelena and his winemaker Mike Grgich; Mary Ann Graf of Simi Winery; and my good friend and mentor, Alex Starling. Then Spurrier smiled and told us about the luncheon we were about to enjoy. An acclaimed chef from France, Philippe Jeaunty, was preparing our meal. Jeaunty is chef at the restaurant owned by Chandon's parent company, Moet et Chandon, in the Champagne region of France.

"Philippe will be coming over to Napa for good soon. He will become head chef at Chandon's new restaurant, Étoile, that is being constructed on the premises. He has prepared a special repast for us that I think will more than adequately prepare our palates for the tasting *après dejeuner*."

With that introduction, four waiters came into the room carrying magnums of Dom Perignon and filled each of our Champagne flutes with the famous sparkling wine. When each guest had a glass of Champagne, Spurrier stood, raised his glass and said, "Bon appetit."

The lunch that followed was truly special, and replete with many foods that were exotic to my plebeian palate. As I had suspected, each course was paired with a complementary wine. We began our lunch with a soup called *Potage Parmentier* which is made with leeks, potatoes, herbs and cream. The soup was paired with Napa Valley's own Chateau Montelena Chardonnay. Our second course was a salad of locally caught Dungeness crab and sliced avocados in a lemon-aioli dressing that we enjoyed with Georges Duboeuf Chablis from Burgundy. This was followed by seared Diver scallops drizzled with a honey, caper and dill sauce and accompanied by Robert Mondavi Fume Blanc. Next was a dish called *lapin à la crème* which is braised rabbit cooked in white wine with smoked bacon and crème fraiche. The course was perfectly paired with Hanzell Pinot Noir from neighboring Sonoma County. Finally, the main course, and something I had actually eaten before: ribeye of prime beef. However, I had never had it grilled, flavored with smoked paprika and covered with wild porcini mushrooms. This dish was deliciously paired with Chateau Cos d'Estournel, a second growth red wine from Bordeaux. Thankfully, the dessert was *crème brûlée* with fresh raspberries. It was light and refreshing, and was served with small glasses of Chateau Y'quem – the world-famous Bordeaux First Growth sweet white wine. Cups of dark roast, expresso-like coffee concluded the meal.

After lunch, we moved outside to a porch adjacent to the reception area while the dining room was reconfigured and prepared for the wine tasting to come. The weather had moderated, and the day was now full of bright blue skies and sunshine. While we stood chatting and breathing in the brisk fresh air, I noticed that half the people on the porch were smoking cigarettes. I had always assumed that people in the wine trade, especially winemakers, would certainly adhere to the universal wine appreciation admonition: never taint your palate with cigarette smoke before a tasting. So much for that viticultural myth. After ten minutes of fresh air and cigarette smoke, we all went back into the winery and to the room which was now was set up classroom-style with three rows of tables. On the tables in front of every chair there were six glasses, each filled with about two ounces of red wine. There were also two other glasses on the table, but they were empty. I knew that one of the glasses could be used to cleanse our palates with water between wines if we wished. But what was the other glass for? There were also small dishes on the table with wafer-like crackers, several pitchers of water and as many silver buckets. The buckets, I knew, served as receptacles to dump or spit into whatever wine was not drunk. There were also note pads and pencils with erasers at each place setting.

Steven Spurrier once again stood and addressed our group of tasters.

"And now to the work at hand. In front of you, are six red wines. Three are from here in the Napa Valley, and three are from Bordeaux. This tasting will be a good way to judge the similarities – if any – among the wines as well as any differences. I want to stress that this is not a contest to judge which country's wine is superior. But, since these wines use some of the same grapes, albeit from different parts of the world, this should be an interesting exercise. I am the only one at this table who knows what wines have been selected for the tasting, but I have no idea into which glass before you they have been poured. In front of you there is a tablet with the wines numbered one through six.

You may wish to take notes on your impressions of the wines. At the conclusion of the tasting, I would ask that you rate them in order of preference from one through six. I must also ask each of you to leave your notes and ratings here before you leave the tasting room. And please, do not discuss any of the results with anyone outside this room. Any questions? Alright then, let's get started."

I took a sip of water and a bite of wafer. I held wine number one up, swirled it and looked at its color. Then I put the glass to my nose and sniffed deeply. Next, I tasted the wine, and I repeated this method of evaluating each of the wines on the table. Then I wrote my impressions of each. After about twenty minutes, Spurrier asked if anyone needed more time and, when no one spoke up, he asked each of us to use a separate sheet of the notepad and rate the wines. He then collected our rating sheets and began tallying the results.

I really liked all the wines. There were no disappointments, but there were definite differences, and I was anxious to find out what we had tasted. After about fifteen minutes, Spurrier stood.

"Well, I must say, I'm not completely surprised, but… Oh hell, here's the order of how you rated the wines, and their names from number one to number six."

When he read the results, I must admit I was disappointed, but like Spurrier, not really surprised. And since there were only two people at the tasting who were not American, we could not claim any national bias in the results.

First Place: 1961 Chateau Mouton Rothschild
Second Place: 1959 Chateau Latour
Third Place: 1966 Chateau Margaux
Fourth Place: 1968 Heitz Cellars Martha's Vineyard Cabernet Sauvignon
Fifth Place: 1966 Robert Mondavi Reserve Cabernet Sauvignon
Sixth Place: 1967 Starling Vineyard Cabernet Sauvignon Reserve

I was not shocked by the results, but I felt sorry for Alex. I suppose there is still a huge difference in quality between Bordeaux and Napa. I thought every wine was very good, but in looking at my scores, I had rated only one Napa wine – the Heitz Cabernet – in the top three – and at number two. Sadly, I had rated Starling wine at number five. Judging from the results, Napa obviously had more work to do. Just then, four wine waiters returned to the room and, from bottles covered in paper bags, they began to pour a final wine into the remaining empty glass in front of each of us.

Steven Spurrier addressed us once more. "I think we can agree that all the wines we tasted here today are exceptional. No one has anything to be ashamed of. And I still think the Napa Valley will become one of the greatest wine regions on the planet. Someday. But we have one more wine to taste. And we have Baron Rothschild to thank for this special wine. Please go ahead and taste it, and then I'll let you know what it is."

The wine was purple. The deepest purple I have ever seen. When I swirled it and put it to my nose, I was astounded by the depth of black fruit, coffee and spicy aromas emanating from the glass. When I sipped the wine, I was overcome by a complex symphony of layered flavors. I tasted nuances of blackberries, chocolate and cola, all seamlessly integrated and supple. The wine also had very soft, silky tannins, but it seemed very young, and I wondered if it had any aging potential. It is without a doubt, though, the best wine I have ever tasted. I looked up at Steven Spurrier who was tearing the bag from the bottle which revealed the mystery wine to be 1947 Château Cheval Blanc. The wine was nearly thirty years old! How could a wine so luscious tasting, with amazingly complex layers of flavor, be so old and yet taste so young? I would read later that this wine from the commune of Saint Emilion, on the right bank of the Gironde River in Bordeaux, is generally regarded as the best wine ever produced in Bordeaux.

As Ginny, Topo and I walked out of Domaine Chandon into the late afternoon sunshine, Alex, who was standing next to his car, waved us over. When we joined him, Alex looked over at Topo, his co-winemaker at Starling Vineyard, and smiled.

"I hope you're not discouraged by the results of the tasting, Topo. Our wine did not win, but it was in very, very good company. I'm not disappointed at all. So just keep doing what you're doing because we are making great wine."

Then Alex looked at all of us. "I have one more piece of exciting news to tell you about. Steven told me that Baron Rothschild and Bob Mondavi have shaken hands on a deal to make a special joint venture Bordeaux/Napa Valley wine. It will be a blend of Napa Valley grapes like the ones used to make Bordeaux reds. As you all know, Bordeaux winemakers use some combination of cabernet sauvignon, merlot, malbec, petit verdot and caberret franc in their final blend. This new wine will be comprised of similar grapes, but the cuvée will vary from year to year based upon the decision of the co-winemakers. They are Tim Mondavi, son of Robert who makes wine here in Napa for Mondavi, and Lucien Sionneau from Château Mouton Rothschild in Bordeaux. Steven said that the first virtage will be in 1979."

"What are they going to call the wine?" Ginny asked

Alex smiled broadly at Ginny "Looks" Loveleigh. "The wine is to be called Opus One."

That day at Domaine Chandon produced one of the most pleasant and memorable wine experiences of my life, and I think of it often. I especially need these pleasant thoughts now to keep me sane while I try and deal with the fact there are two homicidal psychopaths trying to kill me.

Chapter 19
Tubby and Cheech

Tubby and Cheech moved quickly through the ensuing chaos and mayhem precipitated by the incident at the BART Station. They were hustling back to their truck which was parked near the Chronicle building. Cheech was royally pissed off at Tubby after the screwup at the subway. But Cheech was even more worried about how their boss Carmine would react once he found out. First, they had bungled the snatch and grab of Cumpton in the Marina District, and then they had really dropped the ball when Tubby pushed the wrong guy onto the train tracks at the BART Station. Cheech wondered if his partner really gave a shit. He probably didn't care because at least he got to kill someone, and that's all that really counted to Tubby.

Cheech looked at the short, squat, baby-faced man and grumbled in a nasal, whiny voice, as he ran, "Why'd you shove the wrong guy on them tracks? You was standing right next to Cumpton. I know, cause I'm the one that got him there in that spot right next to you. All you had to do was push him. But instead, you shove the wrong guy. Now we gotta let Carmine know. And there will be hell to pay!"

Tubby grinned up at Cheech and said, "The guy I was s'posed to shove moved away from me. I musta shoved the other guy by mistake."

"Bullshit, Tubby. When I seen Cumpton turn away from you and start to leave, I was gonna follow him. But when you pushed that guy onto the tracks, the crowd went crazy and everyone tried to get outta there at once. I couldn't move. We both should have chased him. But no. You had to get your jollies off by wasting someone ... anyone... right? And now, we'll probably never find Cumpton, and we gotta let the boss know we screwed up again. As a matter of fact, you're the one's gonna call Carmine this time. Since you made the mess, you'll have to clean it up."

Tubby stopped suddenly and grabbed Cheech by the arm. He was breathing heavily, and glistening rivulets of sweat streamed down his doughboy face. "Hey Cheech, ain't there nothin' else we can do to find this guy? I mean, the boss warned us not to come back without Cumpton." Tubby was pleading with his partner.

"I don't know how we can ever find him now. He could be anywhere."

Cheech was shaking his head and trying to figure a way to get back on Cumpton's trail. Tubby was right, though. They couldn't go back to Pittsburgh unless they found him and finished the job. And even though it seemed impossible, they had to continue to search for Cumpton. That was for sure. So, Cheech and Tubby drove around the Powell Street BART Station and SOMA for several hours until dusk hoping to spot Cumpton. They stopped at a diner for dinner, and then they returned to the Mission District. They parked the truck a few blocks from Cumpton's place and set up an observation post with a view of his apartment building's front door. They spent the night there, but Cumpton didn't show.

In the morning, Tubby hid near the apartment hoping to spot Cumpton while Cheech took the truck and drove to a parking spot near the Chronicle. He then began patrolling the area around the building hoping to spot Cumpton. Each hour on the hour, Cheech dialed the number of a public pay phone on a corner near Cumpton's apartment where Tubby was on lookout. However, neither one had spotted the man all day, and Cheech returned to the Mission District and caught up with his partner.

It was Wednesday night and they decided to give it one more day. If they couldn't locate Cumpton by this time tomorrow night, they would have to decide: risk going back to Pittsburgh and beg Carmine to forgive and forget; or simply cut their losses, go into hiding, and wait for the old capo to die. Everyone in their crew knew Carmine was not in good health. Maybe when he finally kicked the bucket, they'd be able to return to La Famiglia Vagabonda in Pittsburgh.

Thursday was a repeat of the previous day, with the two of them switching jobs. Tubby took the panel truck and cruised SOMA and the Embarcadero area, while Cheech stayed in the Mission District near Cumpton's apartment. However, the result was the same: no Cumpton sighting.

Cheech was desperate when he spoke to Tubby later that day. "The only thing we ain't done yet is check out Cumpton's apartment. We know he was tryin' to catch the subway to Oakland. Maybe there's something in his place that'll give us a clue about why he was headed there. I think it's worth the chance to break into the place. That's the only thing I know to do." Tubby just nodded his head.

Cheech rubbed the dark stubble on his chin and then he added, "Okay, here's what we're gonna do. We'll sneak over to Cumpton's place right now and see if we can find something. But if we come up empty-handed after that, then you and me are screwed, and we're probably dead meat too if we go back home."

It was nearly 9 p.m. when the two Black Hand men parked their truck along Folsom Street. They walked two blocks south and then turned up 18th Street, strolling casually up to Cumpton's apartment building. They entered the building through a glass door and walked into a foyer. Along one of the walls just inside the entrance were several locked mailboxes with the tenants' names affixed above each. Johnny Harman's apartment was on the second floor. They walked up the stairs and stood before the apartment door. Cheech, who was adept at gaining entrance to places he wasn't supposed to be, used his lock pick to easily gain entrance to the apartment. Cumpton's dwelling had two bedrooms, a bath, a kitchen and a small living room with an RCA television set and an old wooden desk. The desk had three pedestal-style drawers on either side of the knee space. On the desktop was an Olivetti electric typewriter. Cheech began going through the contents of the desk drawers while Tubby checked out the kitchen drawers and the furniture in the bedrooms. The men searched for two hours and found nothing to indicate where Cumpton might have gone. They had torn the place apart, but they were unable to find anything. It was after 11 o'clock and both men were tired and frustrated.

Cheech said, "I guess we're gonna have to call Carmine in the morning with the bad news."

"Maybe he'll cut us a break, Cheech," Tubby said hopefully. "You know, let us come back."

"Yeah, even if he did say everything's okay, you can bet your sweet ass it ain't. Only thing you can be sure of — if we go back empty handed — is a bullet in the head. No, we'll just have to go underground for a while and hope this shit storm blows over. Or the boss dies. In the meantime, I'm bushed. I say we just stay here tonight. Cumpton sure as hell won't be back. We can try and figure something out in the morning." Cheech left Tubby and went into one of Cumpton's bedrooms. He undressed and fell quickly to sleep.

It was Friday morning around 8 a.m. when Cheech woke up. He walked into Cumpton's other bedroom where he found Tubby lying on his back, fully clothed and snoring like a freight train. The little man looked like a soiled and disheveled version of that board game character, Mr. Monopoly.

"Get your ass out of bed, Fatso. I'm gonna take one more look around this dump and see if I missed something. And you might go into Cumpton's bathroom and use his toothbrush. Your breath smells like couple of rats shacked up in your mouth."

Tubby rubbed his eyes and rolled out of bed. "I'm up Cheech. I gotta take a piss, but I ain't using no one else's toothbrush."

Within a couple of minutes, Cheech called out to his partner.

"Hey Tubby, come in here. I think I got something."

Tubby came waddling into the kitchen. "What'd you find?"

Cheech held out a small address book. "I thought you said you looked in the kitchen?"

"I did. I tore the place up. Where'd you find that?"

"It was in the refrigerator freezer in a plastic bag. It has a bunch of telephone numbers and some addresses. Mainly for people back in West Virginia. Probably Cumpton's family and friends. But on the last page, I found a telephone number and a street address for a 'D. M. Smith.' I checked out the whole book and that's the only person in there who's from Oakland, California. It ain't much to go on, but it's the only thing we got. We'll take a drive over there this morning and check this D. M. Smith out. It would be great if Cumpton's staying over at this person's place. If he ain't there, maybe this person will tell us where we can find him. I'll let you work on D. M. Smith, Tubby, to find out. But you can't take all day."

Tubby smiled broadly. He was overjoyed at the prospect of inflicting pain and suffering.

"Don't worry Cheech. If this Smith person knows somethin' about where Cumpton is, I'll find out. I get to do what I do best, right?"

Cheech just shook his head at his smiling little friend.

CHAPTER 20
MENDOCINO JACK

Since Della Mae took the bus each day to her office in downtown Oakland, she let me use her 1973 AMC Gremlin for the trip to Jack's Mendocino County vineyard. She said that Jack, or his partner, could return the car tomorrow.

The drive from Oakland took us on I-580, across the Richmond Bridge and onto US 101 North for the trip to Mendocino County. We followed the road through Sonoma County to just beyond Cloverdale where we turned west onto Highway 128, and into the Anderson Valley of Mendocino County. It was mid-October and some of the leaves on the scattered deciduous Valley Oak trees had turned yellow. However, a more glorious palette of fall colors was on display in the vineyards of Anderson Valley. There, the red, purple and orange grape leaves did their best to mimic autumn back in West Virginia. That made me wonder, wistfully, if I would ever see my home state again.

Lou was the navigator, reading Della Mae's handwritten directions. About three hours into the trip, we made a right turn off Highway 128 onto Yorkville Ranch Road and began the ascent up Hawk Butte Mountain toward our remote destination. Fifteen minutes later, we turned left onto Fruit Lake Drive and drove for another three miles along the narrow two-lane road that was bounded by a forest thick with conifers.

We spotted a sign with an arrow pointing left and reading "Fruit Lake." Della Mae had instructed us to go beyond the sign for one-half mile until we saw a wooden signpost with an arrow pointing to "FLV." We turned onto a rutted, gravel track and very slowly traveled for another two miles until we reached a metal farm gate with a sign proclaiming in large, red letters: Fruit Lake Vineyard and Winery. No Trespassing.

As I turned the Gremlin's engine off and reached for the door handle, two men quickly emerged from the forest and stood – each against a front passenger door – preventing either of us from getting out. The man up against my door was at least six-five with a completely bald head, a barrel chest and biceps that seemed about to burst out of his tightly fitting lumberjack-like wool shirt. I was momentarily startled and speechless. The guy's a dead ringer for Mr. Clean – the caricature who promotes that household cleaner on TV. He even wears a ring in his ear like Mr. Clean. I looked over to Lou who seemed frozen with her hand on the door handle. The man who stood guarding her door was shorter than Mr. Clean by several inches, but he was broad in the chest and looked like a weightlifter.

I rolled the window down but before I could speak, Mr. Clean asked, "Who are you?"

"Are you Jack?" I responded.

"That depends on who's asking," he said.

"I'm Augie and this is Lou," I said, pointing to her.

"How'd you find this place?"

"Della Mae gave us directions." I reached over to Lou who handed me the written directions. I handed the paper to this very large, strange-looking man.

"This sure looks like her handwriting. Tell me, where was Della born. And how does she know this Jack fellow?" He leaned into the car, looking carefully into the front seat. "And hand me the car key," he said sternly. It was not a question.

I removed the key from the ignition and handed it to him. I turned and watched while he moved to the rear of the car and used the key to open the hatch-back rear window. He stuck his head through the window opening and looked from side to side.

"She's from Jeweltown, West Virginia," I said. "She told me she was Jack's lawyer and she helped him with some legal problems a few years back," I added.

"Okay. I guess you're going to be my guests for a while," he said as he walked back to the front door and opened it up. He handed me back the ignition key. "I'm Jack Cosgrove. And I'm happy to help any friends of Della's. You're right. She got me out of a big jam. If it wasn't for her, I'd be busting rocks at some maximum-security prison right now."

I got out of the car and shook Jack's large and calloused hand. He had an angular, almost chiseled face with piercing blue eyes. He pointed to his friend who had opened Lou's door and stood back while she got out of the car.

"That's Artie. He's a good friend of mine. He helps me at the vineyard and winery," Jack said.

"Pleased to meet you both. And this is Lou," I said.

Two large German shepherds suddenly appeared and were on the other side of the gate growling at us. "Those are two scary looking dogs," I added.

"They're Sport and Chelsea. They do a good job discouraging trespassers," Artie said.

I smiled right back. "Good to meet Sport and Chelsea too. I really appreciate you letting us hide out at your place for a while. I suppose Della Mae told you why we're here. And that you could be in some jeopardy if the guys after me track us up here." I looked at Jack for any signs indicating concern or fear, but he seemed completely calm.

"Yeah. Della gave me the quick and dirty. Sounds like you've had quite a ride since you returned from the war. But don't worry about bringing us any trouble. We've had to deal with our share of poachers, druggies and other assorted reprobates looking to steal anything that isn't tied down. If it will make you feel any better, we have a pretty good early warning system in place that alerts us when someone uninvited tries to get past the gate," Jack said and pointed to the dogs.

"Chelsea and Sport are excellent sentinels for us. But I'd sure love to have a few of those claymore mines we had over in Vietnam though," he said and smiled.

I didn't return the smile. I looked directly at Jack. "You need to understand that these guys won't hesitate to use deadly force. A couple days ago, one of them shoved a man onto the tracks in front of a BART train. He meant to kill me. But when I moved aside, he just murdered the poor guy standing next to me... for no reason. So, I really hope the bastards after me won't be able to find us up here. In the meantime, I have some friends back home working behind the scenes to try and get these thugs to back off. Hopefully, we won't be in your hair for very long."

Without missing a beat, Artie, pointing to his bald partner, said "Don't worry Augie, you won't be in his hair."

I smiled, but I doubted very much that these men had ever encountered mob guys before. Made men who didn't hesitate to murder at the drop of a hat. But I had to admit: this place was very isolated, and off the beaten track in a rural location, and I couldn't imagine those city slickers from Pittsburgh being able to sneak up on us.

"Look Augie," Jack said, "you can stay here as long as you need to. Hopefully, this will just be a little inconvenience for you and Lou. And I understand things could get dicey. But if there's trouble, I think we'll be able to handle things. We've had to defend this place before from people who've tried to come up here and take things from us. Nasty people. Kind of like the guys after you."

Jack then moved to the gate and used a key to remove the large padlock. He leaned over and rubbed each dog's head and then he motioned for us to drive through. Jack re-locked the gate, and he and Artie climbed into the back seat of the Gremlin. "Follow the road, Augie," he said.

The gravel road wound through the pine forest for five minutes before we drove up a small rise in the woods just below a ridge top. Jack asked me to stop.

"Let's get out and walk up the road a little," he said.

We all got out of the car, and we followed Jack and Artie as they began walking up the road to a small plateau where the forest abruptly ended. We gazed down on a vineyard valley. The scene before us was almost surreal. Like Van Gogh's canvas *Red Vineyard*, rows of vines with grape leaves painted a palette of colors, filled the area in front of us. A gravel road bisected the vineyard and led gently down to the winery building and living quarters. Fashioned from rough cut redwood, the building sat grandly overlooking Jack Cosgrove's exquisite property. Jack told us the winery was located below the home in a large two-story basement, the bottom floor of which was completely underground and housed the fermenters, stainless steel tanks and barrel room.

"Jack, this is absolutely stunning," Lou said in a reverential tone. "What are you growing up here?"

Jack looked over at Lou and smiled. "Della Mae told me that you're a winemaker too. That you have a vineyard back in West Virginia. So you know how important it is to plant vines in locations that will give you the best chance of producing good wine. We're at about twenty-four hundred feet above sea level, so we planted vines that do best in this microclimate. You know, cool weather grapes. I've got six acres planted to pinot noir and chardonnay. Both grapes do well up here. The soil is rocky and drains well. That makes the vines work harder to find water and, as you know, that produces better wine."

Lou was nodding her head while Jack was speaking. That's good, I thought. I knew that Lou didn't want to be away from her vines, but at least she would be surrounded by a vineyard and have access to a winery, and to folks with whom she could share a common interest.

"Hey Jack, maybe Lou can give you a hand around the winery," I said. "She's got this year's wine already aging back home. I can help out too. I spent a couple of years working at Starling Vineyard, down in Napa, as an all-round cellar rat."

"That's great. We sure could use the help. From both of you. We just finished harvest out here and we're dealing with a lot of new wine that has to be tended to," Jack said.

That was our first view of Mendocino Jack's winery. I'm grateful to Della Mae for arranging this with Jack, and for his generosity and willingness to let us hide out here for a while. I just hope this won't put Jack and Artie's lives in danger.

CHAPTER 21
DINNER AT FRUIT LAKE

Jack gave us a quick tour of the winery and then we followed him upstairs to the living area where he led us to our bedroom. After Lou and I got settled, we stepped out of the bedroom and were immediately intoxicated by the savory smells of something delicious being prepared nearby. The aromas reminded me of how famished I was, and they also seemed very familiar – like something from my childhood that Mom or one of my aunts might have lovingly prepared. Lou and I followed the scent through a long hallway and into the kitchen. There, Artie stood, using a wooden spoon to stir something in a large pot.

"Damn Artie. What's in the pot? Kind of has my mouth watering," I said.

"It's called *ribollita*," he said and turned smiling toward us. "It's a recipe from my Pop's restaurant down state. It's made from cannellini beans, canned tomatoes, bread and cheese. And a whole lot of veggies like onion, garlic, carrots and kale. By the way, my full name is Arturo Passinetti. I'm a second generation paisan."

"That sounds like a pretty fancy dish to me, Artie," Lou added.

"Not really. *Ribollita* means 'reboiled' and it's really an Italian peasant dish... kind of like pasta and beans... only heartier. It's really simple to prepare. I sautéed the veggies in the pot and then added the beans and tomatoes. I also put a half loaf of cut up day-old Italian bread and a wedge of parmesan cheese in the pot too. I let that cook for about an hour and then I topped it off with more pieces of bread and grated parmesan. I did all that this morning and let it sit all day. That way the bread absorbs the flavors of the other ingredients. Right now, I'm reheating, or reboiling, the *ribollita*. When it's hot, I'll grate some more parmesan on top of it, and put the pot in the oven under the broiler for about fifteen minutes. Then we'll eat the stuff, and you can tell me if it's as good as it smells."

"Smells, unlike looks, are not usually deceiving," Lou said, grinning widely. "But what wine are you going to pair it with, Artie? Probably needs a big red, don't you think?

"You know Lou, I heard about the award you won for your sangiovese. That would be a perfect complement to this dish. *Ribollita* originated in Tuscany where the local red wine, usually Chianti, is made mostly from sangiovese. Since we don't have any sangiovese, we'll open a bottle of locally produced zinfandel. It pairs well with *ribollita*, too."

Just then Jack came into the kitchen holding a bottle of white wine. "Okay folks, before dinner why don't we warm up with a taste of our Fruit Lake Chardonnay. You too, Artie. Follow me and I'll pour us some."

Jack led us into the dining room, and we all sat at a long, rough-hewn, redwood table situated perpendicular to a large picture window that presented us with a spectacular vista of the vineyard that was speckled with multi-colored grape leaves. The view looked west over the mountains to where the sun was just about to disappear and complete its descent into the Pacific Ocean. The sunset bathed the dining room in soft, pink light as Jack poured chardonnay for each of us into small stemless glasses. Then he stood and raised his glass.

"To our new friends Augie and Lou. May they live safe, well and long!"

"Hear, hear," Artie said and also raised his glass.

We all sipped the silky, smooth wine and then I rose. "A couple of days ago, I was desperate to get us away from the Bay Area. But I didn't have any idea where to go. That's when Della told us about you and your winery, Jack. And about the trouble she helped you get through. She also told us she had called you, and that you had agreed to let us stay here. Jack, Artie... Thank you so much for your generosity and kindness. Here's to you guys," I said, and lifted my glass to our new friends.

Both men nodded and took a sip of their wine. Then Artie stood up. "Hey Jack, I'll go get the chow and bring it in. Why don't you give them the quick and dirty about us queers," he added, chuckling as he left the room.

I looked over at Jack who seemed to be momentarily flustered and speechless. A crimson glow began to materialize on his face and rose slowly toward his shiny, bald head. He looked over to Lou and me.

"I don't suppose it's very common to discuss personal matters with complete strangers, but Artie is… how can I put it… very direct. He and I are a couple. We've been living together now for about three years. We met several years ago at a gay bar in the Castro District down in San Francisco."

Just then, Artie came into the room carrying a large tureen of steaming *ribollita* on top of which was a perfectly balanced baguette. He placed the bowl and baguette on the table and extracted a ladle from his back pocket which he placed in the tureen. He looked over at Lou and me and smiled. "Sorry for the interruption," he said.

I was trying my best to hide the shock I felt at this personal revelation by Jack and Artie. I had heard and read about homosexual relationships, but I had never encountered anyone who had spoken so openly about being in one. Clearly, my world was expanding. And I also had never heard the term "gay" used to describe homosexuality. I guess I really had led a sheltered life.

Jack continued. "Look, enough said about that. And I'm sorry if I made you feel uncomfortable, but Artie's right. You should know about us and who we are. But that's not all we are. And believe me when I tell you that we're committed to keeping you hidden and safe up here."

We passed our bowls to Artie who ladled the thick and aromatic stew into each of them. Before he passed them around, he drizzled a little olive oil onto the *ribollita* in each bowl. I also noticed that there was a small shaker of red chili pepper flakes and a saucer filled with freshly grated parmesan. I topped my bowl with generous portions of both. Jack grabbed the baguette, tore a piece off and passed it to each of us. Artie then opened the zinfandel and poured the deeply purple wine into a small jelly jar-like glass. Immediately, the aroma of blackberries and spice seemed to fill the room as the Zinfandel was poured into each of our glasses.

"Hey Jack. Where'd you find these little wine glasses? They look exactly like the ones my Grandpa Costanza always used," I said.

Jack smiled and looked over at Artie. "I'll let him tell you about the glasses. He's the one that insists we use them."

Before Artie could answer, Lou asked, "Don't they call them *bacaro?*"

"Lou, you're absolutely right," Artie said. "They are *Bacaro del Veneto*. My folks come from a little village outside of Verona. *Bacaro* means tavern or roadhouse, and the glasses they used in these places were as humble and unpretentious as the wine they poured into them."

Then Artie held his glass up. "Mom packed these glasses in one of her suitcases when she and Pop came to this country right before World War II. Pop was not a fan of Mussolini – or his German buddy Adolph – so he and Mom left Italy and made the voyage to New York. Then they took a train across the country and settled in Monterey, California. Just like most other Italian immigrants, they chose to live in places where other family members had settled. In this case, my father's brother Emilio. He had moved to Monterey some years before to work in the fish canneries there. That's how my family got to California. And these *bacaro* glasses made the trip with them."

Artie explained that his father also worked in a cannery for a few years. Then, right after the end of the war, he opened a small restaurant on the Monterey Wharf. Artie was born in 1946, and he worked in the restaurant all through grade school and high school, and then for two years while he attended Monterey Peninsula Community College.

"After college, it was time for me to get out of Monterey," he said. "By that time, I knew that my sexual orientation would be a problem for me and my family there. So, I moved up to San Francisco. Because of my experience working in my father's place, I was able to get a job as a line cook at an Italian restaurant in North Beach. After work, I hung out in the Castro District. That's where I met 'Mr. Clean,'" he said and smiled at Jack. "Later, I took a job as a sous-chef at a fancy sounding place in Berkeley. You may have heard of it – Chez Panisse..."

Lou nearly jumped out of her chair. "You worked for Alice Waters? Wow, that's amazing! I read about her restaurant in the Washington Post a couple of years ago. According to the Post article, she's kind of a celebrity chef. The story says she's revolutionizing the restaurant industry. And Chez Panisse has become a famous place."

"Yeah, it has become well known," Artie said. "A friend of mine – another cook at the restaurant where I was working – introduced me to her at a bar in San Francisco. Over a few months, we became good friends. Alice is a great gal. Really down to earth. And when she opened her place, she offered me a job. I really learned a lot from her. She's worked hard to keep the place afloat. She buys her produce and meat from area farmers instead of from the large food wholesalers. She pays top dollar for these local products. That goes for fish, too. She buys her seafood right at the docks from Bay Area fishermen. So, it's been a financial struggle to operate the restaurant, but I think she's turned the corner."

Lou asked, "So how did you end up in Mendocino?"

"I worked at Chez Panisse for almost two years until Jack convinced me to come up here and help him at the winery. Later, Alice hired a guy named Jeremiah Tower as executive chef. Her menus have always been based on French food, but this Tower guy really upped the emphasis on *haute cuisine*, you know, the fancy old world French dishes. When I worked there, Chez Panisse was more of a bistro type place with dishes like beef bourguignon, quiches and escargot. But I have to give Jeremiah credit, the restaurant has really become famous. Like you mentioned, Lou. And last year, the menu was completely revised with a total focus on California cuisine. I'm going to stop by and see her when I return Della Mae's car tomorrow." Artie then looked over to Jack.

Jack smiled at his partner. "I guess it's my turn, right Artie? You know, I think we make a pretty good team. Artie's the chef and a good winemaker too. I'm more of the vineyard guy. I'm from a little town near San Diego. After high school, I enrolled at UCLA and ended up with a degree in agronomy. I was in Army ROTC, and when I graduated, I was commissioned as a second lieutenant. Later, I trained for and became a Special Forces officer. You've probably heard of the Green Berets. Anyway, it was 1964 and Vietnam was just heating up. I was with the 5th Special Forces Group up in the Central Highlands. I thought I was going to teach the indigenous people there – the Montagnards – how to grow rice. But all we really taught them was how to use modern weapons of war to kill the Viet Cong. When I got out of the Army, I decided to put my undergraduate degree to work in a more civilized and peaceful way. I started working at vineyards and wineries all over California. Then I went over to Burgundy for a couple of harvests. That's where I fell in love with pinot noir and chardonnay. I wanted to plant those grapes over here. To see if I could kind of replicate what they do in Burgundy. I think Mendocino County is the perfect place to do that. That's why I came up here and bought this land. And thanks to Della Mae, I was able to keep the place through the tough times. She not only represented me and got my record cleared, she also made my mortgage payments while I was in jail and helped Artie with the harvest that year. Quite a gal, that Della."

I looked over at Jack and brushed tears from my eyes. "You're right, Jack," I said, trying to control my emotions. "Della Mae is an incredible friend to have. She's affected both of our lives in major ways. And by connecting us with you, she's literally saved my life – and Lou's too. As if helping us was just second nature. And I'm sure it is to her. I hope we'll get to thank her in person when this is all over."

"Hey Augie, I'll be talking to Della tomorrow," Artie said. "I'll give her your regards. And I'll invite her up here when she can get away."

"That would be great, Artie. By the way, how will you get back here?"

"I'll take a Greyhound from Oakland up to Boonville. That's right down the road on route 128. There's a bus station where Jack can come pick me up."

Dinner was delicious and we lingered afterward for an hour or so to finish the zinfandel. It was a satisfying ending to a long and stressful day. When Lou and I got to our room, we undressed quickly and got under the covers. There was no resistance from Lou this night. We made long and sweet love until we were both exhausted. Then I fell into a deep and, thankfully, dreamless sleep.

CHAPTER 22
NEW SHERIFF IN TOWN

The day that Augie made his way to Mendocino Jack's vineyard and winery, Jimmie Ponza received a very strange telephone call. Mickey O'Shay, the longtime bartender at the Ruff Avenue Poolroom, walked around the bar to the telephone that hung on the wall just inside the front door. He picked up the ringing phone from its cradle on the wall.

"Ruff Avenue Poolroom. Mickey speaking."

A nasal and gruff voice on the phone said: "Let me talk to Jimmie Ponza. I s'pose he's your boss."

"Can I tell him who's calling?" Mickey said.

"He don't know me, but he'll want to talk to me. Put him on the line."

"I need to get him to come down here. He's upstairs in his office. Hold on," Mickey said.

Mickey looked to the back of the room where he could see Jimmie Ponza sitting at his desk in his small, second-story office that looked down through a smoky, glass window to the poolroom below. Mickey caught Jimmie's attention by waving the phone with one hand and motioning for his boss to come downstairs with the other. Jimmie nodded, ran his fingers through his full, white mane and then he came down the steps, and through the poolroom to where Mickey held the phone.

Mickey covered the phone's mouthpiece with his hand and said, "I don't know who it is, but it sounds like one of them guys from Pittsburgh." Jimmie took the phone from Mickey.

"This is Jimmie. How can I help you?"

"I'm with the crew up north. We been doin' business with yinz guys for years. I understand you was calling up here to find out about that kid from down your way. The one who disappeared a few years ago. And now someone spotted that guy alive out west."

Jimmie was puzzled. He had called and talked with the boss, Carmine. He didn't recognize this guy on the other end of the line. "I spoke to Carmine a couple of days ago about Augie Cumpton. He's the nephew of a good friend of mine. I helped my friend do a deal with you guys several years ago where there was an exchange made. Like I told Carmine, we don't know nothin' about him being alive. We all thought he was dead. Did Carmine ask you to call me?"

"No. Carmine didn't ask me to do nothin'. I'm calling on my own to see if you would be interested in passing along some information to that friend of yours. I think his name is Sal. He's the Cumpton kid's uncle you just mentioned, right? Anyway, I might be able to work something out where this kid gets off the hook. Where he can come home without any worries about anyone from Pittsburgh bothering him. You think Sal would be interested in something like that?"

Jimmie was shocked at the boldness of the offer, and he didn't know how to respond. He didn't even know if he should continue this conversation. What if this was a set-up to trap him into admitting he was part of the scam the Costanza family cooked up to save Augie? He definitely needed to find out more about this guy before he agreed to work with him.

Jimmie asked, "Who are you? I've only talked to Carmine about this stuff in the past. I just spoke to him a couple of days ago. And now I get this call from a stranger. I need more information. Tell me a little bit more about why you're calling."

"Okay. Listen up. My name's Vito. I'm one of the guys who came down there to pick up Cumpton back in 1970. We brung Cumpton's girlfriend with us, and Sal was s'posed to give us the kid in exchange. But things didn't go the way they were meant to go. Let's just say I'm now in a position to make sure nothing bad happens to Cumpton. I know there's some guys trying to find him out in California. Your friend Sal has something I want. If he gives it to me, I can get the Cumpton kid off the hook. You talk to Sal and then give me a call. And if you can get a hold of a Pittsburgh Press paper today, check out the story on page B-2," Vito said and recited his phone number. Then he hung up.

Jimmie was puzzled. He needed to think this through. While neither of the two mob guys sent to get Augie were model citizens, the one called Vito The Scar had an especially deadly reputation. He was a brutal enforcer for La Famiglia and Jimmie had heard stories about the man's penchant for mayhem and murder. So, this must be the guy who is now on the run from Carmine, and the one the mob is looking for to explain why Augie is still alive. They haven't found Vito, though, or the guy wouldn't have called me. Which means that Vito must be acting on his own. Carmine had to be fishing when he called and tried to suggest that me or someone in the Costanza family had been involved in a scheme to scam them. It was clear that Carmine didn't have any idea how Augie had survived. Jimmie scratched his head. How could Vito make a deal without the blessing of Carmine? He decided to contact Carmine directly. Jimmie dialed Carmine's private number. He let the phone ring twenty times, but no one picked up. Over the next two hours, Jimmie called Carmine's number ten more times, but still no one answered the phone. Finally, on the eleventh call, someone picked up.

"Yeah," a man with a gravelly voice said.

Jimmie asked, "Can I speak to Carmine?"

"He ain't here. Who's calling?"

"This is Jimmie Ponza down in Jeweltown. I spoke to Carmine a couple of days ago about an issue we're having. I'm calling to talk to the boss about this situation."

There was a long pause on the line and then the man said, "Well, there's a new sheriff in town. Here's a number where you can reach the boss," he said and read Jimmie the number. Then he hung up the phone.

Jimmie read the number. It was the same number as the one Vito had given him earlier. After the shock wore off, Jimmie walked down the street to the newspaper vending machine and bought a copy of the Pittsburgh Press. He quickly turned to Page B-2. Then he went back to his office and called Sal.

Sal answered after the first ring. "Hello."

"This is Jimmie. You're not going to believe this, Sal" he said and explained the strange call from Vito, and then the response he got from the guy who answered Carmine's private number.

"Shit, Jimmie," Sal said, "something must have happened to Carmine. You think Vito got rid of him?"

"It sure sounds like him or one of his buddies did. Because when someone up there finally answered Carmine's phone, he gave me the new boss's telephone number. And it's the same as the one Vito gave me. And, when I talked to Vito earlier today, he said to check the Pittsburgh Press for a story on such and such a page. I went and bought the paper. I'll read you the headline: 'Mob Boss Amato and Associate found Dead in River.'"

"Damn, Jimmie. Vito had to be involved in this, don't you think?"

"Definitely. It sounds to me like Vito is now the capo, and he wants those pictures you have – and probably the negatives too. The ones of him and the other guy that you had someone take. And Sal, if Vito is the new sheriff, you're going to have a serious decision to make. Do you give him the photos and trust that he'll call off the guys that are after Augie? And what about long term? What's to keep Vito and those other Black Hand guys from going back on their promises. To leave Augie and your family alone?"

Sal was quiet for several seconds. Then he said, "If Vito wants to do a deal where he gets the pictures back, then we'll need some assurances that he'll live up to his end of the bargain. A show of good faith. Maybe you tell him to call off the guys that are after Augie right now. When we have proof that those assholes are no longer after my nephew, then we'll set up a meeting where we can discuss the photos."

"That's a pretty good idea, Sal. And it buys us time, too. Let me think this thing through a little bit longer. But I'll need to get back to Vito sometime later today. In the meantime, when will you hear from Augie again? We need to make sure he's safe and hidden until you come to some agreement with Vito."

"Augie said he'd give me a call tomorrow. I won't tell him about any of this because he can't afford to let his guard down. Unless you have any more ideas, go ahead and give Vito a call and let's see how he reacts," Sal said.

* * *

Jimmie spent the afternoon making phone calls to a few trusted friends in Pittsburgh. He wanted to find out if any of them had heard about any changes at La Famiglia Vagabonda. These were not Chamber of Commerce types, but they were as shrewd, calculating and accomplished as any Fortune 500 CEO. All of them had read about the murder of Carmine and his associate, but none of them knew who was now in charge. His last call was to Frankie Silver, a member of La Famiglia Vagabonda who had grown up in Riverview, and who was now Jimmie's "business" contact with the mob. Frankie confirmed to Jimmie that Vito The Scar Scaramungi was now, indeed, the new capo of La Famiglia Vagabonda.

It was 6.30 p.m. when Jimmie Ponza dialed The Scar's phone number. The phone was answered after one ring.

"Yeah. Who's calling?"

"Vito, it's me. Jimmie. I talked to Sal Costanza. Here's what he wants to do. If you get your guys to back off and stop trying to get Augie, and then let Augie come back home to West Virginia, Sal is willing to deal with you on the pictures."

"Okay. Tell him I'll get in touch with our guys out there. The ones tryin' to find Cumpton. I'll tell 'em to stop right now, and to get on the first plane back to Pittsburgh. I'll let you know when they get back here. Then you can get your boy home. Once he's home safe and sound, you call me. Then we'll set up a time and place where me and Sal can meet. Where he can give me those phony pictures and negatives. Then this will be all over. This shit has been going on too long, anyway. And for workin' with me on this, I'll sweeten the pot a little bit for you too, Jimmie. We got some new things comin', like poker machines and dog racin'."

As soon as the call ended, Jimmie phoned Sal with the news. "He agreed to call off his goons. And he promised to let Augie come home to Jeweltown. Then, you and Vito can meet. It all sounds too easy to me, though, Sal. Too good to be true. That Vito would let bygones be bygones. Especially since he knows you're the one whocame up with the idea for the pictures."

"I guess that's a chance I'll have to take. I mean, what else can I do if we ever want to see my nephew again? And, other than revenge, what would Vito gain by continuing this feud? I gotta hope it's water over the dam by now. But I suppose I might have to spend the rest of my life looking over my shoulder. Anyway, we're committed to playing this thing out. I'm expecting a call from Augie tomorrow. I'll let him know the good news. At least, he'll be able to breathe a little easier," Sal said and hung up the phone.

Chapter 23
Harvest Repast

Lou and I rose early Friday morning after our first night at Fruit Lake Vineyard and Winery. The enticing aroma of intensely flavored coffee drew us to the kitchen, where Artie was removing freshly baked croissants from the oven. He looked over at us.

"Morning," he said. "How about a cup of mud and a croissant to get your engine revved for the day ahead?" He pointed to the coffee pot simmering on the stove.

"Sure! It smells like a sip of that stuff could raise the dead. But hell yes, I'll pour us a cup. And those croissants look delicious," I said.

"Help yourself. I've got to get on the road and run Della's car back to her down in Oakland. I should be back late this afternoon. Jack's down in the winery dealing with the new vintage. I'm sure he could use a hand or two," Artie said and smiled at Lou.

"That sounds great," she said. "I am... or was... doing the same thing back in West Virginia at my winery on Rattlesnake Ridge."

Artie looked quizzically at her for a moment. "Explain something to me, Lou. Why do you go to all the trouble of trying to grow grapes back in a place that requires so much more work? I mean, in California, growing wine grapes is simple compared to what you guys put up with on the east coast. Out here, we plant a vine, and the weather is almost always perfect. Hardly any frost in the spring, and the climate is warm and dry during the growing season. And there's hardly any need to spray for mold or bugs. But you guys need to deal with all those issues in a climate that's too humid in the summer, and too damn cold in the winter. Hell, you should just come out here where you can spend most of your time concentrating on making good wine. As a matter of fact, most of the winemakers in California don't even have vineyards. They buy their grapes from growers," he added.

Lou just smiled at Artie. "I suppose you're right. It can be a struggle to get the great varietals like chardonnay, cabernet or sangiovese, to survive our winters. I've learned to do things like hilling up soil over the graft on each vine before winter in case we have prolonged freezing temperatures. This is a good way to save the vine when we get those brutal kinds of weather conditions. And we have to keep up with a regular spray program in the summer. To keep the insects from eating our vines or to keep mold-producing humidity from trashing the vineyard. But you know what, I think it's worth all the extra work. I believe that different geographic locations with diverse soils make distinctive tasting wines. I guess that's why I'm doing what I'm doing where I'm doing it."

"Well, I can't argue with success, and winning that gold medal is proof enough for me," Artie said. "And anyway, we don't need any more competition out here from competent winemakers," he added, smiling at Lou.

We ate croissants and drank our coffee before heading down to the winery to help Jack. As we walked down the stairs to the barrel room, I thought back to my time at Starling Vineyards and the hard, but satisfying, work there with my great friends Alex and Topo. People in the wine industry worked long and strenuous days and, once all the grapes were picked and the new wine was in the cellar, they were ready to party. As was the custom at many wineries, Starling celebrated the end of harvest with a dinner in the vineyard. I smiled to myself as I thought about the first harvest dinner I had attended at Starling Vineyards.

* * *

It was a beautiful evening in late October, and there were about thirty of us sitting at a long wooden table that was situated in the vineyard row nearest the winery building. Earlier in the afternoon, we had stacked cinder blocks four high, about five feet apart, that we used as anchors for a sturdy metal grate that would serve as a grill. Topo had asked his father, Miguel, to be in charge of preparing the dinner for the Starling team, and for a gaggle of winemakers and workers from around the Napa Valley. Miguel is a sous chef at one of the Valley's upscale resorts, and he put together a memorable feast for us that night. The centerpiece of the meal was grilled wild boar roasted over hardwood coals and wine-soaked grape vines. Accompanying the meat were roasted tomatoes, leeks, *tomatillos*, carrots and *poblano* peppers, along with large pans of cheesy grits – a kind of Mexican polenta – dotted with jalapenos and *chorizo*. Fresh fruit and *churros* dipped in caramel and chocolate served as dessert. Of course, the dinner was accompanied by bottles of every wine that Starling Vineyards produced, including riesling, chardonnay, cabernet sauvignon, and zinfandel.

The meal was capped off with a sinfully luscious and sweet late harvest dessert wine made from gewurztraminer. Alex told me he planted less than one-half acre of Gewurztraminer to make this special wine. The grapes for the wine were infected with *botrytis cinerea* – a kind of vine fungus winemakers call the 'noble rot.' This rare condition is occurs when grapes are allowed to hang on the vines into late autumn. When the intensely sweet, raisin-like, shriveled grapes are then picked and fermented, the resulting wine is a concentrated elixir with distinctive honey and apricot flavors. I've also detected nuances of acetone – which adds a very slight taste of vinegar – to these type of wines that I find delectable. We enjoyed several bottles of it after dessert, and late into the night under a star-filled sky. There were several different vintners at the harvest dinner, and they represented a plethora of winemaking styles. However, none of those in attendance could match one winemaker's singularly odd approach to planting grapes and making wine.

Santino Lupini is a winemaker who emigrated from Italy to the Napa Valley to pursue his goal of making world class wine. He came to California hoping to find legions of thirsty customers and a wine industry that was willing to accept his peculiar approach to growing grapes and making wine. His winery is named Zodiac, and Santino refers to himself as a wine astrologist. He uses every available opportunity to advocate, evangelically, for his fervent belief in a celestial/wine connection. When this stargazing winemaker was roundly rebuked by his tradition-bound industry peers in Italy, Santino decided to leave and find a more favorable and welcoming environment to grow grapes and make wine. He had read about California's open-minded attitude toward innovative ideas, and especially in an individual's right to have and promote controversial, even counterintuitive, points of view, so he moved to the Napa Valley. For about a year, though, Santino's unconventional approach to winemaking was met with the same skepticism and outright rejection by almost all of his fellow winemakers in California; however, one entrepreneurial and well-heeled Napa Valley resident – the animal control officer for the county and my friend, Caspar

Dinwiddy, believed in the potential for Santino's winery to be successful. Caspar decided to financially back Zodiac, and within one year, the winery was turning a profit. Santino's detractors were having to eat crow. Once roundly mocked by his winemaking peers, Santino was now something of a minor celebrity in the Napa Valley.

The conversation that evening, fueled by copious quantities of wine, ran the gamut from insightful to outrageous, with occasional interjections of eccentric and even bizarre opinions. I sat back and enjoyed the show, especially the current debate topic, focusing on best practices in winemaking, and whether certain unorthodox methods are effective, or just whimsical marketing contrivances. All eyes at the table were now focused on Santino Lupini. A lively debate ensued when Topo casually commented on the beauty of the evening, and especially the dazzling, star-filled sky. Now, in this awe-inspiring vineyard setting under a sky lit with twinkling stars, Santino Lupini saw his opportunity to address his colleagues on his belief in the absolute key to making world-class wine. Santino stood up unsteadily and, with his wine glass in one hand, he pointed to the sky above with the other and addressed the assembled group in his halting and broken English.

"Thisa sky, she's whata make this vino molto bene. When thema stars get in righta place, thena you planta the vines. Anda later, with stars in gooda position, you picka the grapes."

Topo, raised by family members involved in the wine industry for decades, and a firm and passionate advocate for traditional winemaking, was having none of this. He stood and faced the wine astrologist and protested loudly, "How in heaven's name can you prove that looking up at the stars helps you make good wine?"

Santino fired right back. "That's justa it, Signor Topo. You justa sayed it, 'heavens.' It's whata I been tella you now for longa time. I geta my inspiration from looka up ata the sky. The heavens, asa you say. Anda them stars, they tella me whata grapes to plant. So thena I know whicha ones to put ina the dirt."

"That's bullshit, Santino. We know, by using science and agriculture, what to do. And through years of planting, we know what grapes grow best in a particular type of soil. And which ones do best in certain geographic locations. We also rely on long-term weather patterns. The only time we look up at the sky is to see if it's going to rain. And we sure as hell don't consult our horoscope before we plant, harvest or bottle our wine. So, tell us how the hell you can use astrology to make wine?

And be specific," Topo demanded.

Santino was livid. "Ok, Signor smarty pants, this isa how," he said, leaning back even further and gazing up into the star-filled night. "I looka up and whata do I see? I see Jupiter isa frolic witha Mars. I see Zeus grabba his spear. He looka for Venus. Anda when he finda her, he puta the spear upa close to her special place. Well, thena we know itsa time to planta sangiovese. Ona the other hand, whena Scorpio…

Topo interrupted his fellow winemaker and held up his wine glass. "Stop it Santino. You're giving me a headache. Here's what I think. Let's all make our wine however we want to. But tonight, let's just drink this stuff until it's gone. That way, the only headache we have is the one we'll have in the morning."

* * *

I thought about that night at the Starling harvest dinner as Lou and I worked in Mendocino Jack's winery. It was a pleasant memory, but things were about to change – and not for the better.

CHAPTER 24
OAKLAND

Cheech was grumpy and his back ached as he drove the truck across the Oakland Bay Bridge. The bed in Cumpton's apartment had been as hard as a slab of marble. He glanced down at the bay. The mottled, drab water and the overcast sky matched his dour mood. Small white-caps dotted the murky bay and looked like balls of cotton bobbing in a sea of gray gruel.

Cheech was worried. They would need to call Carmine soon to give him an update on their mission to locate and waste Cumpton. Find-ing the notebook in Cumpton's freezer with the address in Oakland was probably their last hope of getting the man. Tubby was sitting in the shotgun seat of the truck flipping through the pages in the center-fold section of Playboy Magazine. His mouth was opened slightly, and saliva was dribbling onto his chin. Cheech looked over in disgust.

"Jesus H. Christ, Tubby. Why don't you take that magazine in the back of the truck and whack off before you drown in your own spit. Get your head back in the game. We gotta find this guy, or we ain't gonna be able to go back home. You capeesh?"

"What?" Tubby said and looked over at Cheech. He hadn't heard a word his partner had said. Then Cheech's words registered. "Oh, okay," he said. But I have a good feeling about this, Cheech. I think we're gonna find our guy."

"Well first, we need to check out this D. M. Smith. It's a long shot, but it's our best hope of gettin' Cumpton. When we find D. M., that's when you get to do your thing. You gotta make sure D. M. tells us every-thing he knows. Hell, D. M. might even be a woman. Who knows?"

Tubby did his best imitation of a Cheshire Cat, smiling broadly through small teeth that looked like dull yellow kernels of corn. "Boy oh boy! I really hope D. M. is a chick. And you're right, Cheech. I need to think about the best ways to get this person to spill the beans. But remember, it takes more time than you think to get the truth out of people."

Cheech just shook his head. "Open the glove compartment. Get that map out. The one we got when we stopped for gas. Of the Bay Area. I circled the place where this D. M. lives. I wrote down the exact street address. When you find it, look at the map and tell me how to get there."

Tubby fumbled around and was having difficulty figuring out the map. After several moments, Cheech pulled the truck over and grabbed the map from his partner. He quickly found the address in the Elmhurst neighborhood of Oakland and drove to the area in ten minutes. When they arrived, Cheech drove by the place and then parked the truck a block beyond it. It was just after 10 a.m., and Cheech figured that most folks were at work, and kids would be at school. D. M.'s home was a duplex. The street was empty as they made their way to the building. They quickly walked up the stairs onto the porch, and Cheech put his ear to the door. He could not detect any activity inside, so he knocked. No one answered and, after a few minutes, Cheech used his lock pick device to open the door.

They entered and, after quietly checking each room, they determined the place was vacant. Once they started rifling through the drawers and closets, they discovered that D. M. Smith is actually Della Mae Smith. And, within a few minutes, Tubby found a rolodex file with a list of contacts. One of those contacts was Johnny Harman, who they knew was the alias Augie Cumpton now used.

Cheech smiled. "This gotta be the person Cumpton was coming to see. This Della Mae. She's some kinda lawyer. But since no one's here, maybe they're out somewhere together. Or the Smith woman's at work and Cumpton just went out for a pack of smokes or some food. If he don't show up, we'll wait for the chick to come home. Then you can do your thing, Tubby. In the meantime, I'll go in the front room and watch for anyone who might be coming. We'll take turns watching. I'll do thirty minutes and then you spell me for thirty."

While Cheech was on lookout, he thought about how he might handle different situations. What would they do if Cumpton showed up alone? That would be the easiest issue to deal with. They would simply put a gun in his ribs and force the guy to come with them. And then get rid of him. Things could get complicated, though, if both Cumpton and the woman came to the apartment together. They would still take

Cumpton, but they would also need to deal with the Smith woman. And if Cumpton didn't show, and Smith came home alone, he would have to let Tubby work on her until she told them where Cumpton was hiding. In that case, they'd need to whack the woman. Cheech didn't like complications. He hoped Cumpton got to the apartment before the woman came home. He was having trouble thinking straight though, because Tubby had the TV sound turned way up.

"Tubby, turn that fuckin' TV down. I can't hear myself think!"

"Hey Cheech. You gotta see this. Moe just smacked Curly in the head with a two-by-four. Right in the chops. And then Larry came in and…"

Cheech was livid. "You oughta go out to Hollywood. You could be the fourth stooge. Now turn it down so's I can think."

Five minutes later, Cheech saw a guy pull up in front of the apartment and get out of a green hatchback. He watched as the man walked toward the steps to the apartment, and then he ran into the room where Tubby sat watching TV and turned the set off.

"Tubby, a guy's coming up the steps. We'll go into the other room just in case he comes inside. This guy ain't Cumpton either. Let's just play it cool and stay quiet. If he comes in, we'll see what he does. But we gotta hope he don't stay. Anyway, let's just be quiet and listen."

CHAPTER 25
ALICE'S RESTAURANT

The three-hour drive from Fruit Lake Vineyard in Mendocino County to Oakland presented a welcome break for Artie. He and Jack had been working a month full of long days picking this year's grapes, and then crushing, fermenting and pressing them into wine. They were also tasked with moving thousands of gallons of new wine from the fermenters into tanks and barrels for aging. It was back-breaking work and Artie was pleased to get away, if only for a day.

Before he returned Della Mae's Gremlin to Oakland, he stopped by Chez Panisse in Berkeley for a quick lunch, and to check in with his friend and ex-boss, Alice Waters. Artie was anxious to find out about the surprise revision of the menu at the restaurant, morphing from an almost total emphasis on traditional French cooking to one now focusing on regional California cuisine. It was around 11 when Artie climbed the stairs of the converted Arts and Crafts style home on Shattuck Avenue in Berkley and found Alice in the kitchen.

Artie walked up behind his friend. "Hey chef. How you doing?" She turned and Artie gave her a big hug.

"Artie, what a pleasant surprise. What brings you to the big city?"

"Well, I had something to do here in Oakland, and I thought I'd just stop by and see you. It's been a while, and I hoped I might catch you before the lunch crush and visit for a few minutes."

"I'm glad you stopped by. Can I fix you some lunch while you're here? I don't know if you've heard, but we introduced a totally new menu last year."

"Well actually, that's one of the reasons I wanted to come by. I read about it in the paper. I was kind of shocked by the news. And yes, I'd love a bite to eat. But nothing special. Just something you're featuring for lunch would be great."

"I'll fix you something from the new menu. I'm making small, individual pizzas today. We call them 'pizzettas.' I'm topping them with wild mushrooms from Sonoma County and a gremolata."

"Wow, that sounds delicious. But first, tell me how this all came about? I mean, you were totally dedicated to French country dishes when I worked here."

"Well, it was kind of a joint decision between me and my new assistant chef Jeremiah Tower. Jeremiah started here right after you left. Anyway, over time, he took my menu of French bistro-type food and changed it to classic French *haute cuisine*. He drenched everything in cream, eggs and butter. It certainly wasn't my style of French cooking. But people loved it, and it brought a lot of new customers in. Over time, Jeremiah's menu also got us out of debt, and even made us profitable"

"Yeah, I remember the lean times. So, this new guy, Jeremiah, helped put you in the black," Artie offered.

"That's right. But later, I think we both came to the conclusion that, while we were profitable, our food was too rich. Even unhealthy. And since I had always insisted on sourcing my raw ingredients from local farmers, it seemed natural to expand that idea and concentrate on California-produced food. You know, finding farmers in the state who could provide home-grown products. Things like oysters from Tomales Bay, strawberries from the Central Valley, or even garlic grown down in Gilroy. Near where you're from, Artie. We're also sourcing grass-fed beef, heirloom pork and free-range chickens from different parts of the state. I guess we're going to try and create a more regional – and healthy – California-type cuisine. But it's a risky move and there's a lot at stake," she added with a worried look.

Artie just smiled. "I think it's exciting, Alice. You'll do great too. I've never seen anyone more dedicated to doing things the right way than you. I can't wait to bring Jack down for a meal. As soon as we put the finishing touches on this year's harvest."

"You and Jack are welcome here anytime. And Artie, we'll be buying more of your Mendocino wines to pair with the new menu. I especially love your pinot noir. Tastes like Burgundy – only more affordable! Now let me put this pizzetta in the oven."

To accompany the pizzetta, Alice served a simple green salad with garlic croutons in a vinaigrette dressing. As he had expected, the food was delicious, and he was especially pleased he was able to visit with his old friend. As he left the restaurant, he made a reservation for he and

Jack for Thanksgiving Day. Then Artie drove into Oakland and over to Della Mae's apartment to return her car.

It was 1.30 when he parked the Gremlin in front of Della Mae's apartment. He walked up the steps to the porch and found the key under the planter. He entered the apartment and headed for Della's office just off the kitchen. Artie took the car keys from his pocket and placed them on Della's desk. He sat down and picked up the phone on the desk and dialed Della Mae's number. After three rings, the phone was answered.

"Good afternoon. Smith Legal Services. This is Macy, how can I help you."

"Hi Macy. This is Artie – a friend of Della Mae's. Can I speak to her?

"Oh, hi Artie. She's on another line, but she should be getting off soon. Do you want to hold?"

"Sure. I'll wait."

Three minutes later, Della Mae came on the line. "Hi Artie. Sorry I didn't pick up sooner, but it was a client," Della Mae said. "How are things going at the winery with your new guests? I hope everything's okay."

Artie stood up. "Everything's copacetic so far. I just wanted to let you know that Augie and Lou got here okay. I don't think anyone could find us up at the winery. And Augie and Lou seem like good folks. They're down in the cellar today helping Jack with the new wine."

* * *

Cheech smiled as he listened to the conversation. The guy talking on the phone was somehow

involved in this whole thing and he knew where Cumpton was. Cheech thought to himself that when this guy hangs up the phone, I'll have Tubby work on him and find out exactly where Cumpton is hiding.

* * *

"Augie said to ask you to come up and see them when you get a chance," Artie said.

Just then, Artie looked to his right and into the bathroom where there was a full-length mirror. He saw the reflection of two men both holding pistols at their side in the next room. He needed to tell Della not to come home. He quickly said, "Della stay…"

* * *

Cheech was standing next to Tubby, and he could see Artie stand and look in the mirror. Artie had spotted them. Cheech rushed into the room and immediately put his finger on the phone cradle, disconnecting the call, and he put the gun to Artie's head. Then Cheech took the receiver from Artie's hand and set it next to the phone.

* * *

Della Mae heard Artie say quickly, "Della stay…" and then the line went dead. She didn't know why the call was disconnected. So, she called back, but the line was busy. She waited a couple of minutes to see if Artie was trying to call her back. But no one called. For the next hour, she repeatedly phoned her home, but the line continued to be busy. Exasperated, she called Pacific Bell and asked the operator to check for any phone issues with her line. The operator told her that everything seemed normal with the line. Della Mae surmised that Artie had mistakenly left the phone off the hook which caused the line to be busy. But why had he hung up on me – and his last words seemed rushed.

Della Mae was worried. Something was just not right, she thought. She decided to wait a while, hoping Artie would call back. In the meantime, she continued to dial her home phone number every fifteen minutes, but each time the line continued to be busy. After three hours, around 5 p.m., she dialed the number for Fruit Lake Vineyard and Winery. She wanted to know if Jack had heard from Artie. She didn't want to think this telephone issue had anything to do with Augie and the people who were after him, but she had a bad feeling.

CHAPTER 26
ARTIE'S FATEFUL DAY

Tubby held a pistol pointed at Artie's chest while Cheech used chicken wire to tie Artie's hands. Then he used duct tape to bind Artie's upper and lower body to the chair in Della Mae's office. Artie looked at the portly little man holding the gun on him and thought he looked like a comic book character with his handlebar mustache, white suit and his smiling face. Only the small, sharp, yellow, fang-like incisors gave any hint of the menace that lurked just below the surface. The large man who was roughly tying him up seemed to, more stereotypically, embody the visage of how one would think a criminal might look. With long, pock-marked jowls, dark circles around his sunken eyes and breath that would repel a turkey buzzard, the man was the embodiment of a living corpse.

Artie saw his wallet on the table, and he looked up at Cheech and said, "I have about thirty dollars in that wallet if you want it. You can have my watch too."

"We ain't interested in any of your stuff, mac. But we might need a little information on where exactly you're hiding that Cumpton guy. And who is this Lou person?"

"Hey man. I don't know what you're talking about."

Cheech just shook his head "This will go a lot easier on you if you just tell us what we wanna know. We heard you say that 'Augie and Lou are okay.' So, we know you must be hiding them at your place. We gotta get Augie, but we don't know about this Lou?"

"Look guys," Artie said, "I'm not going to tell you anything so go ahead and do what you got to do."

Tubby tapped Artie with the pistol right on his chin. "Hey sport, I gotta hope you keep refusing to help. I just love convincing people to talk," he said, smiling ghoulishly.

"And we don't really need you to tell us nothin', anyway," Cheech added. "All you gotta do is be alive enough to go with us up to where you guys have Cumpton. And finding that place is gonna be a lot easier since we seen that card in your wallet with the address for... let's see... Fruit Lake Vineyard and Winery. The card says the owner is Jack Cosgrove."

"What do you need me for then?" Artie asked. He hoped Della Mae had heard him telling her to stay. He needed to get these guys away from her apartment before, God forbid, she came home.

"Okay, I can get you to the winery, but I don't think you're going to be able to convince anyone there to give Augie up."

Cheech smiled. "Oh, I think we can. And you're the key, Arturo. That's what it says your name is. You're a paisan just like us. So, we ain't gonna kill you. But we gotta make sure you ain't in any condition to be a problem for us. You just need to be alive. Barely."

Tubby looked excitedly at Cheech. "Can I get started now?"

"Yeah, go ahead. But let me put this duct tape over his mouth. We don't need no one hearin' him scream. And Tubby, don't kill the guy. I'm going in the kitchen and see if this chick has any food in the fridge. You want a sangwich or something?"

"Sure. Make me something. I'd love a liverwurst and onion sangwich. But she probably don't have nothing good like that."

"Okay, I'll see. And remember what I told you earlier, this guy's gotta be conscious and be able to walk and talk when you get done."

"Okay. I'll be careful. Hey Cheech, hand me my black bag over there."

Cheech gave Tubby the bag and the little man extracted needle nose pliers and a foot-long, heavy, anvil-like iron bar from it. He put his tools on the table. Then he sat facing Artie, smiled and grabbed the man's left hand, bending it up from where his arm had been bound. He took the needle-nose pliers and began to slowly remove the nails from Artie's fingers and his thumb. Artie tried to scream, but only muffled grunts could be heard through the duct tape covering his mouth. He tried to move his chair, but Tubby had put two heavy lamp tables on either side to hold it in place. Then he began working on Artie's right hand. When he had removed the nails from both of Artie's hands, Tubby paused to go to the kitchen sink. He poured himself a full glass of water and drank it in one gulp. Then he went back to where Artie now sat slumped over, and breathing heavily with both hands dripping blood onto the floor.

Since Artie was right-handed, Tubby now grabbed the iron bar from the table, lifted it up and brought it down heavily onto Artie's right shoulder. Mercifully, he lost consciousness. The vicious blow rendered Artie's right shoulder and arm useless, seriously limiting any possibility that he might be able to escape. Tubby then went back to the kitchen and sat at the table with Cheech who handed him a peanut butter and jelly sandwich.

"Hey Cheech, this ain't no liverwurst sangwich," Tubby said and immediately took a huge bite.

"This is all I could find Tubby. How you doin' in there with Arturo. You didn't waste him, did ya?"

"No. I'm almost done. He's a tough guy, though. Don't seem like I'm hurtin' him enough. He ain't even screamin'. Only thing I got left to do is work his face over. And body punch him. Then we can get out of here."

Tubby wolfed down the rest of his peanut butter and jelly sandwich, and he went back into the other room. He reached into his black bag, grabbed a set of brass knuckles and placed them on his right hand. Then he covered his hand with an oversized leather glove and went to work on Artie, punching him in the face and the side of the head. When Artie's nose was flattened and his eyes were both bloody and closed, Tubby began working on Artie's ribs. After twenty minutes, Tubby was out of breath and sweating profusely. His shirt and face were splattered with Artie's blood. Artie sat with his chin on his chest, his upper body convulsing, as he painfully tried to catch his breath.

Tubby called out to Cheech, "I'm done here."

"Okay. You go up the street and get the truck and park it in front of this place. Then come back here. I'll wake Arturo and clean him up a little bit."

It was 6.45, and night had fallen when they decided to move Artie to the truck for the ride to Mendocino County. When Tubby returned to the apartment, Cheech checked up and down the street in front of the place to make sure the street was empty. Then the two Black Hand men stood on either side of Artie, whose upper body was still bound, and walked him down the steps. Tubby opened the sliding side door of the truck and Cheech shoved Artie roughly into the vehicle. Tubby hopped in after Artie and tied his ankles together with more chicken wire. Then both men got into the front seat, and Cheech took the wheel.

"Okay Tubby, here's what we're gonna do. Once we get up the road a ways, I'm gonna pull over at a gas station and call this guy Jack at the winery. I'm gonna offer him a deal. It's pretty simple. All they gotta do is give us Cumpton and we'll give 'em Arturo. But if this guy Jack refuses to give us Cumpton, then all bets are off."

"What about the girl, Cheech? You know, D. M. Smith, the girl that lives here. We need to waste her, too. She might squeal on us. And I'd like a chance to make sure she don't. I mean, I can make it quick. But I think we gotta get rid of her," Tubby said, grinning in anticipation.

"That ain't happenin' Fatboy. We don't got no time for you to screw around with her. All we're s'posed to do is get Cumpton. If Jack won't do the trade, though, we'll whack Arturo, and then move to the winery and snuff everyone there, including the girl with Cumpton. And we don't have to worry about Cumpton going to the police. He ain't stupid enough to call the cops on us. He don't want no one checking into all the illegal shit that him and his family done. You know, like killin' our guy way back when."

Cheech thought it was a pretty good plan. But he knew that they would need to get the final okay for the operation from Carmine. They hadn't checked in with the boss for a couple of days. He hoped Carmine didn't still want them to make Cumpton's death look like an accident, though. They needed to let him know that things had changed, and how they planned to end things with Cumpton. He thought that the boss would agree, but he wanted to make sure, so they could finish the job and get back home.

Around 8, they stopped at a Texaco station in Healdsburg, in Sonoma County along Highway 101. They needed gas and they had to find a pay phone to call the boss. And that guy Jack at the winery.

"Hey Tubby, I gotta take a shit before I call the winery. But first, I want you to call Carmine and tell him what we wanna do. It's your turn to call the boss anyway."

Tubby's mouth hung open and he looked as if someone had used a chalkboard eraser to powder his face. "All right, Cheech. I'll call Carmine. But I ain't lookin' forward to no ass-chewin' from the boss. He should be happy that we're gonna get Cumpton. Since that's what he sent us out here for. Even if it took a little bit longer to get the job done."

"All you gotta do is just get his okay. If he don't like our plan, he'll tell us what he wants us to do different. But I think he'll let us do it our way. And anyways, we need to check his temperature. Try to figure out what he's really thinkin'. You know what I mean? I ain't goin' back to the Burg if he's still pissed at us. About al. the screw-ups we had tryin' to find Cumpton."

While Cheech went into the gas station, Tubby moved the truck to where the pay phone was located on the side of the building. He dialed Carmine's private number. It rang three times, and then was answered.

"Who's this?" an unfamiliar voice on the call asked.

"It's me. Tubby. You gotta a frog in your throat, boss? It don't sound like you."

"That's cause it ain't Carmine, Dipshit. Hold on while I go get Vito. He's in the other room."

Tubby couldn't understand why the guy who answered the phone wanted him to talk to Vito. In a few moments, another person picked up the phone.

"This is Vito. You won't be talking to Carmine no more."

"What happened? We just talked to the boss the other day. About this Cumpton guy we're trying to find. Anyway, we found him. And we wanted to let the boss know what we was plannin' to do. You know, to get rid of the guy. I was callin' to make sure it's okay with the boss."

"Hey Numb Nuts. I told you. Carmine ain't with us no more. He's gone. I'm in charge now. So, tell me about what you're gonna do," Vito said with menace in his voice.

Tubby was shocked and confused, but he knew not to ask any more questions about Carmine. So, he spent the next five minutes letting Vito know how they were able to track Cumpton down. Then how they planned to get the job finished. There was a long pause on the other end of the call when Tubby finished.

Then Vito said, "Forget about Cumpton. I want yinz guys to leave right now and get on the first plane back to the Burg. We're through with him. Leave him alone and get back here. Pronto. You understand?"

Tubby was puzzled. More than that, he was disappointed, and pissed off too. How could they leave now? They just found Cumpton. He had to think. He had to figure a way to get around what Vito was ordering him to do.

"Tubby. Did you hear me?" The new mob boss growled in a voice that sounded like he had been munching gravel.

"I can barely hear you, Vito," Tubby lied. "Hey, there's a lot of

noise on this line. I'll call you right back. I'm going to hang up now."
Tubby didn't wait for a response. He just disconnected the call.

Cheech returned from his visit to the bathroom and approached Tubby.

"You get a hold of the boss?"

"Yeah. I just talked to him. Told him what we wanna do. Just like you asked me to." Tubby said and just stared up at his partner open mouthed. Tubby was flustered. He was trying to figure out what happened back in Pittsburgh. And how could Vito The Scar now be in charge?

"Well?" Cheech paused, waiting for Tubby to respond. "Goddammit, shit-for-brains. Did he give us the go-ahead?"

"I told him how we was going to do it. Give them their guy for Cumpton. And the boss said… to go ahead," Tubby lied straight-faced to Cheech. "And then he told me we need to whack everybody there. We can't leave no one alive."

"Holy shit, Tubby. Why would he want us to do that? It just complicates things. No one up there is going to the cops on this. He should know that." Cheech was frustrated and worried.

Then Tubby took a chance and said, "Hey Cheech. Give him a call and ask him yourself if you want. But I gotta tell ya, he ain't in a good mood. Matter of fact, he said we might as well stay out here for good if we don't do it his way."

Cheech thought it over. He couldn't imagine that Tubby would bullshit him about something like this. And Cheech knew they were on shaky ground with Carmine. This job had been one fuck-up after another.

"Okay. I guess I gotta think about how we do this. Shouldn't be too hard, though. These people are sheep. They ain't gonna give us much trouble. First, I gotta call that guy Jack and see if he wants to do the trade – Cumpton for Arturo. That would make it easier for us. If he won't deal, it just makes things harder. But we still have to whack 'em all anyway."

Cheech picked up the phone and dialed the number for Fruit Lake Vineyard and Winery.

CHAPTER 27
SeeSaw

It was a cool and crisp October day. But in the humidity of the wine cellar, I had worked up a good sweat helping Jack with the new wine. Lou toiled right along with us and was certainly more adept in the cellar with the work than me. Our main job today was to pump the new wine – the pinot noir which was still in the fermenters – into large, upright stainless-steel tanks. The wine would settle and rest there for about a month before Jack and Artie pumped it into sixty-gallon American white oak barrels to age. Just before noon, we all walked upstairs to the living quarters. Working in the winery had allowed me a short respite from the stress and worries of my predicament, but that was only temporary. I was concerned about how my problem would affect the well-being of Lou and my family back in West Virginia. I was also afraid that Jack and Artie could be in serious danger too.

After a quick visit to the bathroom to clean up, I joined Jack and Lou in the dining room for lunch. Lou had made avocado, tomato and onion sandwiches slathered with homemade buttermilk ranch dressing, and we washed it all down with cold bottles of Anchor Steam beer. It was a hearty and tasty meal, and I felt recharged as we returned to the winery. We worked until around 4 o'clock. When we went back upstairs, Jack told us that Artie had defrosted four elk steak tenderloins overnight which he planned to grill over charcoal for dinner. My mouth was watering at the thought of the meal. Then Jack left to pick Artie up. It was an hour round trip down to the Boonsville bus station and back. The Greyhound from Oakland was due to arrive there at 4.30. When Jack left, Lou and I took turns in the shower, and I offered to scrub her back. She declined.

I needed to call Uncle Sal to find out if he and Jimmie Ponza had made any progress in getting the mob boss to call off his hit squad. I went into Jack's office and placed a collect call to Uncle Sal. After two rings Aunt Yolanda, Uncle Sal's wife, answered and accepted the call.

"Hey Aunt Yolanda, how are you?"

"Augie, I'm doing fine. It's wonderful to hear your voice. It's been so long since I've talked with you."

"I know, I know. But, as much as I wanted to stay in touch with you and the family, I couldn't take any chances that the guys after me might find out I'm alive. I couldn't risk that. I'm sure Uncle Sal explained all this to you. By the way, is he there? I need to speak with him."

"Yes Augie, he's in the downstairs kitchen with Ed Perez. You know him as Easy Ed. Anyway, they're down there grinding up pork butts to make Italian sausage. Wish you could be here to have a taste of the finished product. I remember that Sal taught you how to make that kind of sausage years ago. I'll holler down and let him know you're on the line."

My family back in Riverview was full of very good cooks. One of Uncle Sal's specialties is Italian sausage, and it's one of my favorite family dishes. Thinking about the family feasts from all those years ago is a pleasant, but painfully nostalgic, memory for me. Just then, my reverie was interrupted when Uncle Sal got on the line.

"Augie. I got some really good news for you," my uncle said. He sounded excited. "I told you last time we talked that Jimmie was trying to find this guy Vito to see if he could help us get you back. Remember, he's one of the thugs that came down here to pick you up. Anyway, it turns out that Vito is now in charge of the mob up in Pittsburgh."

"Sure, I remember him. He's one of the jerks that kidnapped Lou. So, what's the good news?"

"Jimmie talked with Vito just this morning. And Augie, he agreed to back his guys off. Vito said he told the guys after you to come back you and leave you alone. And he said he would call Jimmie when his guys are back in Pittsburgh. Then you can come home!"

I felt as if a two-ton anvil had been lifted from my shoulders. I was light-headed and I was trying to speak, but I was momentarily speechless.

"Augie. Did you hear me? This nightmare is almost over. You'll be coming home. Finally," Uncle Sal said and laughed into the phone.

"Sorry, Uncle Sal. This is just so hard to believe. That it's all over. After all these years… I mean, I never thought I'd ever be able to see any of you again. Mom and Dad. Grandma Luisa…" I couldn't finish the sentence. I looked up and saw Lou standing there. She had tears in her eyes. Then she came over and put her arms around me.

I realized I hadn't told Uncle Sal that Lou was out here with me. "Hey Uncle, I need to fill you in on a couple of things. I didn't tell you this the last time we talked, but those mob guys almost got me the other day in the subway. They tried to shove me in front of a train. But I was able to get away, and I don't think they were able to follow me. I think I'm safe for now where I'm hiding. And another thing. I have Lou out here with me. After all these years, I was able to get in touch with her. I warned her about me being found by the mob, and that she should be careful. Next day, I called to check on her, and she told me her apartment in Romney had been torn apart. Now it's obvious they're looking for her too. I told her that she would be safer out here with me, and she agreed to join me."

"Okay Augie. That's a real surprise. I thought you and her were old news. That she wouldn't even return your calls."

"Long story, and I won't bore you with the details now. Except to say, we reconnected right before all this bad stuff happened. Sorry, I just haven't had a chance to fill you in on everything that's going on. So, how did you get the Black Hand guys to back off? And why are you dealing with Vito? I thought Carmine was the boss."

"Yeah. It's strange. Jimmie called up there yesterday to speak with Carmine. Called his private number, but no one answered. Then he called again, and the guy that picked up said Carmine wasn't there. He said, 'there's a new sheriff in town' and he gave Jimmie another number to call. Turns out it was Vito's number."

"Holy shit, Uncle. You think Vito did something to Carmine?"

"Yeah, that's what Jimmie thinks. Especially after Vito told him to take a look at a story in the Pittsburgh paper. The headline read: 'Mob Boss Amato and Associate found Dead in River.' Then he said that if we give him those photos and negatives that I have, they'll leave you alone. That he'd get the guys who are after you to back off. And he'd leave the family alone, too. Jimmie did some checking and he confirmed that Vito is the new boss. Then Jimmie and I talked, and we felt like this was the best deal we could make to get you back home."

"That sounds great, but how do we know Vito will keep his word after you give him the pictures?"

"You're right Augie. That's our main concern too. But if we refuse to give Vito the pictures, his guys won't stop until they find you. I don't like having to depend on this guy's word either. But do we really have any other choice? I can't think of any other way that will give us a chance to settle this thing once and for all. I guess we'll have to trust that Vito will keep his promise."

"I suppose we have to take that chance. Anyway, the longer this goes on, the more I'm concerned about the safety of the guys who are hiding us. Not to mention, having to worry about anything happening to our family or Lou. And here's the phone number and address for Fruit Lake Vineyard and Winery. This is where I'm staying," I said and read him the information.

Then I tried to keep the emotion out of my voice and said, "Uncle Sal, I don't know how I can ever thank you enough for all you've done over the years to keep me on this side of the ground. You, Jimmie and everyone in the family have been my lifeline since I came back from Vietnam. And please, tell Jimmie how much I appreciate all he has done for me too."

"I'll give Jimmie your message. But there's no need to thank me or anyone else. You would have done the same for any of us. Anyway, you saved your Uncle Giorgio's life when you smacked that mob guy back in 1970. But you need to stay hidden up there until we hear back from Vito. That his guys are back in Pittsburgh. Then we can arrange to get you home. You know Augie, we can't wait to have you finally back here with us. And Lou too. Take care, son," Uncle Sal said and ended the call.

Lou and I just held one another. I was overwhelmed by the news. Then I heard the front door open, and Jack walked into the office. His face had taken on a slightly ashen pallor, and his voice seemed distant when he spoke.

"Artie wasn't on the bus. Did he call while I was gone?"

I shook my head. "No, he didn't."

With this new alarming development, I didn't feel it was appropriate to share the good news I had just received from Uncle Sal.

Just then the phone rang, and Jack quickly picked it up. "Artie," he said hopefully. "Oh, hi Della. I was just about to call you. Have you heard from Artie?"

Jack listened for about thirty seconds before responding to Della Mae. We could only hear Jack's end of the conversation.

"So, let me get this straight," Jack said. "Every time you called your apartment, the line was busy? Yes, it's strange that he would hang up on you. He must have thought the problem was on his end of the line. But knowing him, I'm sure he would have tried to call you back. No, he hasn't called here yet. He wasn't at the bus stop either. I expect a call anytime, so I better hang up. One more thing, Della, don't go home until you hear back from me. And don't call the police. This is a complicated situation and Augie said calling them would be a major problem for him. So, stay there in your office and I'll call back within the hour. Okay, bye."

Lou and I looked over at Jack. He seemed lost in thought. Then he said: "Sorry, I should have put that call on speaker. Anyway, it's weird. Della was speaking with Artie earlier this afternoon, and the phone was suddenly disconnected. She tried calling back several times, but each time, the line was busy. She even called the phone company, but they said there was nothing wrong with the line. They thought someone just left the phone off the hook. But that's not like Artie to hang up and not call back. Della's worried, especially with what's going on now with you Augie. She said the last words from Artie were 'Della stay.' And then the line went dead."

Lou and I sat on the couch in the office while Jack sat at his desk. All we could do was wait for Artie to call. Just when Lou and I got the best news we could ever hope for, this issue with Artie cast a dark shadow over our situation. I tried to think positive thoughts, but there were too many 'what ifs.' What if the bad guys had grabbed Artie, and what if they're hurting him or... God forbid... worse. If they have him, they'll probably find out about us up here. They could be on their way here right now. It's so frustrating to me because since this nightmare started, I've had to depend on others to bail me out, and this was another situation where someone else would be in danger, or dead, because of me. In Vietnam, my friend Rooster dove on a hand grenade to save my life. When I got home my good friends, JDP and Johnny Hambone Harman, were both tortured and killed because they wouldn't tell the mob guys where I was hiding. Then another friend, a giant hermit-like cowboy named Spud, hid me, and then helped me get rid of the mob guy who murdered Johnny. And now Artie might be another friend who was unlucky enough to make my acquaintance.

I fought the panic that was about to consume me. As I had feared, Jack and Artie's lives are now probably in jeopardy because they chose to help me. I could not help but think that from the time I served in

Vietnam until this moment, I have been both cursed and blessed. I was cursed to have some pretty awful experiences in the war, and then with the mob when I came home. But I've been blessed by the love and assistance of my family and friends to whom I owe my continued existence. Nonetheless, it pains me terribly to know that some of those people are no longer among the living, and that I am the reason for their untimely exit. I pray that Artie does not suffer that same fate.

I could only hope that if the Black Hand had taken Artie, they might release him now that Uncle Sal and Jimmie had worked out a deal with the new boss. Maybe those thugs hadn't gotten the word yet. Or maybe they had, and they already let Artie go. I had to hang onto the hope that this nightmare is really over.

Like so many other times over the past week when fear and stress have pretty much dominated my consciousness, I forced myself to think pleasant thoughts. The gourmet lunch and extraordinary wine tasting I was invited to attend at Domaine Chandon is one. The other, a little over a year ago, was an international tasting that I am convinced will be recognized as the single most important day ever for California wine.

Chapter 28
Judgment of Paris

I'm convinced my job with the San Francisco Chronicle came about as a direct result of the stories I wrote for The Grapeline. My relationship with the newspaper developed gradually over a period of two years. In addition to the membership of the winery association, The Grapeline was mailed out to more than one hundred other recipients, including major newspapers, magazines and wine critics in California and around the country. I always mailed a copy of The Grapeline to the Chronicle's Lifestyles section two days before the general mailing went out. I let the editor at the paper know that he was getting a heads-up on what was to appear later in the newsletter. This worked, because almost every month the Chronicle used one of my newsletter stories in the paper. Eventually, I was offered a part-time job as a stringer for the paper, and I wrote stories for them about wine with my own by-line. I continued editing The Grapeline, and that allowed me to supplement my income too. More importantly, I was recognized as a credible source for information about the wine industry in the Napa Valley, and other parts of northern California.

Caspar Dinwiddy had introduced me to a number of wine industry titans over the years. He knew just about anyone who was anybody in the California wine business. He counted among his friends such vintner luminaries as Robert Mondavi, Myron Nightengale of Beringer and August Sebastiani. These folks and their wineries were widely recognized and respected among wine lovers across the US. I used the introductions and countless others from Caspar to interview and write stories for the Chronicle.

Two other Napa Valley winemakers Caspar introduced me to, Warren Winiarski of Stag's Leap Wine Cellars and Mike Grgich of Chateau Montelena, were about to turn the wine world upside down because of an event which took place in the spring of 1976. I was invited to attend that international wine tasting known as "The Judgment of Paris" and I was one of the few journalists to report on the event. It was also at the tasting in Paris where my relationship with Ginny became more than I ever expected.

Caspar's friend Steven Spurrier has introduced Caspar to some of the most famous vintners in Europe, particularly those in Bordeaux and Burgundy. Spurrier is a graduate of the London School of Economics, but his love of the fruit of the vine led him to purchase a wine shop in Paris called La Cave de la Madeleine. He also operates the Académie du Vin, a wine school whose six-week courses are attended by French oenophiles, chefs and sommeliers. Over the years, Spurrier has developed an especially close relationship with winemakers in Bordeaux whose wines he enthusiastically sells in his wine shop. Unlike most European wine experts, especially those in France, Spurrier recognized the potential quality of California wines, and he quietly kept up with happenings in the Napa Valley through Caspar Dinwiddy. But Spurrier had to be circumspect because it is widely known that the French, and particularly those in Bordeaux, have nothing but contempt for the nascent American wine industry. They are especially disdainful of the upstart vintners in the Napa Valley.

It was December of 1975 when Steven arranged that impromptu wine tasting at Domaine Chandon that pitted a few Napa Valley cabernets against some of the best reds of Bordeaux. Those Napa Valley wines, including one from Starling Vineyards, did not fare well against the wines of Bordeaux. I had attended that tasting, but I had given my word not to report on the event at Chandon. That decision would serve me well because I later learned that the December tasting was a precursor to another event that Steven Spurrier was planning for the spring of 1976.

He was organizing a competitive tasting of the wines of Bordeaux and Burgundy. Spurrier planned to assemble a panel of French wine experts who would taste and evaluate wines from those two storied appellations. It would be a blind tasting where the judges would not be able to see the labels on the bottles, thus ensuring objectivity. Since the tasting would take place in 1976, and America would be celebrating its Bicentennial, Spurrier's American partner, Patricia Gallagher, thought it would be appropriate to include wines from the new world. So, Spurrier asked Caspar and a few others with knowledge of the wine industry in Napa to recommend the best red and white wines from California that Spurrier could add to the tasting. Specifically, Spurrier hoped to select a few cabernet sauvignons that would be placed in competition with the greatest reds from Bordeaux; and California chardonnays that would compete against the most famous chardonnays from Burgundy.

I remember the day in the early winter of 1976 when Caspar told a few of us about the upcoming event. We were in the Starling Vineyards tasting room, and Alex had asked Caspar to join Topo, Ginny and me to evaluate his 1974 Starling Cabernet Sauvignon Reserve. We had been monitoring and tasting the wine now for over a year and had shared our opinions regularly with Alex since we comprised his in-house tasting team. Alex also wanted an outsider with a good palate to assess the wine, and so he invited Caspar to the tasting. The wine had been aging in small oak barrels for thirteen months, and we were asked to evaluate the wine at this stage in its development. After an hour of sniffing, swirling and sipping, the consensus of our group was that the wine would need at least another year in the barrel before bottling. At the end of the tasting, Caspar stood up and addressed our group.

"First of all, I'd like to thank Alex for letting me be a part of this tasting. I think the wine is going to be excellent, but I agree it needs more time in the barrel. But I wanted to tell you about a special wine event that will be held in May. It's about a tasting in Paris, and I'd like to invite you to attend the event with me. As my guest. I'll pay for your airline tickets and for your lodging and meals. I hope you'll join me. This should be a one-of-a-kind event."

I was stunned and I could see that Topo was too. We both looked over at Alex, but before we could say anything, he said, "You guys can have the time off – with pay – if you decide to go. Unfortunately, I have a conflict and won't be able to make the trip." It was obvious that Caspar had spoken with Alex ahead of time about the invitation and got his buy in. We gratefully accepted the offer.

Caspar then addressed Ginny. "If you don't mind being in the company of a bunch of dirty old men, I hope you'll accompany us too. It should be a good time and I bet you can flash your nun card and get us a private tour of Notre Dame. And don't worry, the cathedral has withstood visits by some very disreputable people throughout history. I don't think it will collapse if a few amateur scoundrels like us enter the building. Will you join us?"

Even dressed in old blue jeans, a work shirt and wearing flip-flops, the woman most of my friends called Looks, was truly a lovely rose among we motely and homely male thorns. She gave us her best, stern, Catholic grade school nun look, and then she grinned from ear to ear. "Hell yes. I'll go. I even speak passable French. And I've certainly had to put up with nastier dudes than this motley-looking crew."

That statement, I thought to myself, was certainly true and Ginny had the scars from Viet Cong shrapnel to prove it. She added, "But I don't think the folks in charge of Notre Dame will do any favors for an ex-nun. In fact, if they knew about my hasty exit from the Sisters of Penance, they might dust off the old guillotine."

Over the next few months, we met with Caspar to give him our thoughts on the wineries and the wines he might recommend as California's entries into the Paris tasting. Finally, during the third week of May, we flew from San Francisco to Paris to attend what would turn out to be the most consequential tasting in history for the California wine industry.

The event was held on Monday May 24. The judges on the tasting panel consisted of some of France's most famous sommeliers and restauranteurs who had been told shortly before the event that several California wineries would be entered in the competition. The French did not consider any country's wines – even the bottles their European neighbors produced – to be the equal of what was being made in France. They were openly contemptuous and dismissive of American wine, and they scoffed at the suggestion that the California bottles would have any chance against the wines of France.

Six cabernet sauvignons and six chardonnays – all from California – competed against some of the greatest of all Bordeaux and Burgundy wines. For example, one of the world's most highly acclaimed Bordeaux reds– 1970 Chateau Mouton Rothschild, and one of the world's most famous White Burgundy – 1972 Puligny-Montrachet Les Pucelles – were among the French bottles against which the California wines would compete.

To the shock of the wine world, when the results were tallied up: Napa Valley wines were awarded first place in both categories! The 1973 Chateau Montelena Chardonnay won first place in the white wine category, and the 1973 Stags Leap Vineyards Cabernet Sauvignon was judged first among all the reds. The fact that two upstart Napa Valley wines were voted the best in each of the two categories, and by a tasting panel composed of all French judges, astonished everyone in France and across the world. Once news of the wine tasting was widely disseminated, California wines gained universal respect and acceptance.

A reporter from Time Magazine was the only credentialed journalist who attended the event, and his story did not appear in the magazine until the next week. When I returned to California to write a story for the Chronicle, the Time article had already appeared. Nevertheless, my editor was impressed that I had attended the event, and he asked me to write a feature story and a first-person account of what Time called "The Judgment of Paris." Within a few short months, I was offered a full-time position with the newspaper, and I'm convinced that the trip to Paris and my story about the tasting sealed the deal.

That historic event was not the only unforgettable memory for me that week in Paris. Two days before the tasting, my Starling Vineyards traveling companions and I were invited by Steven Spurrier to attend a pre-event meet and greet party at the Intercontinental Hotel in Paris, where the tasting would take place. It started out as a nice evening, and we were treated to an impressive array of gourmet hors d'oeuvres, and an open bar. We also had access to a plethora of famous wines from Bordeaux and Burgundy that I could never have afforded, otherwise, to taste. And I made the most of the opportunity! I suppose that's where things went south. To be honest, I don't remember much after about the first hour. The last thing I vaguely remember is taking a bottle of wine off the bar and going to my room. Maybe I was suffering from jet lag, maybe a combination of a lack of sleep and too much good wine, but something triggered a flashback.

* * *

I was in an elevated guard bunker ten feet above the ground and along the basecamp perimeter. We were under attack from a large force of North Vietnamese Army soldiers who were firing rocket propelled grenades and AK-47s at us. Their comrades behind them were lobbing barrage after barrage of mortar fire at our positions. It was 3.30 a.m. and hurricane force wind was blowing monsoon rain horizontally into our bunker. My friends, Elvin "Rooster" Washington, Calvin Vendetti and Toby Chang, were in the bunker with me, and we were all attempting to repel the waves of enemy soldiers who were dead set on overrunning us. Toby was firing his M-16 and Rooster was engaging the North Vietnamese with an M-60 machine gun. Calvin assisted Rooster by feeding belts of ammunition into the machine gun. I was firing an M-79 Grenade launcher out into the murky blackness at the attacking enemy. Suddenly, there was a bright flash followed by an explosion, and our bunker was engulfed in flames. I was deafened by the explosion, but otherwise unwounded. I looked at my friends, all of whom were horribly on fire. I could see, in their distorted faces, their mouths working to form screams of hellish agony that I could not hear. There was nothing I could find in the bunker to put out the flames. I could only watch them die a horrible death. I screamed over and over and over "I'm sorry, I'm sorry, I'm sorry…"

"Johnny, Johnny. Wake up. Come on, open your eyes. You're having a nightmare," I heard a distant voice beckon to me. I was lying on my back in bed. The pillow under my head was soaked with sweat and tears. I looked up into the face of Ginny, and then past her. I could see there was a man standing by my door. Ginny turned and addressed the person in French, and then I watched as the man closed my door and left.

"Where am I?" Then I remembered. I was in Paris with my friends for a wine tasting. "What the hell happened to me?"

Ginny smiled and then said, "We were all having a pleasant evening sitting at a table and enjoying the food and wine. You seemed fine. After about an hour or so, I noticed that you got up and followed one of the waiters to the bar. It looked to me like you were talking to him. He was Asian. It seemed like you two were having an animated conversation. That was about two hours ago, and that's the last time I remember seeing you until just now. I was concerned when you didn't return. So, I came here looking for you. I heard this awful thrashing and yelling coming from your room. After knocking on your door for five minutes, I called the front desk and asked them to send someone up who could unlock your room. What's going on Johnny? Were you having a nightmare?"

"Let me think. I know I was pretty buzzed. I hadn't eaten much, and I know I got more than my share of wine…" Then I began to remember. "It was the waiter guy. Something about him. I remember getting up and following him. And then we began to talk. He could speak English. I asked him if he was Vietnamese. He nodded and I told him that I had been in Vietnam with the Army. I remember he tried to turn away from me and leave. But I grabbed his arm to stop him. He turned around and said something to me. He was angry. He said we Americans had killed his family. That their village was hit with napalm dropped on them by an American plane."

I rose to a sitting position on the bed and just stared straight ahead.

Ginny said, "Augie, you don't have to go on. I can see this is painful for you."

I looked over at Ginny and shook my head and continued. "This man said his mother, father and little sister were burned to death. Oh God. That's what happened. I remember grabbing a bottle of wine and coming back here. I drank the wine pretty quickly, and that's the last thing I remember until you found me just now. I'm sorry Ginny. I feel like a fool. I haven't had one of these bad Vietnam flashbacks for almost two years now. In this dream, I was with the three Army friends of mine who were killed over there. In the nightmare, they all were burned to death, and I couldn't help them. Jesus, Ginny. I thought I had finally turned a corner. I thought our veterans' meetings at the Railcar in Yountville were helping. But this awful dream makes me think I'll never get past what happened to me in Vietnam."

Ginny shook her head. "Johnny, you know it's a process. We've talked about this many times. There isn't any quick fix for what we experienced in that awful place. I still dream about what happened to me at Cam Ranh Bay. Less and less. But sometimes I have this particularly graphic nightmare. I see Viet Cong running through our hospital and killing my friends and patients. Then I can almost feel the pain of the hot shrapnel in my back from the exploding satchel charge. Just like it just happened yesterday. So, maybe none of us will ever be able to completely erase the terrible things we saw and experienced over there. But I'm convinced talking about those things in our meetings helps. We just need to keep at it. To be there for each other. And that's why I'm here now."

I looked up at this beautiful woman. I considered her one of the best friends I've ever had. "Ginny, thank you for being here for me. And I'm sorry for all this drama. For months now, I've wanted to tell you something about me. That only one other person in California knows. I'm not the person you think I am." She seemed surprised, but she just nodded her head and looked at me.

Then I told her my true name, and about the real-life soap opera that Augie Cumpton has been living for almost a decade. Ginny listened patiently as I explained the issues with my family and the thugs who had threatened them. I told her how I had, unintentionally, killed one of them defending my Uncle Giorgio. Then I told her about how they had murdered two of my friends in their relentless search for me. When I finished my story, I watched her wipe tears from her eyes. Then she took one of my hands in both of hers and looked into my eyes.

"Johnny… I mean Augie… I am so sorry for all that you've had to endure. We both have some very upsetting memories of our time in Vietnam. But things have just gotten worse for you since you've been back. I can't imagine the pain you must be living with. To think you can never go back home to be with your Mom and Dad, and your family…"

"Look Ginny. I'm not telling you this because I want sympathy. I just feel we have a real bond, and I really trust you. And I've wanted to tell you the truth about me. Especially since you're someone I feel so connected to in so many ways. From our Catholic school upbringing to the time each of us spent in southeast Asia, I really do consider you an important part of my life."

Before I could say another word, Ginny bent over and took my face in her hands. Then she kissed me long and passionately.

"Do you mind if I stay here with you tonight?" she asked.

We spent the next five nights together sharing the bed in my room. We comforted each other with soothing words and acts of love. The bed was like a safe harbor that we could retreat to. A place where we could help each other exorcise the demons of the war that still haunted us.

But in that same bedroom, on the morning we were to leave France, Ginny looked at me and said, "Augie, I have something to tell you. And like you, there's only one other person who knows about this. It's a very personal and heartfelt decision. And it would mean the world to me if you would understand and accept what I'm about to tell you…" she seemed hesitant to continue.

"Look Ginny, I'll support any decision you make. And you certainly don't need my approval for anything."

"But I do. I really do. Especially after what we've just shared the last few days," she said, and paused once more. Then she added: "Okay then, here it is. I'm going to return to my order – The Sisters of Penance. To the monastery up in the hills above St. Helena. I've spoken to Mother Superior – Sister Joretta – and she has agreed to accept me back. She said I can continue working at the hospital, but I'll probably need to give up my weekend job at the winery. But the hardest part of my decision, though, is that we'll need to have a less personal relationship in the future," she said and looked away from me. I watched as she brushed tears from her eyes.

I was speechless, and I was hurt. I wanted to ask her why she had allowed our relationship to advance to this point if there was no future in it. I was falling in love with this woman, and for a fleeting moment, I thought I had found someone who could make me forget about Lou. An intelligent person, a passionate and ardent lover, and someone who understood and shared with me the soul-searing and life altering experiences of war. I didn't know what to say.

"I know this must be hard for you to understand. But for the last two years I've been thinking about my decision to leave the convent. I was upset with the turmoil and conflict among the sisters back then. Our religious order was divided over the changes made by Vatican II, but instead of staying and trying to find compromise, I took the easy way out and just left. I believe now that was a mistake. And I really do miss the work and our mission of ministry to the community we serve. That probably sounds pretentious, but it's the absolute truth."

Then Ginny stopped talking. She just looked at me for a few seconds. Just as I was going to respond, she held her hand up to stop me. When she spoke, her voice was filled with emotion.

"Augie, these last five days with you have been wonderful. I know you must be hurt, but believe me, I love you. And I didn't sleep with you because I felt sorry for you or wanted a last hurrah before recommitting to lifelong chastity. I needed the comfort and love you gave me. I think we both needed that. And I hope you'll feel that what we've just experienced was mutually beneficial. But it can't be in that way anymore."

I didn't say anything for a moment, and then I simply said: "I understand, Ginny."

And so, when we departed France, we agreed that our corporeal union in Paris would forever stay in Paris, but the emotional and spiritual healing from those sweet days will always reside in my heart.

CHAPTER 29
LET'S MAKE A DEAL

It was 8.15 p.m. and very dark when Tubby pulled the truck up close to the pay phone on the side of the gas station in Healdsburg. He had just gotten off the call with Vito, and now it was Cheech's turn to call the winery. First, though, Cheech opened the truck's sliding side door and helped the still bound and gagged Artie out onto the pavement next to the phone. Cheech then dialed the number for Fruit Lake Vineyard. The phone was answered after the first ring.

"Hello. Artie?"

"No, this ain't Arturo. But I'll let you talk to him in a minute. Who's this I'm talking to?" Cheech said.

Jack put the phone on speaker and then replied, "My name is Jack. Let me speak to Artie, please."

"Hold your horses there, Jack. You can talk to Arturo in a minute. But first, I wanna know if you still got Augie Cumpton up there with you. And don't try and bullshit me. I know he's there. And his girlfriend's there too."

Jack looked over at Augie and Lou and shook his head. "Why do you want to know about Augie Cumpton?"

"Look Jack. I don't have no time to waste. Here's the deal, I'll trade you Arturo for Cumpton. You can keep the girl. If you don't want to make the trade, I'll just send Arturo back to you a piece at a time. And then we'll come over there and kill everyone. So, what's it gonna be, Jack?"

Jack put the phone speaker on mute and spoke quickly to Augie, "I'm not going to do this. I won't trade you for Artie. But I'm going to play along with the guy. We'll try and figure a way to get Artie back," Jack said, and then activated the speaker phone.

"Okay, but I need to speak to Artie right now. I need to know you haven't hurt him. Then we can discuss making the exchange."

"I didn't say we didn't hurt Arturo. But he ain't dead... yet. He will be, though, unless you give us Cumpton," Cheech said and roughly pulled the tape from Artie's mouth. Then he held the phone next to Artie's mouth. "Tell him you're okay, Arturo."

Artie's voice was hoarse, and his speech was slurred as he tried to speak through his swollen lips and tongue. "Jack. I'm okay. Just a little busted up. But don't even consider doing this trade. I'm going to..." Tubby slapped the phone away from Artie and knocked him to the ground.

Cheech picked up the phone. "If yinz ever want to see Arturo again, then you better give us Cumpton. I'll give you a call tomorrow morning when we get up closer to where you're at. Then you better be ready to make the trade," Cheech said and hung up the phone.

* * *

Lou was holding her hand over her mouth. Then I turned to Jack.

"This is what I was concerned about all along, Jack. That you and Artie would be drawn into this. I don't know what else to say except that I'm sorry. But I don't understand how this could go so wrong. I haven't had a chance to tell you this yet, but I got a call from my uncle while you went to the bus station. My uncle is using a friend of the family, Jimmie Ponza, to communicate with the mob. Uncle Sal said Jimmie told him that this mob guy, Vito, was willing to make a deal that would guarantee my release. But he wanted something that Uncle Sal had in return." I gave Jack a quick overview of the compromising photos.

"Anyway, Vito told Jimmie that he had already ordered his men – the ones out here looking for me – to leave us alone. To go back to Pittsburgh. That was less than an hour ago. Uncle Sal said it was a done deal, and that we would be left alone."

"Well, the guy that just called apparently didn't get the message," Jack said. "Or maybe there never really was a deal. As far as I'm concerned, we need to find another way to get Artie back. There's no way I'd ever agree to give you to them, Augie. And what assurance do we have that they'd honor the agreement anyway? If we gave you up, they'd probably just kill you and Artie during the exchange. Then they would come up here and kill Lou and me. No, we need to come up with something that buys us time."

I looked over at Lou. I was concerned that the emotional roll-er-coaster we were on would send her stress level off the rails. She looked back at me. Then in a calm and resolute voice she said, "Augie, you should call your uncle and tell him about this. How these thugs are still after us. See if he can find out if this guy Vito is just trying to get us to let our guard down. To make it easier for his animals to surprise us. I can't imagine they would disobey their boss if he actually told them to back off. Jack is going to call Della and tell her what's going on and to stay put. She can't go back to her apartment until this is resolved. And Augie, I know you don't want to hear this, but if all else fails, you really need to consider calling the police and get them up here. That may be the only way we'll be able to survive this."

I was proud of Lou. She was cool as a cucumber and I appreciated her logical suggestions, including calling the police as a last resort. However, getting the cops involved would peel back a seven-year scab and cause a lot of legal trouble for me and my family. I would almost certainly be charged with murder or, at best, manslaughter, for killing the mob guy. The one who was about to murder my uncle at the bakery. Then there was also the issue of another Black Hand guy who was hunting me down back then. The one who had tortured and killed Johnny Harman. I had accepted the offer of another friend to help me ambush and abduct this thug. We took him to a remote mountain area where we left him bound and blindfolded in the middle of nowhere. I hadn't learned if this guy ever made it out of the mountains alive, but I would be shocked if he had. So, getting the police involved would have to be a last resort.

I reached for Lou's hand. "Sure, I'll call the police if that's the only way for us to survive. But there's another option. Say we agree to their terms. An exchange of me for Artie. But between now and then, we might be able to come up with a plan to save both of us. I have an idea that I'll share with you after I talk with my uncle again."

"Augie, I'll consider anything that would end this thing with no casualties. But there's no way I'll agree to a straight up deal to exchange you for Artie," Jack said firmly. "That's completely out of the question. And I don't want to call the cops either. I haven't exactly had a positive relationship with the local constabulary. Look, I'll call Della and warn her, and bring her up to speed on this. Maybe she has some ideas too. Then you can call your uncle and see where things stand."

"Okay, Jack. But something's not adding up here. Why would this

Vito make a deal and then immediately break it? Maybe this is just some miscommunication. At least, I hope so. Go ahead and give Della Mae a call, and then I'll phone Uncle Sal."

Jack immediately walked over to the phone and called Della Mae. I took Lou's hand, and we walked back to our bedroom. We sat on the bed, and I looked at Lou. After all she had been through with me, including some very good times and a few extremely harrowing days as the victim of kidnappers, she was unwavering in her love and support for me. It was all I could do to keep my voice steady.

"I keep saying this, and I know it must sound pretty lame, but I'm so sorry you've been dragged into this mess again."

"Augie, I know you feel guilty. But if we hadn't run into each other a couple of weeks ago in San Francisco, we might never have gotten back together – ever. Remember, I wasn't accepting any calls from you, and I had pretty much cut you out of my life. So yes, this is a bad situation, and it might get worse. But despite all that, I'm happy we found each other again."

Of course, Lou was right. It was, indeed, fortuitous for us to meet in San Francisco. Maybe it was good Karma? I hoped us getting back together was a sign of positive things to come and that God – or whomever else was in charge of Divine Providence – had a master plan that was being played out, and that plan would have a happy ending. There was one thing, though, that I knew for sure: I wasn't going to just sit around and accept what fate had in store for us. I began to formulate a plan. It would be risky and involve a lot of moving parts. First, however, I would call Uncle Sal and let him know that the bad guys hadn't gotten the message to back off – and that's assuming they had ever been given that order by Vito. Then he or Jimmie Ponza needed to contact the new mob boss and ask him what the hell was going on. We were running out of time.

CHAPTER 30
WHO'S ON FIRST?

When Lou and I returned to Jack's office, he had just hung up with Della Mae. She told him she would be staying at a friend's house for the night, and she gave him the phone number. She also agreed to stay away from her apartment until she received word that it was safe to go home. As soon as Jack got off the phone, I called Uncle Sal. He answered after the first ring.

"Hi, it's me. And things are all screwed up." I told him about the call from the mob guys and the exchange they wanted to make. Then I asked my uncle, "Do you think Vito was bullshitting you when he said he contacted his men. And ordered them to back off and leave us alone?"

"Augie, I can't imagine he'd lie to us about this. Jimmie said Vito seemed relieved when he talked to him earlier. That his guys hadn't gotten to you. That's when Vito told Jimmie he had called them off. He really wants those pictures we have of him. Especially now that he's the new boss. I'll have Jimmie give him a call right now. This doesn't make any sense. He knows that if anything happens to you, I'm going to make sure the guys in his outfit get copies of those photos."

"Okay, but we don't have a lot of time. The mob guys are going to call Jack tomorrow morning to set a time to make the exchange. We're playing along like we're going to do it, but we think they're just using Artie as a way to get us to let our guard down. If we tried to make the exchange, I'd be an open and easy target and they'd just shoot me. And Artie too. We need to get Vito to contact his guys and get them to back off. For real! I have to go now. Call me as soon as you know something," I said and hung up the phone.

I couldn't count on Uncle Sal or Jimmie Ponza getting Vito to call his guys off again. I had to assume that Vito was lying, and that he hadn't really instructed his mob minions to leave us alone. If he was telling us the truth, then his guys had gone rogue on him. Either way, I had to assume that the Black Hand thugs were coming after us, and I needed to come up with a plan to deal with the situation. I had begun developing a strategy, but its success would depend on the assistance of a friend. Unfortunately, my idea would put that person at risk; but I could think of no other way that would give us a fighting chance of survival. This would be a difficult call for me; not only because I would ask my friend to put himself in jeopardy, but also because I would need to tell him I was not Johnny Harman. I had to hope that he would understand why I had to live this lie when I told him my story. I dialed Topo Rojas' telephone number. It was Friday evening, and I hoped he would be home.

"Hello."

"Topo, this is Johnny. Do you have a minute to talk?"

"Hell yes, bro. What's up?"

For the next half hour, I told Topo my story, including my real name, and I hoped he would understand why I was forced to deceive him. When I finished, there was silence for a few seconds on the line. Then Topo spoke.

"Hey Johnny, I mean… Augie… that's some story. I hope I'm not being disrespectful here, and that you won't be offended, but as you were telling me your story, all I could think about is that guy in the TV show – 'The Fugitive.' Richard Kimble was his name, and he was being hunted down by a US Marshall."

"No. I'm not offended at all. That's a pretty good analogy except the guys chasing me don't want to just capture me, they want to put me in the ground."

"I hear you. But why don't you just call the cops?

"I know that seems like the logical solution, but getting the police involved would require me to reveal some things that most likely would put me in prison. I'm willing to do that as a last resort to save Lou, and the guys who are hiding us, but I'm hoping I can find another way to resolve the situation that doesn't involve the cops. I have a plan and I'd like to run it by you. I might also need your help to make it work."

"Just let me know what you want me to do. And Augie, I know you're under the gun – literally. So, I can help you right now. Anyhow, it's the weekend and I've got a lot of free time. What's your plan?"

I spent the next ten minutes outlining my idea with Topo, and he chimed right in with his own thoughts which improved the plan substantially. This was going to be a dicey operation and I had to make sure that he understood the risks involved.

"Topo, you have to know that the guys we're dealing with are mob-connected. Like the mafia. I wouldn't ask for your help, but I didn't know who else to turn to. Especially since you've been in tight situations before. No pun intended. And you have skills that no one except maybe law enforcement guys have."

"Hey Augie, I understand there are risks. But I also know that you don't have a chance of surviving this situation without help. So, count me in. Now, let's go over your plan again. I just had an idea that might improve our odds."

Topo and I spent another quarter hour refining the plan. I asked him to come up to the winery early tomorrow morning and he agreed. Jack had told me about a little-known forest service road that also led to the winery, but from another access point along the main road. It would get Topo to us without being confronted by the mob guys. I gave him the directions and hung up.

It had been more than an hour since my conversation with Uncle Sal, and I was anxious to find out if Jimmie Ponza had been able to speak with Vito. I called my uncle, and he picked up right away.

"Uncle Sal, any news from Jimmie?"

"Yes, Jimmie just called me. He said that Vito sounded shocked. He swore to Jimmie that he had given his men the order to leave you alone and to come back home. Vito said the guy he spoke to on the phone agreed to do what he was being asked. Then Jimmie reminded Vito that if anything bad happened to you, the embarrassing pictures would be circulated around Pittsburgh. Jimmie said Vito went ballistic. He told Jimmie to warn me to keep those pictures private or bad things would start happening to the Costanza family. Vito said he would contact his guys again and find out what was going on. He said he'd get back to us and then he hung up."

"So, we really don't know if he's telling us the truth. And even if he's not lying, what are the chances he'll be able to track his guys down out here before tomorrow afternoon? We need to assume the worst and try and figure a way to get through this alive," I said.

"Damn Augie. I can't believe this has taken another turn. Just when I thought we had it all going in the right direction. Hey look, you gotta call the cops. I know it will unravel a lot of things, and it might cause us some legal problems. But at least you'll survive this. Please promise me you'll call the police."

"I can promise you that if it looks like we can't get this solved any other way, I'll contact the police. But I have a plan that has a chance of working. We'll see what happens. In the meantime, let me know what, if anything, you hear from Vito."

"I will Augie. But you need to get the cops involved if that's your only way of getting through this in one piece."

When I got off the call, I asked Jack and Lou to join me in the dining room. We sat around the table, and I explained what Topo and I had put together. Jack offered additional tweaks to the plan. I was amazed at how calm he seemed. He had to be devastated knowing that Artie's life hung in the balance, but he never showed any sign that he was distressed.

"Jack, Lou. Listen, if either of you think this plan doesn't have a chance of working, you need to tell me right now. We probably have until tomorrow morning. Then we'll reach the point of no return. We either go ahead with it, or we call the cops and get them up here right away. What do you think?" I looked at each of them and tried to read their expressions. Then Lou spoke.

"Augie, I really want this to be over, so I'll go along with what you want to do. It seems like you've thought this through, but I don't know how much help I can give you if things go bad. But I say we go ahead with your plan. I know it's risky, but it seems to me to be the only choice that offers you and me any future together. And as you pointed out, getting the police involved will probably mean jail time for you. We've waited so long to be together… And, of course, there's Artie to consider. Your plan seems to be the only hope we have of saving him."

I looked over to Jack. "What do you think?"

Jack's expression was uncommonly neutral, but I could see tears welling up in his eyes.

"Augie, I hate to depend on the police to rescue Artie. I agree with Lou, particularly as to how our decision might affect his well-being. And your potential jail time. So, I say let's go with your plan."

We continued discussing our strategy at the dining room table for another half hour. At one point Jack left the room for a short while. When he returned, he was carrying a rifle with a large scope attached on top, and a tripod affixed to the barrel of the gun. Jack placed the rifle on the dining room table and looked over at me.

"Augie, you probably recognize this contraption, right?"

"Sure. That's a Starlight cope attached to what looks like an M-14. We used that rifle during Basic Training."

"Exactly. I shipped the scope and rifle home, piece by piece, through the mail right before I left Vietnam. This is the M-84 scope. It's a first-generation Starlight scope, but it does a pretty good job as long as there is some ambient light in the night sky – like a few stars or the moon."

"How does it work?" Lou asked.

"Simply put, it amplifies any light through the lens – even from the stars or moon at night. The images can look a little green and sometimes they're blurry, but you can spot targets pretty far away. Out to about two thousand feet. That's the good news. Unfortunately, the weight of the M-14 with the scope is more than nine pounds. The tripod helps, but it's still hard to hit a moving target unless you're an expert marksman. But for our purposes, we just need to be able to spot any bad guys trying to sneak up on us. I think we should take turns pulling guard duty overnight, and this scope will be a big help. Follow me out on the deck and we can take turns looking through it."

Jack opened the glass French doors in the dining room and stepped out onto the deck. We followed and watched as he placed the gun, with its tripod, on a wooden picnic table. He positioned the rifle so it pointed out into the vineyard and toward the ridge about quarter mile from us. He then demonstrated how to use the Starlight Scope, and we took turns familiarizing ourselves with the otherworldly-like images it magnified. When it was my turn, I spotted a deer walking leisurely through a row of vines, and I suggested to Jack that he might want to take a little target practice.

"If this was spring or during times when the grapes are mature, I might consider doing just that. But now that the grapes have been harvested, I might welcome any help Bambi might give me in cleaning up the vineyard," Jack said and chuckled.

"Any questions? Okay then. Augie, let's you and me take turns tonight on guard. I'll start at midnight, and you can spell me at 3 a.m."

"What about me?" Lou said. "I can take a turn too."

Jack looked quickly over to me, and I nodded. "Okay then. Let's do three two-hour shifts from midnight to 6 a.m. That's when the sun comes up around here. Lou, you take the first shift and Augie will spell you at 2 a.m. Then, I'll take over at four. If either of you sees anyone creeping around during your time on guard, just come wake me up. If necessary, I can fire a few rounds out there. That should be enough to discourage anyone with bad intentions."

"That sounds reasonable to me," I said and looked over to Lou. She nodded in agreement.

It was nearing midnight when Jack left us to get a few hours of sleep. Lou and I sat for a few more moments on the deck under a clear, but moonless, night with a universe of stars twinkling above us. I reached for Lou's hand and pulled her to me. She sat on my lap, and we embraced. Neither one of us spoke for several moments. Then I leaned back and smiled at her.

"Louise, what have I gotten you into?" I said and looked into those lovely green eyes of hers. Then I pointed to the stars above. "Under normal circumstances, this would be the perfect time and place to crawl under this table and ravish each other. But who cares about normal circumstances? Damn, I don't think we ever had times together that could be described as normal or routine."

"Augie! You're not serious, are you? I don't think it would be much fun pulling redwood splinters out of my butt." Lou flashed me her best crooked smile, and I laughed out loud.

"You wouldn't have to. I'd love to volunteer for that job. But we both might be more comfortable in the bedroom. What do you say? We have about fifteen minutes until your guard duty begins."

Lou slapped my hand, but quickly pulled me close and we kissed. We kissed again and then I gently took her shoulders, nudged her forward and looked into those dazzling green eyes.

"We're going to get through this. I promise. Even if it takes calling the police. We'll have time to get them up here if it looks like our plan won't work. We'll make that decision after our call with those thugs tomorrow morning."

"Augie, I know you'll make the right decision. One way or the other, this nightmare will be over, and we'll at least have a chance to be together. Even if you have to... God forbid... go to jail. But let's just think positive thoughts."

Even though our situation was precarious, I couldn't help but smile at Lou. I was so lucky to have her in my life now, but I wondered if our relationship would survive tomorrow.

Chapter 31
Nocturnal Surprise

After hanging up with Jack, Cheech leaned over and helped Tubby pick Artie up from the ground directly under the pay phone. He looked at Artie and said, "You tryin' to be some kinda hero, Arturo. You must wanna die, otherwise you'd want your buddy Jack to make the trade."

Artie's speech was slurred and hoarse, but he said, "I'm no hero. But I heard you and your midget psychopath buddy talking about how you're going to kill everyone anyway. I was trying to let Jack know you won't keep your word."

"I think you're wrong, Arturo. Your buddy Jack wants you back. He won't have no problem giving Cumpton up for you. Anyway, even if he decides to keep Cumpton and screw you over, he has to know we'll be coming after all of 'em. And I know you're hopin' they'll call the cops. But guess what? They can't risk callin' the pigs for help. Cumpton would end up in jail if he did. And Jack knows the only chance he has to get you back in one piece is to make the trade. He knows you're dead meat for sure if he calls the cops."

Tubby looked over at his partner. "Maybe you could let me git in the back of the truck with this tough guy before we start up the road. I'd like to have a little talk with him. What do you say?"

"The answer is no. We ain't got no time for you to beat on Arturo again. We still might need him to be able to talk. To his buddy Jack."

Cheech roughly slapped a strip of masking tape over Artie's mouth, and both men shoved him into the back of the truck. Cheech and Tubby climbed into the front seat. Cheech fired up the truck and pulled out onto Highway 101 north.

"Hey Cheech, how far is it to that winery place? And why do we gotta wait until tomorrow to get the job done?"

Cheech looked at Tubby and smiled. "You know, sometimes you surprise me little man. I always figured you was dumber than a sack of rocks. But maybe you're not as stupid as you look. Cause we ain't waitin' till tomorrow. That's what those sheep at the winery think. But we're gonna pay them a little visit before then."

Cheech drove through the California night for another hour. It was 10 p.m., and he was looking for a gas station, restaurant, or some other business that would be closed, but would have lighting in its parking area. He wanted to get out of the truck, spread the map on the hood and find out where he needed to exit Route 128 for the last leg of the trip to the winery. The business card they had taken from Artie did not provide directions. It simply listed the winery name, identified Jack as the owner and provided a phone number. Tubby had tried to extract more information from Artie, but the bloodied and battered man refused to give them any information, despite the beating he had taken.

Cheech had just driven past a sign for Yorkville. Within a mile, he spotted an illuminated area ahead and pulled into the parking lot of Billy's Gas and Grub. The place was closed and Cheech maneuvered the truck next to a twenty-foot-tall light post and stopped. He grabbed the map, and Tubby followed him out into the parking lot. Cheech spread the map out on the hood of the truck and peered down on it.

"Tubby, look at this. We gotta take that road right there." Cheech pointed a long, thick index finger to a spot on the map. "That's Yorkville Ranch Road. It's about six miles up ahead and that's where we need to turn. It goes up to Fruit Lake. So, the winery's gotta be close to it. When we find the place, we won't wait till tomorrow. We'll see if we can get things over with tonight. And hey Tubby, bring me that black case that's in the truck."

Tubby went around to the back of the vehicle and opened one of the double doors. He grabbed a long, black case that looked like it could contain an electric guitar or some other large musical instrument, and he brought it around the truck to his partner. Cheech took the case from Tubby and slowly turned in a 360-degree circle, checking to make sure they were completely alone. Then he placed the case on the hood next to the map and opened it. Inside was an AK-47 automatic rifle with three fully loaded magazines of 7.62 caliber rounds. There were also two handguns, one of which was equipped with a silencer, additional ammunition clips for both pistols and various tools, including a twelve-inch-long bolt cutter. These armaments and tools had been provided to them by Black Hand associates in California, and Cheech had retrieved them from a rental storage facility near San

Francisco International Airport.

Cheech handed one of the pistols to Tubby, took the other one and affixed the long silencer to it. He also removed the AK-47 and slapped a magazine into the rifle. "Okay, this should be more than enough heat to take care of business. Put the case back in the truck and let's get going."

When both men returned to the truck, Cheech placed the rifle on the floor of the vehicle at Tubby's feet and started the engine. He then drove through the clear, star-filled night for a few miles until he spotted the sign for Yorkville Ranch Road. He turned onto it and began climbing up Hawk Butte Mountain for about fifteen minutes until he saw a sign and turned left onto Fruit Lake Drive. Cheech drove for another five minutes until he arrived at the entrance to a large lake. A square wooden sign read Fruit Lake and indicated that the road ended right there in the parking lot. Cheech turned the truck around and back-tracked to Yorkville Ranch Road, and then he continued following the road up the mountain until it seemed to flatten out onto a plateau. He sensed that he was getting close to the winery, and he began driving slowly, looking for any indication they were nearing their destination. A half mile further down the road, Tubby spotted a wooden signpost.

"Hey Cheech, stop! There's a sign. It has an arrow pointin' to the right and it says 'FLV.' But them letters don't make no sense."

Cheech just shook his head and turned onto the rutted, gravel road that would most likely take them to Fruit Lake Vineyard. He drove very slowly, trying to make as little noise as possible. Two miles later, the truck reached a metal farm gate with a sign that proclaimed in large red letters: Fruit Lake Vineyard and Winery – No Trespassing.

They men got out of the truck and walked up to the gate. Cheech was carrying the silenced pistol at his side. He could see that a large metal padlock on a thick steel chain secured the gate.

"Tubby, go back to the truck and get them bolt cutters. Then come back here and use 'em to cut this lock off." In a few moments, Tubby came waddling back carrying the heavy tool.

Just then, two large German Shepherds emerged from the forest and leaped up onto the gate just opposite Cheech. They were growling and snapping their fang-like teeth against the gate, trying to reach the trespassers. Cheech was paralyzed by the sudden attack. Tubby screamed, dropped the bolt cutters and fell onto his back, nearly impaling himself on the tool. He covered his eyes and began to moan. Finally, Cheech reacted. He lifted the silenced pistol and fired a round into the face of each dog, killing them both instantly.

Cheech looked down at his whimpering partner and whispered loudly, "Shut the hell up, Dipshit. You want them people at the winery to hear us." He reached down and jerked Tubby to his feet.

Cheech picked up the bolt cutters. Then he went to the gate and successfully snapped off the chain securing the padlock. Tubby opened the gate widely, and both men returned to the truck. Cheech drove slowly for another ten minutes until he reached a small rise. Before they reached the top of the hill, he stopped the truck and both men got out of the vehicle. Cheech walked to the crest of the rise and peered over. He stared down at a vineyard some twenty yards directly in front of him. He turned and motioned for his partner to join him.

"This is it Tubby," he whispered. "We gotta creep through all those grapevines till we see the winery. It should be straight ahead. At the end of them rows of vines. But we need to keep real quiet. You capeesh?"

The little man nodded, grinning. "This is where we start havin' fun, right Cheech? Let's go. I'll follow you."

Cheech went back to the truck and grabbed the AK-47 and the silenced pistol and returned to where Tubby was waiting. He handed Tubby the pistol and then he bent over and began to creep through the darkness down the road toward the vineyard. When he got to the first row of vines, he moved silently into the vineyard and Tubby followed.

* * *

The sky was full of shimmering stars that gloriously illuminated the heavens. However, the vineyard to the front and below Lou's post on Jack's deck was still shrouded in darkness. Lou could look down and see the first few rows of vines, which were situated perpendicular to her position. However, the area beyond that where the vineyard rose up the hill would have been murky and visibly indistinct without the aid of the Starlight scope. Lou was amazed by how using the scope magically brightened the area with a kind of fuzzy, green visibility. She would lean forward on the picnic table and lift the back of the rifle up from its stabilizing tripod, sight through the scope and scour the vineyard for anyone who might be out there. Lou would gaze through the scope for a minute or two and then rest for about the same amount of time. Scanning the vineyard with the heavy M-14 rifle and scope left her arm and shoulder sore, and her neck stiff. She had been at her post now for an hour and a half and soon she would go and wake Augie for his turn on guard duty.

Suddenly, Lou spotted movement at the far end of the vineyard just below the ridgetop some four hundred yards to her front. Two figures – one tall and full-bodied and the other short and pudgy – were making their way slowly down through the vines toward her position. Instead of walking directly along the gravel road that bisected the vineyard, the two figures were slowly zig-zagging down one row, and then into the next one, in a pattern that would eventually bring them to the base of the winery.

Lou quickly rose from her position at the picnic table and rushed into the house. She ran down the hall to the guest room where Augie slept, fully clothed, on top of the bed spread. She roughly shook him.

* * *

Someone was shaking me. I heard a voice say, "Augie, wake up. I just spotted two guys in the vineyard. They're coming this way."

I looked up. It was Lou. I rose quickly, now completely alert. "Okay, I'll go roust Jack. You stay inside the house." I ran down the hall toward Jack's bedroom.

Before I could get there, Jack met me in the hallway. "Lou saw two men creeping around in the vineyard," I said.

Jack didn't say a word. He just rushed by me. I followed him into the dark dining room, and then stopped next to him at the glass doors that led to the deck.

"I don't think anyone can see us on the deck unless they're real close to us. But we need to be really quiet now," he whispered.

I heard movement behind me, and I felt Lou grab my hand. Jack turned and looked at both of us. He pulled what looked like a .45 caliber pistol from his back pocket and handed it to Lou.

"You probably won't need this, but just in case," he said, and handed Lou the gun. "You can stay in the dining room on the floor, but don't get near the windows."

Lou nodded and I followed Jack onto the deck. I crouched near the picnic table while Jack put the Starlight Scope to his eye and began to sweep the vineyard beginning where the rows of vines began in front of us. He swept the rows very slowly for about five minutes. Then suddenly he stopped.

"I see movement. Two figures. They're almost crawling. I'm going to wait until they move to the next row. Then I should have a clear shot," Jack said.

I was confused. "Jack, you aren't going to shoot them, are you? We can't be sure they're the ones after us. I mean, they probably must be the bad guys. But you can't be sure."

"Augie, I hear what you're saying. But you told me the one guy you remembered seeing at the BART station was short and heavy. Well, one of the people out there right now fits that description to a tee. And if I put them down, we can go and find Artie. That's the only way to guarantee I'll ever see him again. Alive. But if they're trying to ambush us tonight, chances are they've already killed him."

Jack was whispering to me, and he was trying to remain composed, but I could still hear the anger and desperation in his words.

"So, I'm willing to take a chance those are the guys who're after you. If I'm wrong, then I'll have to deal with the consequences."

I knew what Jack was saying was true. And I didn't have any qualms about killing those murdering bastards. If they were, indeed, the scumbags after me. But if they weren't those guys, then we both would have to live with it. I didn't say another word to Jack. I thought to myself. Whatever happens, happens.

Jack continued to track the men with the rifle and scope as they slowly made their way down one row. Then he quickly said: "That's definitely them 'cause the tall one is carrying a rifle, and he's about to come into the open."

Just then, I saw the muzzle flash and was momentarily deafened by the roar of the M-14. I watched as the rifle recoiled into Jack's shoulder. In another second, Jack fired again. He looked back into the scope.

"Damn! I don't think I hit either one of them. You better lie flat on the floor," Jack yelled. Then I heard a whizzing sound, immediately followed by a volley of automatic fire that struck the glass doors on the deck and the redwood siding above them. The panes in the doors shattered, sending shards of glass onto both of us. Jack grabbed the M-14 and rolled onto the deck floor beside me. He was sighting through the scope, desperately trying to locate the men who were shooting at us. Then he returned fire, squeezing off three more rounds into the vineyard. Once again, automatic weapons fire erupted and impacted onto the siding and into the house. I knew after the second volley that the weapon being fired at us was an AK-47. Its distinctive sound brought back bad memories of Vietnam. Then I panicked. I thought about Lou.

* * *

Cheech looked over at Tubby who was lying face down with his hands covering his head. He was whimpering. Cheech shoved Tubby with the stock of the AK-47 and whispered loudly, "Get your shit together, fat boy. We gotta move and get outta here right now."

Then Cheech slung the rifle onto his shoulder and lay prone on the ground in the vineyard. Tubby quickly mimicked his partner, and both men began belly-crawling. Like slithering serpents, they scurried under the horizontal trellising wire to which each of the grape vines were tied in the six-acre square matrix that was Fruit Lake Vineyard. They crawled underneath the wire and through foot-high grass that served as a cover crop in the vineyard between each row of vines.

"Holy shit, Cheech," Tubby said breathlessly. "Them guys back there was tryin' to kill us." The deranged little hit man was wheezing and gasping as he followed Cheech, clambering up through the vineyard to escape the unexpected rifle fire from the winery.

"Keep it down, doofus! If they hear us out here, they might drill us with a lucky shot."

After twenty minutes of exhaustive effort, Cheech and Tubby emerged from the vineyard and crawled into the pine forest just above the last row of vines. They scurried down through the trees and made their way to the gravel road where the panel truck was parked. Cheech opened the side door and checked on Artie, who was still bound from head to foot with masking tape and chicken wire.

"Looks like you get to live another day, Arturo. Your friends at the winery seen us coming. So, I guess we gotta go ahead with trading you for Cumpton. Like we was gonna do," Cheech said, and slammed the side door shut.

"Okay Tubby, get in the truck. Let's go for a little ride. I gotta figure out how we're gonna do this tomorrow."

Cheech climbed into the driver's seat and started the engine. He turned the truck around and headed toward the main road. He stopped the truck about a hundred yards before they reached the highway.

"It should be light in about an hour. We'll catch some zz's here for a while and then I'll go into that town… I think it's Yorkville. I'll call Jack and tell him he can still get his buddy back if he gives us Cumpton. Then I'll find a diner or some fast-food joint and get us some chow. And I'll bring something back for Arturo too. A Coke or some water. He needs to be alive and well enough to walk. While I do that, you wait here with the rifle just in case them guys try to get past us. You can hide here in the trees and be on guard."

"I don't know, Cheech. Them guys got guns. And they ain't afraid to use 'em. What if they try to come after us? Like we did to them. I don't want no civilian jamoke wastin' me."

"They ain't gonna do shit as long as they think Arturo's still alive. There's only three of them. And one of them is a broad. We can still get this done. No, we BETTER get this done, or else. You remember what Carmine told you, right?"

Tubby did not reply. He knew that Carmine hadn't said a thing. Carmine was probably dead. However, he did know what the new boss – Vito The Scar – had ordered them to do. To stop trying to get Cumpton and come back home. Tubby was tempted to tell Cheech the truth. He thought it over. If he came clean and Cheech didn't kill him, Tubby feared that Vito might have him whacked for ignoring his direct order. On the other hand, Tubby knew that going ahead with Cheech's plan would be dangerous, and that he might get killed anyway. He was in a tough spot. But now that they had Artie, it was probably too late to stop what they had started. One thing was for sure, though: he and Cheech could not go back to Pittsburgh now. Finally, he decided to keep quiet and go along with Cheech's plan. It was risky, but it offered him the best chance to do what he loved to do more than anything else in the world: torture, maim and then kill. He became excited and aroused at the thought of how he would participate in the massacre at the winery. And then his mouth began to water at the thought of the ways he would inflict slow and agonizing pain on Cumpton's chick.

* * *

I stood and began running across the broken glass that covered the deck, and then I flung the door open and crossed the threshold into the dining room.

"Lou, Lou. Are you okay?" I yelled. When there was no immediate response, I looked over and saw her huddled in a corner of the room.

She was lying in a fetal position and her back was to me. I crawled over to her and gently touched her shoulder.

"Lou, are you hurt?" No response. I leaned in and felt her carotid artery. Her pulse was rapidly pounding. Thank God, she's alive, I thought. "Lou, can you hear me?"

Lou did not reply. Then I gently turned her toward me. The upper portion of her blouse was darkly stained. I looked in horror as the stain seemed to be expanding by the second.

CHAPTER 32
FLORENCE NIGHTINGALE

Lou's shoulder had been penetrated by a five-inch shard of glass from the shattered windows on the deck doors. She must have been kneeling when she was struck. Then she rolled onto her side and lost consciousness. After examining her closely for any other wounds, Jack and I carried her as gently as we could to the bedroom where we laid her onto the bed. Thankfully, Jack's training as a Special Forces officer included extensive classes on battlefield emergency medical care. He was able to stanch the flow of blood from Lou's wound, but he didn't want to risk trying to remove the glass from her shoulder. He feared that action might cause the wound to bleed profusely. Lou needed more extensive medical treatment than Jack or I could provide, and she needed it soon. She had not regained full consciousness, but she would stir and try to move occasionally, and that could get the wound bleeding again. It was almost too much for me to bear. I felt helpless, and I knew that we had to get Lou professional medical care soon. However, I didn't know if it was safe to move her, especially since we would need to use the rough, forest service back road that led to the paved highway. Then I thought about Topo. He might be able to bring us some medicine or medical supplies that would help us to stabilize Lou until we could move her.

I immediately left the bedroom, went into Jack's office and I dialed Topo's number. It was after 3 a.m. when he answered the phone, and I quickly filled him in on the earlier attempt by the mob guys to ambush us. I also told him about what happened to Lou. When we had spoken earlier, I had asked Topo to come to Jack's place around mid-morning. However, we needed help now, but not the kind of assistance Topo would have been trained to provide.

"Sorry, Topo. I didn't know who else to call. We're afraid to move her, or we would have already left this place by the back road I told you about. But we don't think Lou would be able to survive a trip to the hospital. We really need some medical supplies to treat her, though. Jack said we need bandages, antibiotics and an IV kit with saline solution bags. And anything else you can think of to treat a puncture wound. I know this is the middle of the night, but do you think you can get some of this stuff and bring it up here as soon as possible?"

"Hey Johnny. I mean Augie. I think I can help. And if I leave now, I should be able to get up there in three… maybe four hours."

I thanked him and hung up. Then I rushed back to the bedroom. Lou's eyes were open and she was trying to speak to Jack. I quickly moved to the bed and reached for her hand. The one opposite from her shoulder wound.

"Lou. Don't try to speak. Just rest. You have a piece of glass in your shoulder, and you really need to lie still. I know it hurts, but you shouldn't try to move." I was trying to keep my emotions in check. I had put Lou in a situation where she might lose her life. "We have someone coming soon with medical supplies to take care of you."

Lou tried to smile and then she seemed to fall asleep. That was three hours ago. Now, as she lay there unconscious, her breathing became shallow, and I feared the worst. Just then I heard voices and muffled conversation. I could hardly believe my eyes as Topo and, surprisingly, Ginny walked quickly into the room followed by Jack.

Without a word, Ginny moved to the bed and looked down at Lou. Then she asked where the bathroom was located and left the room. When she returned, Ginny was wearing sterile surgical gloves and she gently felt Lou's forehead. Next, she took her temperature. Then she moved to the other side of the bed, took Lou's uninjured arm and placed a blood pressure cuff on it, and took a measurement. She moved back around and removed the thermometer from Lou's mouth.

"One oh two," she said. Ginny grasped a tall floor lamp by the bed. With Jack's help, Ginny used the lamp as a stand to hold the IV kit, and quickly started the drip into Lou's arm. Then she removed the gauze Jack had used as a bandage and examined the wound.

"It's a good thing you didn't try to remove this glass. It's jagged and could have really done some serious damage. The fatal kind. I'm going to need to do a little surgery here, so we'll have to make this area as sterile as possible."

At Ginny's direction, we enclosed the area around Lou by sealing it off with clean bed sheets that we taped to the ceiling. I used a mop to scrub the wooden floors around and under her bed with disinfectant. As we worked around her, Ginny cleansed the area around Lou's wound with isopropyl alcohol. Then from a black bag, Ginny withdrew a syringe and injected it into Lou's arm.

"This is Ketamine," she said. "It's used now instead of morphine to treat battlefield wounds. It will have to serve as a substitute for anesthesia while I work on her." Then Ginny looked at me, and said, "So, this is Lou. I would have preferred to meet her under more favorable circumstances. Anyway, I'll do my best here. But we'll need to get her to a hospital as soon as possible."

I wanted to reach out and embrace Ginny, but I just nodded. "Thanks for coming, I really appreciate you getting here right away. I don't know what we would have done if…" I couldn't finish the sentence. I just turned and left the room.

I sat on the floor in the hallway just outside the bedroom and said a silent prayer for Lou. I also prayed that God would give Ginny the ability and steady hands to successfully treat her. I know that Ginny is extremely competent. She's a surgical nurse. Still, I was concerned. The bedroom is not a sterile hospital operating suite with all of the latest equipment, medicine and complement of other health care professionals. But I had faith in Ginny. In her excellent medical skills, and also in her compassionate understanding and treatment for the emotional and psychological toll physical wounds can trigger.

I thought back to how she had so lovingly ministered to me just a year ago in Paris when I had that Vietnam flashback. That was before Lou came back into my life, and I could have very easily fallen for Ginny back then. But there was a complication. Ginny had decided to resume her life as a nun. So, I have bittersweet memories of those few special days I spent with her in Paris. It was the end of the physical part of our relationship, but Ginny still remains as one of my closest friends. And now, at great personal risk, she arrives here like Florence Nightingale to salve Lou's wounds and hopefully save her life.

After about fifteen minutes, I rose and walked down the hall and into the dining room where Jack and Topo were nailing sheets of plywood over each of the two doors where the windows had been shot out. It was 7.30, and the day had dawned cold and overcast.

Jack turned to me. "Any word yet?"

"No. Ginny told me that she wouldn't know how long it will take to remove the glass. She needs to be careful that she doesn't do any more damage to Lou's shoulder. She did tell me again that if she's successful in stopping the bleeding, and if the sutures hold, we have to get her to a hospital as soon as possible."

Topo added, "Hey guys, you think those mafia assholes are still going to want to make the exchange? You think they're going to stick around?"

Jack answered, "I can only hope they want to. Otherwise, that means they've probably killed Artie. Anyway, deal or no deal, we need to get Lou to the hospital as soon as she's able to be moved. In the meantime, we'll wait for a call."

"Okay," I said. "While we wait, let's talk about how this changes – if any – the plan we discussed yesterday. Let's go ahead and assume that they still want to do the exchange. That way, we're ready."

We spent the next half hour going over our strategy to deal with what we knew would be a risky plan. But all I could really think about was Lou. Will she make it through surgery? And if she does, will she survive? I tried to think positive thoughts. I've been so fortunate over recent years to have good friends come to my aid when I needed help most. And when I reflect on the traumatic events of the last decade, I am beyond grateful, particularly for the love and friendship of three special women. Della Mae, Ginny and Lou have always been there for me when I needed them most. They've not only provided me with love and understanding, but they have all put their own lives in jeopardy to protect me.

Just then, the telephone rang. Jack quickly walked across the room and pushed the button on the speaker phone.

"This is Jack."

"How you doin' Jack. You still wanna see Arturo?" Cheech said.

CHAPTER 33
DEAL REDUX

Topo and I looked over at Jack. He took a moment to gather his thoughts, then he replied, "Is Artie still alive?"

"Yeah. Arturo's still with us. But he won't be much longer unless you give us Cumpton. You still want to do it? The trade? Cumpton for Arturo?"

"First, I want to talk to Artie. I need to make sure he really is alive. Then we can talk about how we'll do the trade."

"You can't talk to Arturo right now. But he's alive. Anyway, if you agree to give us Cumpton, you'll see for yourself that your friend is still with us."

"How do I know that you'll keep your word? You double-crossed us last night. You thought you could just ambush us. Kill us all while we slept."

"Hey Jack, you know you shouldn't trust us. We're the bad guys. We ain't gonna play by the rules. But now that we know you got guns, we'll have to do it the way we said we was going to."

"Okay, I talked to Augie, and he still wants to do the exchange. On two conditions. One, that you don't hurt Artie anymore, and two, that you leave us – me and Augie's girlfriend – alone. But I don't believe anything you say. So, here's how we're going to do this if you want Augie." There was an edge to Jack's tone, a kind of menacing inflection.

"Oh, so now your gonna play tough guy. That right Jack? You think you scare me?" Cheech said and chuckled.

Jack took a deep breath. "Here's how this is going to work. Your guy and Artie will come out into the open and start walking down the gravel road that splits the vineyard. When I have a clear view of them, I'll send Augie out and he'll walk toward them. When they meet, you'll let Artie walk back to me at the winery. Your guy can take Augie to where you're hiding. And if you try and shoot Artie or Augie during the exchange, I'm going to put a round right through the head of your fat little friend."

"That's some plan, Jack. I gotta admit, if I was in your shoes, I'd probably do it the same way. But there's a couple a things you gotta do too. First, you gotta let my guy frisk Cumpton. We can't take no chance he'll be packin' heat. And second, we gotta do it today. You agree to them things, and we got a deal."

"Okay, I agree. Let's do it early this evening. I say we do the trade at 6 o'clock."

"You ain't tryin' to pull a fast one on us, are you Jack? I mean, you know Arturo is a dead man if you try and fuck us over."

"I think you know you have us outgunned. And you know we can't afford to call the police, or we would have already done that. So, no. We'll do it the way I told you".

"Alright then, Jack. See you at six," Cheech said and hung up.

When Jack pushed the button on the speaker phone ending the call, I looked at him and asked, "Why did you want to wait until six to do the exchange? It'll be twilight then, and visibility won't be as good as if we did this thing earlier in the afternoon."

"Augie," Topo answered before Jack could respond, "it probably has something to do with the sun's position at that time of day. Am I right, Jack?"

"Yeah, that's the main reason I suggested 6 o'clock. My deck faces directly toward the west. The sun's position most of the afternoon would be right in my eyes then. But it goes down behind the mountains right before 6. There will still be enough light to see then, but the sun won't be in my eyes. And twilight won't be as good for the guy aiming at us from out there," he said, pointing toward the vineyard. "We need every little advantage we can find."

Then Jack looked at me. His face radiated concern. "Augie, we don't have to do it this way. We could call the cops right now and tell them what's going on. Maybe they would get these thugs before they can hurt Artie anymore. What do you think?"

I knew that Jack meant what he said. That he would risk Artie's life to save mine. But there was no way I could agree to that.

"I appreciate your offer, but no. We can't take the chance the police will get here in time to save Artie. And anyway, getting the cops involved will probably get me a long prison sentence. There's no statute of limitations on murder. So, I say we go ahead with the plan we just discussed. I think it has a good chance of working. And Jack, and you too Topo, I don't know how to thank you guys for helping me. I hate that this situation is putting your lives in danger..."

Jack cut me off. "Augie, we already discussed this. I promised to keep you and Lou safe and secure. We didn't think there was any way those mob guys would find you up here. But they did. And when they took Artie, this became very personal for me. So, let's go ahead and do this."

I looked at Topo. "What about you? I hate to drag you into this. You and Ginny should leave when she patches Lou up. We'll take care of Lou until she can be moved. There's no need for you to risk your lives. You've already gone above and beyond."

Jack looked over at Topo and nodded. "That's right. We can execute our plan without your help."

But the ex-Tunnel Rat just shook his head. "Augie, you know I wouldn't leave you in the lurch. Besides, you really do need me if this plan has any chance of working. And we can't abandon Lou now. She'll need a day or so, at least, to recuperate. I know Ginny will want to make sure there are no complications. So, I'm in. All the way."

I left Jack and Topo and walked back to the bedroom where Ginny was sitting next to Lou. I stood in the doorway and looked over at Lou. Lou seemed to be sleeping peacefully. Ginny got up and we walked out into the hallway.

"How's she doing?"

"The good news is she survived the surgery – such as it was – with no more loss of blood. And the Ketamine kept her comfortable as I removed the glass from her shoulder. But she still isn't out of the woods. I put an antibiotic in her IV to prevent infection. We'll see how she is tomorrow. If the wound is clean and the sutures are holding, we'll need to get her to a hospital."

I didn't want to tell Ginny that there might not be a tomorrow. But it was like she read my thoughts.

"What's going to happen next? I mean, are those criminals going to try and come and get you again?" Ginny face was full of concern and worry.

I hadn't told Ginny about any of what was going on now. I assumed that Topo had on the trip up here. She obviously knew that the thugs had somehow found us at Jack's winery. But she knew nothing about the exchange of Artie for me, and I didn't want her here if our plans failed.

"Look Ginny. You need to take Topo's car and leave as soon as possible. Use the back road you guys came here on. We can nurse Lou over the next few days. When she's well enough, we'll call for an ambulance to take her to a hospital. I don't know if those guys who are after us will try to attack us again. But I can't take the chance that you might be hurt. So, tell me what I need to do to keep Lou stabilized until she's better. And then, please, get out of here."

Ginny shook her head. "Lou needs professional medical monitoring around the clock right now. And that's not something you or anyone here is qualified to provide. So, I'm not leaving until I think she's ready to be moved. And you're not telling me everything, Augie. Now, will you level with me so I can be prepared for anything that might happen. I'm a big girl, and I need to know how you're planning to keep us all safe."

Ginny was right. And I knew she would never abandon Lou. So, if she was going to stay here, she deserved to understand the risks involved. I told her what we planned to do. I also pleaded with her, once again, to leave. She just smiled at me and shook her head.

"Whatever happens, I'm not leaving here. And from what you tell me, when this is all over it sounds like Arty is going to need some medical attention too."

I had to turn away from her. I was about to lose it right then and there. I was able to compose myself just enough to say, "Thank you, Ginny."

CHAPTER 34
CHEECH'S NEW PLAN

After the call to Jack, Cheech found a diner outside of Yorkville. He ordered a couple of bacon, egg and cheese biscuit sandwiches to go. He also bought three large bottles of Coca Cola. He drove back up toward where he had left Tubby along the gravel road leading to the winery. He stopped the truck and got out of the vehicle when Tubby emerged from the pine forest carrying the AK-47.

"Hey Cheech, you git us some food?"

"Yeah, it's in the truck. I got a couple a sangwiches and a few Cokes. We'll give one of them Cokes to Arturo and we'll split the rest of the food and drinks."

"You only got me one sangwich? That ain't enough to keep me strong. How my s'posed to do my job with only one sangwich. Hey, can't I just go into town and git me some more grub?" Tubby pleaded with Cheech.

"No godammit! You ain't gonna go nowhere. We gotta stay outa sight until we git this job done. When I call Carmine, I wanna be able to tell him we finally took care of business. And hey, piggy, you ever pass a mirror and take a look at yourself? You look like someone shoved one of them helium pumps up your ass and forgot to turn it off. If you wasn't such a porker, you'd a prob'ly already floated away."

Cheech calmed down and looked at his partner. The little man was pouting. Cheech swore to himself that he would never work with this asshole again. But in the meantime, he needed to keep him focused and ready. So, he relented.

"You can go ahead and eat both them biscuit sangwiches. I had a candy bar at the diner where I got the grub. I ain't hungry anyway."

"Thanks a lot, Cheech. Did you bring me one of them candy bars too?"

Cheech was so enraged that he almost bit his tongue off. Instead, he turned and went to the truck. He opened the front door, grabbed the bag with food and drinks and removed one of the Cokes. He handed the bag to Tubby and walked around to the side door of the panel truck and slid it open. Cheech put the Coke down and then he grabbed Artie by the feet and dragged the battered and bruised man to the door opening. He pulled Artie up into a sitting position, roughly ripped the masking tape from Artie's mouth and stared at him.

"You don't look so good, Arturo. I bet you're hungry. And thirsty too, right? Well, here's a Coke. But I ain't gonna undo the tape around your arms. So, you're gonna have to let me help you drink it."

Cheech used a bottle opener attached to his key chain and popped the cap off the bottle. Then, with one of his hands, he grabbed Artie's face and forced the man's mouth open and, using the other hand, Cheech poured a little of the soft drink into Artie's mouth.

Artie promptly spit the liquid back in Cheech's face and hoarsely mumbled, "Fuck you, and your Coke too."

Cheech immediately back-handed Artie, and then he dumped the remainder of the liquid in the bottle over the top of Artie's head.

Cheech used his coat sleeve to wipe the expectoration from his face and chest, and he scowled down at Artie. "I guess you don't like Coke. You shoulda told me what your favorite pop is. Anyway, you'll be happy to know that we'll be tradin' you for that Cumpton guy soon. But I gotta say, Arturo, I'm gonna miss you. In fact, I'm gonna miss you so much, I promise to come back sometime when you ain't expectin' it. For a surprise visit. That's if you make it past today. And if you do make it, then you got my visit to look forward to," Cheech said, smiling evilly at Artie.

Cheech grabbed a roll of gray masking tape from the vehicle floor and tore off a large piece. He quickly slapped the tape back over Artie's mouth, shoved him back into the truck and slammed the side door shut. Cheech walked over to Tubby, who was sitting on the forest floor with his back up against a tall pine tree devouring the second bacon and egg biscuit. He had already inhaled the first large bottle of Coke, and he had drunk most of the remaining one. Bacon, egg and biscuit residue was flecked all over the front of his dirty white suit.

"Holy shit, Tubby. Did you get any of them sangwiches inside you? You look like you got caught in a food storm. Now, listen up. Let's talk about how we're gonna handle things at that winery."

Tubby looked up at Cheech. "Okay Cheech. How we gonna do

this? I got some ideas if you wanna hear 'em. But you go first."

Cheech forced a smile and patiently presented Tubby with the plan. They would drive up the road toward the winery just before it reached the top of the hill where the vineyard began. Cheech would set up in an area that offered him cover from anyone that might be shooting at him from the winery. He had spotted a large boulder at the top of the hill just behind the last row of vines that might work. That site would provide Cheech with a clear field of fire toward anyone walking along the road that bisected the vineyard. That's where the exchange would take place. Tubby would appear first with Artie and walk in clear view of Jack who would surely be training his rifle on the little man. Then Cumpton would start walking toward Tubby and Artie, clearly exposing him to Cheech. When they meet, Tubby would frisk Cumpton, release Artie and walk Cumpton back up the road toward Cheech. The deal would be done.

But that's not what Cheech had in mind. Cheech explained the real plan to Tubby for the better part of an hour to make sure he understood his role. Tubby's job was simple. When the little hit man heard the shot from Cheech that was intended for Artie, that would be his signal to shove Cumpton into the vineyard and kill him too. That way, Jack wouldn't have time to shoot Tubby. But Tubby didn't like that assignment. He was concerned that he would be the one at greatest risk to be killed or wounded if things did not go as planned.

"Hey Cheech, how come you git to stay where that Jack guy can't see you? And I gotta be the one in the most danger. How 'bout we switch jobs? You go get Cumpton and I'll stay back here with the rifle and cover you?"

"First of all, Tubby, you ain't good with a rifle. If the shit hits the fan, you'd prob'ly shoot yourself or me rather than hit what you was aimin' at. And Jack won't have no clear shot at you. You'll be in the vineyard. Look, you'll be fine. I guarantee it. And if you do it my way, I'll let you take your time with Cumpton's girlfriend when we go up to that winery to finish the job."

Tubby looked up at Cheech and smiled. Saliva was forming along the corners of his mouth. "You promise? You'll let me have a couple of hours with that chick?"

Cheech wanted to kill the little pervert right then and there. But he needed Tubby – for a while at least. The plan he had discussed with Jack involved Tubby exchanging Artie for Cumpton. He'd need Tubby for that, and to help him when they went up to the winery to kill Jack and the girl. He would also need Tubby to help him clean things up and dispose of the bodies. Once that was done, Tubby was expendable, and Cheech vowed to get rid of the man and bury him with the other casualties at Fruit Lake Vineyard. Then, when Cheech called the boss in the morning to give him the news that they had finally gotten Cumpton, he would simply say that Tubby had been caught in the crossfire and had been killed.

Cheech looked at his partner in disgust. "Yeah. I promise. You can have lots of time with the girl. Now, repeat for me what you're s'posed to do."

CHAPTER 35
THE LONG WAIT

After I tried unsuccessfully to get Ginny to leave Lou and escape this place while she still could, I walked back to the dining room. It was mid-morning and Jack was bent over, holding a dustpan with one hand and using a broom with the other to sweep up the broken glass and splintered wood from the deck doors. He stood up when he heard me come into the room.

"Where's Topo?" I asked.

"He's out on the deck jerry-rigging an observation post and a defensive position. Kind of setting up like we did in Vietnam when we knew "Victor Charlie" was coming."

"Yeah, I heard that. I guess the three of us have some experience with digging in before the VC hit the wire." I thought of the last time I prepared for battle at my basecamp in Vietnam. Unfortunately, on that occasion, two of my best friends were killed, and I was wounded during the attack. I hoped the outcome later this evening would not be as calamitous. But I needed for Jack to be prepared if our plan failed.

"Jack, I want to speak to you about something. And I hope you'll consider what I'm going to suggest. It's some things I hope you'll agree to. To make the best out of a possible worst-case scenario. I mean... "

"Hey Augie. Just spit it out. What're you're trying to tell me."

"Okay. Here it is. Let's say those thugs get the upper hand somehow. You know, if our plan fails or they shoot me, Topo or Artie. If something like that happens and it becomes obvious to you that things have gone south. If that happens, I want you to immediately call the cops. Even if you get Artie back, you need to call the cops right away, and get them out here. I think we both can agree that the mob guys aren't going to be satisfied with just getting me back. They'll come right after you and anybody else here. They'll wipe everyone out. I'd ask you to leave here right now and take the women with you, but I know you and

Ginny would never risk Lou's life by moving her. So, please promise me you'll call for help as soon as Artie's back, or as soon as you know he's not coming back."

"Where's that leave you, Augie? We can't just abandon you. They could keep you and take you with them somewhere. I hate to be this blunt, but I don't think they would execute you right away."

"Okay, even if they do take me alive, I still want you to call the cops. At that point, our plan would have failed, and my only chance at surviving would be if the police get after those bastards. Right away. So, what do you say, Jack?"

"I can't argue with your reasoning. But I just can't stand the thought of abandoning you. Back in the Central Highlands, we would never leave a brother behind in Indian country. That's a vow we all took. So, if I do what you're asking, it would be like I was violating that pledge."

"Jack, you know that doing what I'm asking will save the most lives. I'm talking about Ginny and Lou. That's your primary responsibility in this situation. You can't jeopardize them, especially when you know staying here would serve no practical purpose. Because once the exchange is made, there's nothing you can do to save me. Or Topo, if he doesn't make it back."

"Okay Augie. I'll call the cops as soon as I know there's nothing more I can do to help you. Given the circumstances, you're right about where my responsibilities lie. I just wish there were other options."

"Look, you shouldn't feel guilty about this. Think about it. I'm the one who put you in this awful position. If I hadn't come up here and complicated your life – and caused Artie to be taken – none of this would have happened. So, please don't think any of this is your fault. It's all on me. But I'll feel a hell of a lot better knowing you'll be able to save Ginny and Lou."

In a little more than eight hours, we would execute our plan. I yelled out to the deck for Topo to join us in the dining room. For the next two hours, the three of us looked at our strategy from just about every angle, critiquing and refining it until we had exhausted all possible permutations that might improve it. Then we agreed to spend the remainder of the day alternately resting and pulling guard duty. Around 2 o'clock, I went into the dining room. I wanted to call Uncle Sal once more before this evening's events. He answered after the first ring.

"Uncle Sal, you or Jimmie hear anything more from that mob guy in Pittsburgh?

"Augie, Jimmie called up there again this afternoon. He couldn't even get through to Vito. But he really believes what the guy told him yesterday. That he – Vito – did give his guys an order to leave you alone and come home. Jimmie thinks he's telling the truth. Not because Vito gives a shit about you. It's because he's desperate to get the pictures and negatives. You know, Augie, I could have Jimmie tell Vito where the winery is. What do you think? Should I have Jimmie call up to Pittsburgh again?"

"I actually thought about that this morning. But even if we had enough time, getting another group of bad guys to come and help us would only complicate things. And probably end badly for all of us. Really, at this point, I think we're better off dealing with the problem ourselves. And hey, Uncle Sal, I've got a couple of friends up here with me. They're both Vietnam vets, and one of them is a former Army Special Forces officer. We've all been in tight situations before, so we know how to defend ourselves."

"Jesus, Augie. It sounds like you're preparing for war. I wish I could do something to make this all go away. I feel so helpless back here. But remember what you promised me yesterday. You'll call the police if it looks like you won't be able to handle what those assholes are going to try. Will you keep that promise?"

I hadn't given Uncle Sal any of the details about how the mob guys had tried to ambush us last night. Nor did I tell him that Lou was seriously injured. If he knew about those things, he might go ahead and call the cops himself right now.

"Absolutely, I will. If I think we won't be able to handle things ourselves, we'll call the police immediately. I promise." And I really did mean it.

When we hung up, I went back to our bedroom. Lou was still sleeping, and Ginny had nodded off too. I gently shook her.

"Ginny, let's go down the hall to the living room. There's a couch there and you can try and get some sleep. I'll sit here with Lou. If she comes to, I'll come and get you."

"Okay. I do need to recharge my batteries. But come get me right away if she stirs or wakes up. And Augie, I know you must be worried about us. But you guys need to concentrate all your energies on getting us safely out of this place. We need to get Lou to the hospital no later than tomorrow. I'm down to my last two IV's, and she really needs a blood transfusion."

I walked Ginny down the hall to a mahogany-paneled room. There was a brown leather couch with two cream-colored fabric cushions. I waited until she lay on the couch, and then I covered her with a blanket that was draped over a chair.

"Get some rest," I said and left the room, closing the door quietly.

I returned to the bedroom and Lou. Her eyes were still closed, and her breathing seemed slightly labored. I hoped that she was sleeping, and not simply unconscious from the anesthetic Ginny had administered. I sat in the chair next to her bed and covered her hand with mine. I wanted to tell her that everything was going to be okay. That we would get through this. But even if she was fully conscious, I could not assure her that anything would ever be okay with us again. If I'm able to survive tonight, and she recovers from her wounds completely, I'm afraid this latest challenge to our relationship will result in her leaving me again. And I really couldn't blame her.

In reality, though, all I can hope and pray for is that Lou will survive the events which are about to unfold tonight.

CHAPTER 36
DÉNOUEMENT

It was 4.30 p.m. when Cheech shook Tubby awake. Like a large orb of grizzly bear scat, the rotund and filthy little hit man was curled up under a Ponderosa Pine. He looked like a brown stain on the verdant and pristine Mendocino National Forest.

"Hey Fat Boy! Get your ass up. Time to get to work."

Tubby rubbed sleep from his eyes, rolled onto his side, and struggled to his feet. "I'm up, Cheech. You ready for me to do my thing? Can't wait to get a little time with that girl up there," he said pointing in the direction of the winery.

"No, shit-for-brains. Not yet. But we gotta get ready. We'll drive up real close to where the vineyard starts. Then, I'll pick that spot that gives me cover. And also gives me a clear shot at Arturo. And Cumpton too – if you don't do your job right."

"Hey Cheech. Don't you worry none. I'll take care of Cumpton. I remember what you said. When I hear you shoot the gun at Arturo, I get to do Cumpton. Just like you told me to," Tubby said.

"Ain't you forgettin' somethin'? What are you s'posed to do before you whack Cumpton?" Cheech was trying to remain calm, but he wanted to strangle Tubby.

"Yeah. I know. I ain't s'posed to shoot him. I gotta use the K-bar knife on him. Right?"

Cheech bit his tongue. "No. Think about what I told you, Tubby. And I don't give a fuck how you kill him. Shootin' him would be the quickest way, though. But I know you like to use that big knife. To get your jollies. And I don't care. So, what are you s'posed to do first?"

Tubby looked puzzled.

Cheech screamed at him. "If you do it out in the open. What's gonna happen to you, Dipshit?

Still, Tubby seemed flummoxed.

Cheech toned it down a bit. "You wanna get killed? That what you want? If you waste Cumpton right out in the open, that guy Jack's gonna drill you."

Finally, Tubby understood. "Oh yeah. Right Cheech. I gotta shove the asshole into them vines first. Then I can take him out. But I don't want to shoot him. It'll make too much noise. So, I'll just shove that K-bar in him. That's the best way. Dontcha think?"

Cheech ignored the question. He just stared at the little asshole and nodded.

"Okay then. Let's go ahead and git up there a little bit early. I wanna get things set up. We gotta do this right and whack Cumpton. And when we get that part done, we can go up and finish things at the winery. Then, if you done your job right, you can go and have some fun with that chick."

Tubby gave Cheech his widest, yellow-fanged smile, and then he rubbed his hands vigorously together in salacious anticipation.

* * *

Jack, Topo and I all agreed on how the exchange scenario would likely develop, and where and when that would occur. We expected the inflection point to be when the actual exchange takes place, and when both Artie and I would be open targets for the guy with the rifle pointed at us. It would be critical for us to act swiftly and decisively at that point if our plan had any chance of succeeding.

Topo's role in the plan would kick off the operation. We needed to get Topo in position. He was our ace in the hole. The mobsters didn't know about him. To make our plan work, Topo would be required to belly crawl from the front of the winery building up and through the vineyard for about four hundred yards. He would then conceal himself and hide out until the mob guys revealed their location. That would be the spot where they would have a clear shot at both Artie and me. It would be Topo's job to find, prevent and possibly eliminate any threat to our lives, and to the people in the winery building. Everything depended on Topo's ability to react swiftly and decisively when the time came.

* * *

It was 3.30 when Topo Rojas surreptitiously left the winery building by a small side door. He was dressed in a Tiger Stripe camouflage uniform, matching boonie hat and a pair of combat jungle boots. He had brought all these Army-issue clothing items with him when he returned home from Vietnam. It was the same outfit that he often wore during daylight operations as a First Infantry Division "tunnel rat." Today, he was lightly armed with a short-barreled .38 caliber special, and a six-inch, sheathed, Bowie knife. He secured the weapons in a small, Army-issue canvass bag he wore strapped over his shoulders on his back.

It had taken Topo forty-five minutes to get to his objective in the vineyard. It was a cool fall afternoon, but Topo was sweating profusely from the strenuous climb, and he was happy to finally find a place in the last row of vines that afforded him a good hiding spot where he would be able to hear anyone approaching. His position faced the road which bisected the vineyard. He removed his weapons from his back-pack and began covering himself with grass, twigs and grape leaves as he lay prone on his stomach. He extended both his arms out, pointing the Bowie knife and the pistol in front of him. Now, he would need to wait patiently for circumstances outside his control to dictate when the next part in the event would begin.

He had been lying completely still now for thirty minutes. Waiting was always the most challenging part of any mission. Suddenly, he heard the engine of an approaching vehicle. It sounded like a small truck or van, and it seemed very close. Then the engine stopped, and Topo heard two doors being opened and shut. Next, he heard what sounded like another door being opened, and then muted rustling as if someone or thing was being jostled or moved.

* * *

"You gotta be real quiet now, Tubby," Cheech said firmly to his partner when he stopped the truck.

"And don't slam the door when you git out."

Both men exited the vehicle and walked around to the side of the truck. Cheech slid the panel truck side door open. "Okay Arturo, we gotta git you ready for your big day. I'm gonna undo the tape wrapped around your legs so's you can walk. But I ain't gonna take it off your mouth or your arms. I don't want you tryin' to be some kinda hero."

Cheech pulled Artie roughly out of the truck, stood him up and then he had to steady the man so Artie would not fall to the ground. "Tubby, use your K-bar to cut the tape from Arturo's legs while I hold him so's he don't fall."

After Tubby cut the tape binding Artie's legs, Cheech grabbed the man under his armpits and lifted him up into a sitting position on the floor of the truck so that his legs dangled out of the vehicle.

"Listen up now, Arturo. In a little bit, Tubby here is gonna walk you out into your vineyard. Don't try and run away from him or he'll kill you before you git five feet. And then I'll shoot that Cumpton guy. Nobody wins if that happens. You capeesh? Nod your head if you understand me."

Artie's response was to grunt and dip his head down. Cheech looked quizzically at the bound and beaten man. He couldn't figure out why the guy kept grunting and looking down. When Cheech followed Artie's downward glance, he saw that, even with his arms bound, Artie was able to extend the middle fingers of both his hands toward Cheech.

"I gotta hand it to you, Arturo," Cheech said while trying to swallow a smile, "you're a feisty little wop. But I think you heard me. When the time comes, all you gotta do is walk with Tubby to Cumpton. When Tubby has him, you can walk on down to the winery and to your buddy Jack. Pretty simple, right?"

Artie just stared coldly through swollen eyes at the sagging jowls and badly pock-marked face of Cheech, while continuing to give him a double dose of the bird.

* * *

It was 5.50 p.m., and I stood with Jack in the dining room behind the doors that were now boarded over with sheets of plywood. Topo had set up the M-14 rifle with the supporting tripod outside on the floor of the deck. Using a blow torch, Topo had cut a triangular hole in a steel garbage can lid that was measured precisely to cover the daylight scope attached to the rifle that rested on the tripod. Then he used metal screws to attach the contraption to the wooden cross braces of the deck. The opening in the garbage can lid would provide Jack with a clear view of the road where the exchange would take place, and at least, some protection from any incoming fire directed at him.

Topo had been gone now for almost an hour and a half. There

had been no signs that he had been discovered, and now it was my turn to assume my role in this dangerous and risky undertaking. I kept going over the plan in my mind, trying to develop alternative strategies to counter any unanticipated actions by the mob guys. I knew it was impossible to prepare for every eventuality, and I wondered if I was poring over the plan so much to avoid thinking about the consequences of failure for Artie, Jack, Topo, Ginny and Lou. But now it was time to stop thinking and start doing.

"You okay, Augie? You ready to do this?" Jack asked. "You know, it's not too late to call things off, and get the cops up here. What do you say?" Jack and I were lying on the floor of the deck.

"There's no way to turn back now. We can't leave Topo out there. And anyway, if things start to go bad, you'll still have time to call the police and save yourself and the women. Either way, I'm going through with this," I said emphatically, but not feeling as confident as I sounded to myself.

"Okay, but before you go, would you take this and give it to Ginny," Jack said and handed me his old Army Colt .45 caliber handgun that he had earlier given to Lou. "I don't want to leave the deck now. I know the gun is heavy, but it has great stopping power, especially at close range. Hopefully, she won't have to use it, but it's a great tool to have if you need it."

"Sure."

I was very familiar with that particular handgun. I had had an up close and personal familiarity with the weapon when I was attending supply school at Fort Lee, Virginia. Illogically, the Army required supply school candidates to spend the last week of training learning to repair small arms, including M-16 rifles, .50 caliber machine guns and several other deadly weapons of war. The final exam required us to completely disassemble, and then reassemble, a .45 caliber Colt pistol, blind folded! To this day, I'll never know how I was able to successfully complete the requirement.

I walked down the hall and stuck my head in the doorway of the bedroom where Ginny continued to monitor Lou. I motioned for Ginny to come out into the hallway. When she joined me, I handed her the gun.

"I'm sure you didn't expect to see one of these again, but Jack thought you should have it just in case," I said awkwardly to her.

Ginny smiled sadly at me. Then she shook her head. "Augie, I would never be able to shoot another human being. It goes against everything I believe in. I spent a year over in Vietnam, and I never once fired a gun. Even when the Viet Cong attacked the hospital."

"Look Ginny, there's a chance, hopefully a very slight one, that the guys we're after could get the upper hand. If that happens, they'll come here and kill everyone, including you and Lou. And they'd probably do unspeakable things to you both first. I'm sorry to be so blunt, but those guys out there are not like any human beings you ever met. So, please take this gun and use it if it will save you or Lou."

I took the gun from Ginny and racked a round into the chamber.

"This is a pretty heavy gun, but it's very accurate in close quarters. The magazine holds seven rounds, and it will shoot seven bullets as fast as you can squeeze the trigger. I know you don't want this, Ginny, but please take it. And I'll pray that you won't need to use it. I really need to go now," I said and handed the gun back to her.

It was just 6 o'clock when I went down the hall, opened the door and walked downstairs to the vineyard level of the winery. I opened the door and walked quickly outside. Jack would soon call to me from his perch on the deck above when it was time for me to move out to the vineyard road. I would then start walking toward Artie and the Black Hand guy with him. I said a silent prayer as I waited.

* * *

Topo heard muffled sounds nearby like the footfalls of more than one person moving quietly above, and to the right, of his position. The sounds continued for about half a minute, and then stopped. Topo figured that the mob guys were setting up in a location that would give them a protected and clear field of fire at the spot where the exchange of Artie for Augie would take place. Topo knew he had to move to a position as close as possible to the road that bisected the vineyard, and to the men who had Artie. Somewhere near them where he could strike quickly if he needed to. But it was critical for him to move very quietly. And since the .38 Special had no safety mechanism, he needed to be very careful to keep his finger outside the trigger guard to avoid the possibility of an accidental discharge. If he made any kind of sound, he would be discovered and have little, or no chance, of surviving.

Once again, he heard stirring and a slight jostling from above. He used those sounds to cover any noise he made as he began to move.

Using the heels of his hands and his combat boots, he advanced slowly forward almost to where the row ended and met the vineyard road. Suddenly, the sounds stopped. Topo froze in. The only sound now was the wind rustling through the vineyard. Topo lay silent for what seemed like an eternity. The silence was broken by a loudly whispered invective which seemed to come from just a few feet away.

"Get your fat ass down, Numbnuts," Topo heard a gravelly whispered voice declare.

* * *

"And let's get behind that big rock right there," Cheech said in a loud whisper to Tubby. He pointed to the back of a large boulder at the top of the vineyard, and where the row of vines on the left side of the road began. Cheech was holding on to Artie, and shoved him quickly behind the boulder. Tubby followed, waddling over, and joined them.

"It's almost over, Arturo," Cheech said to the bound and bedraggled man as he leaned Artie up against the boulder. "All you gotta do is just walk with Tubby down the road. Once Tubby has Cumpton, you can go see your friend Jack. You'll be a free man."

Cheech liked the spot he had chosen. It provided a clear view of the road that bisected the vineyard, and especially the midpoint of the gravel track where the exchange would take place. And he could use the boulder to steady the rifle, and that would improve his aim. Cheech also had a clear view of the winery deck, a quarter mile away, where he assumed Jack was perched with his rifle. There was an odd, round piece of metal that seemed attached to the lower portion of the deck, and it had a triangular opening at the bottom. Cheech thought this must be some kind of defensive shield that Jack had fashioned. And then, when he looked closely at the bottom of the oval, he could just make out a long, cylindrical piece of black steel protruding from it. That had to be the barrel of Jack's rifle sticking out of the hole.

"Okay Tubby. It's almost game time. You ready?"

Tubby didn't reply.

"Hey, you hear me? You remember what you gotta do, right?"

"Yeah, I remember. But I still don't like it none. I mean, my ass is hangin' right out there in the open. You got a good hidin' place here. What if that Jack guy starts shootin'? He don't have no clear shot at you," Tubby said.

"Look, we talked about this. You ain't got nothin' to worry about... if you do what I told you. Just wait for me to shoot the gun. When you hear the shot, all you gotta do is push Cumpton in them vines and blow him away. That's it. Then we can go up to the winery and finish off Jack. And that's when you get to do your thing to the girl."

Tubby nodded. "Yeah, I guess that's why I'm gonna do it your way, Cheech. The girl," he repeated, and his eyes glazed over as he thought about the fun he was going to have with her.

"Okay Tubby, it's a little after 6 right now. Time to go. You gotta help Arturo and make sure he don't fall down."

Tubby grabbed Artie roughly by the left arm, and they moved slowly out onto the vineyard road.

* * *

Jack was lying prone on the floor of the deck sighting through the scope on his M-14 rifle. He had replaced the nighttime Starlight scope on the gun with a daylight M84 scope. The M84 provided Jack with excellent visibility, making targets as far away as the top of his vineyard seem like they were only a hundred feet away. Suddenly, he spotted two men emerge from behind the large boulder at the top of the vineyard. As the two began to walk down the gravel road, Jack scanned their faces and bodies, and then he focused on the taller of the men. He was shocked, and then enraged, by what he saw. Artie's face was swollen and distorted with bluish, black lumps and rust-colored streaks of dried blood. His mouth was covered with a strip of masking tape, and his upper body was bound with wire and more tape. Artie was limping badly, and in the grasp of a squat, rotund and disheveled little man who was nearly dragging him down the road. Jack had to compose himself. He wanted to fire a round right through the face of the grotesque little man. He took a deep breath, and then quietly, in a halting and unsteady voice, he said:

"Augie, I've got Artie and the bastard walking with him in my gun sights. You can move out now."

* * *

"Okay Jack" I said and began to walk toward the vineyard road. I was as ready as I would ever be, and I tried to obliterate any thoughts other than those that fully focused on the task at hand. Once I started up the road, I could see the men walking toward me. They were at least a hundred yards up ahead, and I could begin to see the cartoon-like facial features of the ogre who had tried to murder me just a few days ago at the BART station. He was nearly dragging a person along with him, but that man didn't look at all like the one I had just recently met here at Fruit Lake Vineyard and Winery. As he got closer, I could see that Artie's face was full of bruises, and his eyes were nearly swollen shut. I could only imagine the emotions Jack must be dealing with right now seeing the person he called his partner – his lover – badly beaten and abused by the evil little man accompanying him. Right then and there, I vowed to do everything in my power to make sure this little insult to mankind never saw the dawn of another day. When Artie and his captor were within twenty feet of me, they stopped.

"Okay, Bud. That's far enough," the little man said and stared blankly at me. It was like he had no affect... no human expression I could identify. "I'm gonna walk this guy over to you now," he added. Then you gotta come with me. Don't try no funny stuff or I'll gut you and him right here," he added, and drew a large K-bar knife from one of the inside pockets of his dirty white suit jacket.

"Okay, come on," I said and motioned for them to come to me. I was trying not to show any emotion or shock, but I'm not sure I was succeeding. Artie was a mess. A bloody and beaten mess at the hands of this Neanderthal, and I wanted to strangle the thug and send him to hell with my bare hands.

"Hey Artie," I said, and nodded. "Jack's waiting for you. Just go ahead and walk to him. And don't worry, Jack has his rifle aimed at this little fat fuck's head. This guy's buddy knows it too. We worked things out..."

Artie started grunting. He was trying to say something. I couldn't understand him, but I could tell he was emotional, and then I saw tears running down his damaged face. I wanted to tell him not to worry. That we had a plan and that everything would work out. But I couldn't. So, I just moved up to Artie and hugged him, and whispered in his ear, "Don't worry. We got a plan." Then I released Artie and smiled at him.

"Hey, you ain't s'posed to touch him?" the little man said. "And now you gotta let me check and make sure you ain't carryin' no gun."

I lifted my arms over my head while the guy patted me down. Having this disgusting subhuman touch me, made we want to throw up. When he finished, I turned away from him and started walking up the road. The little bastard caught up with me and grabbed my arm. Without thinking, I rammed my elbow into his solar plexus. He bent over and tried to say something, but he couldn't catch his breath for several seconds. Then he stood, grabbed the K-bar from his coat and flashed it at me. He was smiling wolfishly at me through tiny yellow teeth.

"When we get up there," he said, and pointed to the top of the road, "I'm gonna start cuttin' you in little pieces. Prob'ly take a day or two for you to die. You got that to look forward to tough guy."

"Go ahead. Try and stick me, you piece of shit. You'll be dead before that blade gets anywhere near me."

* * *

"What the fuck," Cheech said out loud when he saw Cumpton elbow Tubby in the stomach. Cheech stood up. Then he was shocked as he watched Tubby pull out the K-bar knife from his coat pocket. 'Don't do it, Tubby,' he thought to himself. He knew that if Tubby tried to knife Cumpton, Jack would react immediately, and blow his partner away. Cheech couldn't let that happen, because he needed Tubby alive to help him finish the job. Otherwise, Cheech would have welcomed the idiot's demise. If Tubby lunged at Cumpton, Cheech would need to kill Cumpton first because he was the main target of this screwed up job. Then, he would turn his gun on Arturo, and hope that he still had a shot at the man.

* * *

Jack saw the fat little man pull the knife. He would kill the man if he made a move toward Augie. He sighted through his scope on the center of the short man's chest. He would have to be very accurate because his target was standing just a few feet directly in front of Augie. His rifle was ready to fire as he put his finger on the trigger and waited.

* * *

Cheech pulled the charging handle on the AK-47, sending a round from the banana-shaped magazine into the rifle's chamber. He bent over, steadied the rifle once again on the boulder and used the gunsight to target Cumpton's chest. He put his finger inside the trigger guard.

* * *

Topo was just across the vineyard road and no more than fifteen feet from where the man with the rifle was set up. He could see the barrel of the gun resting on the boulder. Suddenly, Topo saw the side profile of a tall man stand up and pull the charging handle on what appeared to be an AK-47. Then the guy squatted down again and placed the rifle on the boulder. Topo knew it was now or never.

* * *

Cheech saw Tubby move toward Cumpton. He had to shoot Cumpton right now. Cheech held his breath and was squeezing the trigger when he heard movement to his right. He looked to where the sound was coming from and saw a small man in a camouflage uniform running toward him with a gun extended in his hand. Cheech immediately turned with his rifle and fired a shot at the man.

* * *

Topo rose up and sprinted across the road toward the man who was about to kill Augie. He held his small pistol directly in front of him. He saw the tall man turn toward him and bring the AK around. He heard a shot, and he knew he was going to die.

* * *

When Jack heard the gun shot, he immediately squeezed the trigger on his rifle and fired a round into the chest of the small, round man in the dirty white suit. Then Jack heard two more shots. He looked to where Augie was standing and saw him now on the ground. Then he looked to where Artie had been walking along the vineyard road. He gasped and was horrified at what he saw. Artie was lying face down on the road. Oh Christ, he thought, I was too late and now both Artie and Augie are dead.

* * *

Topo felt the bullet whiz by his right ear, and he immediately fired two shots, and then fell to the ground. He expected to die right then, but nothing happened. He turned his head to the left and stared into the lifeless eyes and pock-marked face of the man who had just tried to kill him.

* * *

As soon as I heard the gunfire, I dove onto the road, and lay there frozen. I couldn't move. When there were no other sounds or movement, I scrambled on my hands and knees into the vineyard. Then I turned and peeked out onto the road. I saw the carcass of the little murderer lying spread-eagle, on his back. There was a scorched black hole on the front of the man's white suit coat, and a widening red stain blooming out from the hole. Then I looked down to where Artie had been walking. He was also lying face down, but I could see him trying to crawl to the safety of the vineyard. He was alive!

Chapter 37
Postmortem

Topo and I carried Artie from the vineyard into the winery and then up to Jack's bedroom. We watched as Ginny cut the masking tape and the dirty and bloodied clothes from Artie's body. Artie tried to speak, but Ginny put an index finger to her lips to silence him.

"Sshh Artie," she said softly. "There will be plenty of time for you to tell us what happened, but right now you need to conserve your energy and rest. My name is Ginny. I'm a friend of Augie's and I'm a nurse."

Jack stood across the bed from Ginny with his hand resting on Artie's upper arm. He looked down at his beaten and battered partner with love, but also with a kind of barely repressed anger at what Artie had been forced to endure. I knew how he felt: I had similar emotions when we got Lou back after she had been kidnapped by the mob guys years ago. I motioned for Jack and Topo to join me in the hallway.

"Hey guys. I just want to thank both of you for all you've done to keep Lou and me alive. And Jack, I feel terrible about what those animals did to Artie. I know things got a little dicey out there but thank God things worked out."

Topo looked at me and smiled. "Yeah. I thought I was a goner when that ugly fucker fired his AK at me. But what the hey! We got some payback, and them guys won't be bothering nobody ever again."

Jack added, "Hey Augie, I know you feel guilty about all this. But we got Artie back alive, and Ginny thinks both Artie and Lou will be okay once we get them out of here."

I stared at Jack for a few moments. I was trying to compose myself because I knew that if I tried to speak now my voice would crack. Like winding paths of misery, there were parallel tracks of dried tears descending from both of Jack's bloodshot eyes. He looked haggard and completely exhausted. And I knew it was all my fault! Like so many others who had been victimized because of me, Jack and Artie had paid a terrible price. But unlike two of my wartime buddies and another two friends who helped me later when I was on the run from the mob, at least Jack and Artie had survived.

I finally found my voice. "No, Jack. I should, and I do, feel guilty. I hardly got to know you and Artie before all this horrible stuff happened."

Jack did not respond. He seemed distant and he fixed me with a look I had seen on combat veterans' faces after an intense firefight in Vietnam. We called it the "thousand-yard stare." Then he spoke. "Augie, Topo, let's talk about what we have to do right now to clean up the mess out there," he said and pointed out into the vineyard.

Jack was right. We needed to get rid of any evidence that the mob guys had ever been to the winery. "How do you want to handle this?"

"Well, we need to get to work right away. While it's dark. Here's what I think we should do."

We spent the next four hours cleaning things up. First, we located the bad guys' truck, and then I found the keys to it in the trousers of the big goon who Topo shot. Jack drove the truck to where the bodies of the mob guys were lying along the vineyard road, and we loaded them into the truck. We also gathered all of the weapons and put them in the trunk of Topo's car. Then I joined Topo in the car and followed Jack as he drove for about forty-five minutes. We had wound our way through a maze of forest service roads to a remote trailhead parking area in the Mendocino National Forest. Jack got out of the truck, opened the side door and retrieved a large ten-gallon metal can of gasoline. He climbed into the truck and used all the fuel to douse the interior of the vehicle and the bodies of the mob men. Then he lit and tossed a matchbook into the truck, and we watched as the vehicle exploded in flames and burned until only the smoldering skeleton of the metal frame remained. We waited there for another hour until Jack was sure that the smoking wreckage posed no danger of starting a forest fire. Then we all piled into Topo's car for the ride back. When we got to the turn-off for Fruit Lake, Jack told Topo to drive to the parking lot next to the lake. Jack got out and retrieved all the weapons that had been used, including his own rifle and Topo's pistol. Topo and I helped Jack carry the weapons down to where a rowboat sat in the grass next to the lake. We put the guns into the boat, and then Jack got in and rowed out about two hundred yards. He tossed the firearms into the lake and rowed back to shore.

It was nearly midnight when we returned to the winery. I immediately went to the bedroom to check on Lou. She seemed to be sleeping peacefully, so I walked down to Jack's bedroom. Artie was under the covers, snoring loudly. His face was slathered with some sort of antiseptic ointment that looked like Vaseline. Jack was sitting next to the bed and speaking softly to Ginny who sat on the other side of Artie. They looked up when I entered the room.

"How's he doing, Ginny?"

"I can't really evaluate what internal injuries he might have without x-rays. But it's pretty clear that his right shoulder is at least dislocated. I hope it's not a broken collarbone because that might require surgery. He's got some serious facial contusions that I've treated with a salve. Later he'll need to use ice on his face to reduce the swelling. The good news is that he doesn't seem to have a concussion, but Jack will need to take him to a doctor for a more complete check-up."

Jack said, "I'll take him to a friend of mine over in Little River. On the coast. This guy's a family doc and a Vietnam vet. He has an x-ray machine too. He'll check him out and he won't ask any questions."

"What about Lou?" I asked.

"Augie, she came around a little while ago and asked for you. That's a good sign. Now that you guys seem to have resolved our problem, we should try and move her to a hospital first thing in the morning. I think she's stabilized, but she'll need more professional care."

I wanted to hug Ginny. It was like a great weight had been lifted from me.

"I don't know how to thank you, Ginny. Lou would not have survived without you. And Topo and Jack, none of us would be alive now if wasn't for you guys. But Ginny, I have one other favor to ask. Would you go to the hospital with us? I would just feel a lot better if you were there to let the staff know what you had to do. To patch her up when she fell and hurt her shoulder," I said and smiled sheepishly.

"No problem, Augie. I'd like to take her to St. Helena Hospital. That way I can keep an eye on her. Hopefully, we can get her patched up and out of there in a week or so."

I thanked Ginny again and then I went into the living room and plopped down on the leather couch. I needed to call Uncle Sal, but it was too late on the east coast so I decided to get a couple of hours of sleep. I woke at around 5 a.m. and went into Jack's office and dialed Uncle Sal's number. The phone rang twice and then Uncle Sal answered.

"Uncle Sal. I have some good news. Those Black Hand guys won't be bothering us any longer. The situation out here is… okay."

"Augie, what happened? Did those guys get the message from Vito? To leave you alone?"

"Let's just say they won't be a problem for us now. And I think you need to ask Jimmie to contact Vito and explain the situation. You know, that we didn't have any choice in how we resolved the problem. I'm worried that Vito might be upset when he understands what happened. But he has to know that his guys either didn't get his message to back off, or they went rogue. Either way, it really doesn't matter because those guys are gone. The fact is, Vito didn't deliver on what he promised. And because of that, Jimmie can tell him that we'll need to hold on to what we have. It's our insurance policy. But Jimmie can assure Vito that those things will never see the light of day as long as nothing bad happens to anyone in our family."

I'm sure Uncle Sal understood why I was being vague. While I didn't think that my call was being recorded, I didn't want to take any chances.

"Okay Augie. I understand. I'll give Jimmie the information and ask him to go up to Pittsburgh today and have a conversation with Vito. You're right. It doesn't sound like those employees of his got the message. In the meantime, you need to stay where you are until I get back to you. About what Jimmie finds out."

"Uncle Sal, please don't call me. We have a lot of things to do today, and I don't want to miss your call. I'll phone you later this evening," I said and hung up.

I couldn't give my uncle any of the gory details about what really happened in the vineyard last night. And I couldn't stick around the winery either. I needed to get Lou to the hospital today! Actually, all of us, including Jack and Artie, would be leaving here too. Getting out of here now would be the most prudent thing we could do, especially if the Black Hand guys had given Vito the address of the vineyard. And I'll advise Jack to stay away from the place until we're sure it's safe for he and Artie to return.

I waited until around 7.30, and then I woke everyone up. I told Jack and Topo about the call to my uncle, and then we discussed how we would move Lou and Artie. Jack was going to wait until noon to get Artie up and then drive him to the doctor's office in Little River.

Around 10, Ginny and I walked Lou slowly and very carefully to Topo's car and we helped her into a sitting position. Ginny sat in the back seat with Lou and used pillows to protect her injured shoulder. Topo drove especially slowly and carefully over the gravel road that led to the paved highway. Lou was awake and she seemed to be in good spirits. I gave her a sanitized version of yesterday's events, and I told her there was a good chance that we didn't have to hide anymore.

"Are you sure Augie? You think it's over. That we can go home?" Lou said and looked hopefully at me.

"I think so. Uncle Sal will let me know later today. But you just need to get better. Ginny will be taking you to a hospital where she works in St. Helena – in the Napa Valley. I'll bunk in at my old stomping grounds with Alex at Starling Vineyards while you recuperate. But I'll be with you every waking hour. I'm hopeful you'll be well enough to fly back home sometime next week."

When I convinced Lou to come out here a week ago, she had told her parents that she was going to attend a wine conference in California.

"Maybe you should call your Mom and Dad and tell them you decided to spend a little more time out here. That you met an old friend and decided to have some fun."

Lou laughed out loud. "Augie, I have to say the last week has been exciting, but I wouldn't say it's been fun."

CHAPTER 38
LA PASTICCERIA DI ALDO

Sal Costanza called Jimmie Ponza early that morning to give him the latest update from Augie. Jimmie was relieved to hear that the threat to Augie in California had been eliminated. Now, however, Sal was asking him to meet with Vito and convince the mobster to end further violence and threats directed at Augie. And Sal had insisted that the meeting take place this very day. So, Jimmie called Frankie Silver, his business contact with the mob, and asked him to contact Vito immediately with the meeting request.

Sal hoped the meeting would put an end to all the troubles that the family had been dealing with for nearly ten years. Jimmie didn't think Vito would agree to what Sal was proposing, but he would do his best to make the case for peace. Within the hour, Frankie called Jimmie back.

"Hey Jimmie, the boss seemed like he was almost happy to hear you was wantin' to meet. But he said to tell you to make sure and bring the stuff you guys promised him. He said you'd know what he was talkin' about."

Frankie gave Jimmie directions to a confectionery on the southside of Pittsburgh where the meeting would take place, and then he added, "Oh, and when you get to the place, tell the guy at the counter who you are. His name is Aldo, and he runs the joint."

It was early afternoon when Jimmie found a parking spot near the address Frankie had given him on Pittsburgh's Southside. He parked his car in front of a one-story faded, red brick building that housed La Pasticceria di Aldo. Aldo's Confectionery was a small Italian bodega-like store that provided confections like candy-covered almonds, flavored nougat called Torrone, and an assortment of cannoli, fruit-filled panettone and biscotti. In addition, the business also stocked a large selection of Italian cheeses, olives and salumi, along with freshly baked focaccia, ciabatta, bread sticks and small round crackers called taralli. Aldo's Confectionery was also noted for its opaque, paint remover-like espresso. Patrons of Aldo's, many of whom were members of La Famiglia Vagabonda, would often sit in a back room of the store and delicately sip their coffee from demitasse cups.

When Jimmie entered the dimly lit shop, the air was scented with aromas of dark roasted coffee and pungent cigar smoke. Jimmie immediately identified the acrid and distinctive burning tobacco as emanating from small, potent, black cigars made by a company called Parodi. Parodi's were the cigar of choice for many of the old Italian guys who frequented his poolroom. Jimmie walked up to the counter and waited while a short, fireplug of a man handed change and then a paper bag filled with sweet treats to an elderly Italian woman.

The woman smiled and said, "Grazie, Aldo."

"Prego," the man replied and then he looked at Jimmie.

"Can I help you?" he asked in a voice just above a whisper.

"Yes. I'm here to meet Vito Scaramungi. My name is Jimmie. Is he here?"

"Yeah. Vito said he was meetin' someone. You must be the guy. He's in the room straight back there," Aldo said, using his thumb to point back over his shoulder.

Jimmie walked to the back of the store and into a room with four small card tables. Vito was the only person in the room, and he was smoking a Parodi. He motioned for Jimmie to take a seat at his table. Jimmie tried not to stare at the ugly scar which snaked from below one of Vito's ears, over the bridge of his nose, under an eye and across the other half of his face.

Vito got right to the point in his raspy voice, "So, I guess my crew in California got the message after all. You know, to lay off your guy. That right, Jimmie?"

"Well, Vito, that's what I'm here to talk to you about. Actually, your guys didn't back off. In fact, they tried to ambush Augie and the people he was staying with out there. And I hate to tell you this, but your guys won't be coming back."

"What do you mean, they ain't comin' back?" Vito's voice rose and he stared daggers at Jimmie.

"I don't know exactly what happened, but Augie told his Uncle Sal that your men either didn't get the message to stop, or they just decided to go ahead and try to kill him anyway. Apparently there was a shootout. Again, all Augie would tell Sal was that they were attacked, and they had to defend themselves. He didn't want to go into details over the phone. Sal said to tell you that, since you weren't able to keep your end of the bargain... well anyway, he feels like he needs to keep those pictures for protection. So, you or your guys will leave his family alone. He told me to tell you that he will never let anyone see them unless you guys try to harm them – the Costanzas – or Augie."

Vito's face was crimson, and he slammed his fist down on the table. He stood up and walked around the room for a full minute. Then he sat back down and looked at Jimmie, snarling.

"Look, Jimmie. I don't know why them guys did what they did. I swear to God, I told 'em to stop and come back home. But you gotta tell Sal that I want them pictures, or there's gonna be big trouble for him and his family. Here's why. If I tell my crew here in Pittsburgh that Cheech and Tubby ain't comin' home and that Cumpton and his friends whacked our guys, they'll go nuts. They'll wanna go down there to Jeweltown and get some serious payback. You understand me? You tell Sal that I want them pictures. If he gives 'em to me – and the negatives too, I'll make sure he won't ever have no problems with us. I'll forget that I heard anything about a shootout. I'll just tell my guys that I don't know what happened to Cheech and Tubby. That they must have decided not to come back. But, if Sal don't give 'em to me, then I'll let my crew know what Cumpton done. And I'll let them have their vengeance. I wouldn't be able to stop 'em – even if I wanted to."

Jimmie had expected Vito to react this way. He had told Sal the same thing earlier in the day. He was also concerned that he and his business at the Ruff Avenue Poolroom might get caught in the crossfire.

"Hey Vito. You understand that I'm just the guy in the middle here, right? I don't have any interest in this problem other than to be the go-between. Sal's an old friend. Since I've been doing business with you guys for years, he thought I might be able to give you their side of the story. And help get this mess ironed out." Jimmie wanted to tell Vito 'Don't shoot the messenger,' but he just sat silently waiting for any last words from The Scar.

Vito finally spoke, "We're done here. Call me soon as you talk to Sal. All he's gotta do is gimme them pictures."

Jimmie left and drove home. On the way, he thought about the meeting he just had with Vito. Sal had been naïve to think that Vito would go for his proposal. The only way for the problem to go away for the Costanzas would be to comply with Vito's demands. If they gave the mobster the photos, they would have to depend on Vito to keep his word. But there was no guarantee. However, Jimmie didn't see any other way that would give the Costanzas at least a chance to reconcile the problem.

When Jimmie got back to Riverview, he stopped at Sal's. He went up the stairs and into the house without knocking. Sal met him just inside the door.

"Sal, he wouldn't buy it. He wants those pictures, and I don't see any other possible way to end the trouble with those guys. If you don't give them to him, he said to tell you that he's gonna tell his crew what happened out there. That Augie killed his two guys. Then Vito said they would come down to Jeweltown and have their vengeance. I know you don't want to have to trust Vito. But what other choice do you have that has a chance of making this problem go away? It seems like this is the only way to get them to back off."

"I know, Jimmie. But I hate to trust that son of a bitch. On the other hand, I don't know what else we can do. Maybe you can stall him for a while and give me some time to think of another way out of this mess. But I'll tell Augie what we think when he calls tonight. He won't like it, but I think he knows he doesn't have much of a choice. I just hope when we give Vito what he wants, Augie will be able come home. I hope Augie doesn't just stay out there or go somewhere else to hide. Again Jimmie, you've gone above and beyond to help us. I don't know how I can ever return the favor."

"Hey Sal. I told you a couple times before. If it wasn't for your old man I wouldn't be alive today. Your Pop made me quit my job. That was just one week before the coal mine I was working in blew up. He saved my life. From that day on, I promised myself I'd do anything I could to help the Costanza family. The truth is, I don't feel like I've been able to help much with this situation."

CHAPTER 39
HOBSON'S CHOICE

It's been a week since I agreed with Uncle Sal that we didn't have any alternative other than to accept the terms forced on us by Vito The Scar. If we don't give the man the damning photos, he'll tell the members of La Famiglia Vagabonda that I had killed two of his soldiers, and then there would be a war. The vengeful retribution they would mete out would extend beyond me to the lives of my family in Riverview, and to the most important person in my life – Louise Erickson. Unfortunately, there are no guarantees that Vito will keep his promise to forgive and forget and leave me and my family alone. Will I always wonder if the person walking behind me at night is carrying a garrote, knife or gun to hasten my exit from this life? Will some "accident" befall Uncle Sal, one of my other family members or – God forbid – Lou?

Paranoid thoughts such as these, like shadow companions, haunted my waking moments, lurking always just on the margins of my consciousness. Unfortunately, when I'm asleep, there are no filters to my dreams. Like the nightmares I frequently experienced after my return from Vietnam, violent and horrific apparitions of the incident at Fruit Lake Vineyard dominate my subconscious – in living color. So, I try and concentrate on what's good in my life, and of course, that's Lou. I spent the days she was convalescing in the hospital by her side, and we discussed all aspects of the future we hoped to have together. We have a lot of great plans, but the reality is that we can't be sure if they will ever be realized.

I met with Ginny and Topo every day at the hospital while Lou was healing, and we agreed to be on the lookout for any public information on what happened up in Mendocino. It's been over a week now, but none of us has seen or heard any news reports about the incident. I also called Della Mae the day after the event to let her know that the problems with the mob had been resolved, but I didn't give her any details about what happened. I wanted her to have plausible deniability if that information ever became public. I simply thanked her for all she has done to help me over the years, and I pledged that I would stay in touch.

After a little more than a week, Lou was released from the hospital, and she flew home. She agreed to move in with her parents in Washington to continue her recovery. I convinced her she would be safer there if things with the mob were not resolved. Lou is ambulatory, and she plans to spend a few days each week managing the work at her vineyard and winery on Rattlesnake Ridge. At my suggestion, though, Lou has agreed to book a room at a local motel rather than move back into her apartment in Romney. Her small work crew is doing all the (literal) heavy lifting at the winery, and in the vineyard, that's required after harvest. The new wine is being pumped from large, stainless steel holding tanks into small oak barrels for aging. In the vineyard, the vines need to be prepared for the cold winter to come. We continue to talk by phone every day and we're making plans to get together as soon as possible at her family's cabin in Canaan Valley. Of course, that depends on our comfort level that it is safe to do so.

I returned to San Francisco and my job at the Chronicle after Lou went home, and I try and go about life as if the recent traumatic events never happened. I also stay in touch with my friends who were directly affected by the confrontation at the winery. I'm amazed at the resilience of Artie! After all he has been through, Jack tells me the man seems to be recovering miraculously – at least physically – from his injuries. I know I'll never be able to repay Artie and Jack – or Topo and Ginny either – for their sacrifices in saving Lou and me from certain death.

I needed to contact Uncle Sal. I'm anxious to know when Jimmie will meet with Vito. He's asked our friend to put off scheduling the meeting as long as he can. My uncle has been trying to come up with a counter proposal that Vito might accept. I picked up the phone and dialed Uncle Sal's number. The phone rang three times and then was answered.

"Hey Uncle Sal, did Jimmie set the meeting"?

"You know, I've been trying to think of something we could do to keep from giving him the pictures. But time has run out. I don't think there is any other way, Augie, except to give 'em to him and hope for the best. Anyway, Jimmie told me earlier today that Vito called him and gave him an ultimatum. He said to bring the photos tomorrow or the Costanzas would start paying in blood."

"Oh shit. You gotta tell Jimmie to go ahead. We can't afford to stall any more. It's obvious that nothing but those photos will get him to back off."

"I know. I told Jimmie the same thing. About an hour ago, Frankie Silver called Jimmie and told him where the meeting will take place. I told you before about Frankie. Remember, he's Jimmie's contact with the mob? Anyway, Frankie said the meeting is set up for tomorrow. It's going to be held at a place called The Twin Coaches Supper Club. The place is south of Pittsburgh about halfway between there and Jewel-town. I gotta think Vito wants the meeting there cause he doesn't want any of his mob buddies around when Jimmie gives him the pictures."

"I've been to The Twin Coaches a couple of times when I was in college. It's a great old place. I saw The Temptations there once, and later I went up to see the Four Tops. It makes sense he would schedule the meeting there though. The place is in the middle of nowhere and it's rumored to be connected to the mob," I added.

"Yeah, I heard the same thing too. You know, Augie, once I resigned myself to the fact we'd have to give Vito what he wants, I thought about the chances that he would keep his word. I asked Jimmie to check with Frankie to see how things are going now that The Scar is in charge. Frankie told Jimmie everything was going smooth with Vito as the capo. He got the impression the mob guys were happy to see him replace Carmine."

"I suppose that's good news, but it's still hard for me to trust any-thing that bastard says. Especially after what happened out in Califor-nia. But I know that at some point, I'll need to either decide to stay on the run, or bite the bullet and take a chance that things will work out."

"Augie, I know it's a tough decision for you to make. But you've been away now for almost ten years, and this offer from Vito seems about the best chance you're going to have to put this stuff behind you. And, of course, we would love to see you, and Lou too, back here in Riverview."

"Me too, Uncle. I want to come home in the worst way. I'm having a hard time believing that this could actually be over. I guess I never thought that day would come. But there's another reason I want to come home. It's something I'd like to announce to Mom and Dad, and then to the rest of the family. Lou and I are planning to get married.

Soon. But please, keep this under your hat, okay."

"That's great news, Augie. I'm so happy for you." My uncle's voice was husky with emotion. "I know your parents will be thrilled when you tell them the news. I promise, I won't tell a soul. So, you've decided to come home? Soon, I hope."

"Yes. I'm tired of running. I'll try and be there in a few of weeks. I need to figure out what I'm going to do. You know, things like whether I'll stay out here, or try and get a job back there. Lou and I have talked about it but we haven't really ironed anything out yet. I'll give you a heads-up, though, when we plan to be there."

"Give me at least a week's notice. I'd like to plan a big homecoming celebration. Your parents, Grandma Luisa, Aunt Lia, Dante, Giorgio... everybody in the family will be so excited to welcome you and Lou back."

When I got off the phone, I just sat and thought about it all. I would be going back to Jeweltown and to my old Riverview neighborhood. A place I didn't think I'd ever see again. And to the people in my family who mean so much to me.

CHAPTER 40
THE TWIN COACHES

Vito Scaramungi's smile was so wide that it painfully stretched the earthworm-like scar that traversed the mob guy's face. But Vito didn't mind. In fact, he was elated! Soon he would take possession of the fake photos purporting to show him engaging in degenerate sex acts with his now deceased mob partner Guido Mancini.

Today, at last, he would finally get the damning pictures and negatives back. The tables had been turned, and now Vito would be able to plan his retribution. He would need to wait for a time until Sal Costanza and Augie Cumpton assumed that he was honoring his promise to let bygones be bygones. Then Vito would find a way to eliminate them that would not point back to him or his organization. But he would have his revenge, and Cumpton and Costanza would pay with their lives for the worry and misery they had caused him over the years. However, he couldn't let anyone in his organization ever know what he intended to do. After all, he had convinced the leaders in La Famiglia Vagabonda to authorize him to take out the old mob boss, Carmine Amato, largely because of that guy's obsession with his years-old vendetta against the Costanza's and Cumpton. Vito would also need to get rid of the guy who had brokered the deal – Jimmie Ponza. He could not afford to allow anyone who had knowledge of what had transpired to live.

To avoid any possibility of encountering someone from his crew, Vito had chosen to meet with Ponza at The Twin Coaches Supper Club located in the rural hamlet of Rostraver Township. He had reserved a private room at the club where Jimmie Ponza would be handing over the photos and negatives. Vito arrived a half hour before the 2 p.m. meeting, checked in at the office and then walked back down a dark hallway to a door marked private.

Vito The Scar opened the door and entered a small room. He

flipped the light switch on and walked toward a deeply burnished mahogany desk, behind which was a brown leather executive office chair. Vito sat in the chair and looked at his watch. It was 1.56 p.m. He sat there quietly waiting, gleefully anticipating the return of the bogus, but compromising, images of him engaged in homosexual acts.

There was a knock at the door.

"Yeah. Come on in Jimmie. For your sake, I hope you brought them pictures," Vito said loudly.

The door opened and a person walked in. It was not Jimmie Ponza.

CHAPTER 41
RIVERVIEW

It had been three weeks since I had spoken to Uncle Sal about my decision to return to Riverview for a reunion with the family. There were also significant life-altering decisions to be made that I was pondering and working through with Lou. At my suggestion, Lou had moved back in with her parents in Washington, D.C. right after our adventure in Northern California. She would continue to live with them until we felt it was safe for her to return to her apartment in the city.

Lou and I spoke on the phone every day, planning our future together, and we had finally decided where we would make our home. Since neither one of us wanted a bi-coastal relationship, we had decided that I would leave California and find a job somewhere in the D.C. metro area. Initially, I would move in with Lou at her apartment until we could find something larger and more permanent in the area. Her work at the vineyard and winery on Rattlesnake Ridge was seasonal, so she would continue to commute there on an as-needed basis. During the busy times of the year, especially during harvest, she would stay at her apartment in Romney near the winery. And since the winery was just a couple of hours away from the D.C. metro area, we would try and find a home in the region that would be convenient for her, and for me whenever I landed a job. To that end, I had contacted editors at both the Washington Post and the Washington Star, and my prospects of landing a job at one of those newspapers seemed good.

Over the last few weeks, I also stayed in regular contact with my uncle regarding the issues with the mob guys in Pittsburgh. Was Vito honoring his pledge to leave us alone now that he had been given the racy photos? Uncle Sal told me that everything seemed normal to him, and that he had asked Jimmie to keep his ear to the ground for any signs that trouble might be coming. Jimmie had not heard or detected anything alarming. He told my uncle, "Everything seems to be working out so far."

I decided that now would be a good time to make a quick visit to Riverview and finally reconnect with my family. This would give me the opportunity to thank them all personally for the unconditional love and support they had given me over the years. First, providing me with support and understanding, as well as a job, during those dark days when I came home from the war. Later, when I was on the run from the Black Hand guys, for hiding me and eventually coming up with a plan that saved my life.

I was also excited to share some good news with them about my future. I would tell them that Lou and I planned to get married. After all that had transpired over the past seven years, I was beyond excited to be going home. I never thought the day would come when I would ever be able to see my family again. Unfortunately, we couldn't chance staying in Riverview for more than a day or two on this visit. I didn't want to push my luck now, but I hoped that over time we would be able to feel comfortable enough to visit regularly.

I had taken a red eye flight out of Oakland, and I arrived at Washington National Airport a little before 6 in the morning. I slept fitfully on the flight. During my few moments of slumber, I experienced troublesome dreams, reliving the violent events of the past month that had culminated with the showdown at Fruit Lake Vineyard and Winery. Then I spent my waking moments wondering if I might be exposing myself and my family to harm by visiting them now. It was a calculated risk I was taking, and I prayed that everything would be fine.

Lou greeted me at the airport. She smiled at me and we embraced. Just seeing her lifted my spirits. We ate breakfast at the airport and discussed the day ahead. Then we boarded a mid-morning Capitol Airlines DC-3 for the short hop down to Jeweltown. It was fall in West Virginia, and the scene out the cabin window was awe-inspiring. It had been years since I had seen the mighty Alleghenies. And now that it was fall, those green mountains were gloriously ablaze with brilliant brushstrokes of red, yellow and orange.

I am as excited now as I ever remember being. The prospect of finally being reunited with Mom, Dad and my family seemed like a dream come true. I'm also looking forward to having them meet Lou who will soon take my REAL name and join our family. I looked over at her sitting next to me, and I gently squeezed her hand. She smiled and then winked at me with one of her mesmerizing green eyes as the plane gently landed at Jeweltown Regional Airport.

As we walked down the gangway stairs from the plane, I looked toward the fence where a crowd of people were lined up waiting to greet us. There seemed to be a large number of people waving their hands toward us, and I could see that the majority of the greeters were my Costanza relatives. I stopped on the stairs for a few seconds trying to compose myself. Lou nudged me and we continued down onto the tarmac. I was trying to hold back tears as I began walking quickly toward my family. I went first to Grandma Luisa, and I hugged her for a long while. Then I moved to my parents, Uncle Sal, my favorite Aunt Lia and everyone else. And to each of them, I also proudly introduced Lou. She had only very briefly met my uncles Sal, Dante and Giorgio on the day she was released by her kidnappers seven years ago. I was overwhelmed with emotion as I looked into the faces of the people who meant so much to me.

When we got to the family enclave along Williams Avenue in Riverview, I smiled nostalgically as I looked at my grandparents' home that sat right across the street from the Chestnut Bakery. We would be having an Italian feast in the large side yard of the house, and I could see many in the family already gathered there. They were sitting at picnic tables and nibbling on a mouth-watering assortment of antipasti. I glanced over at the bakery where I had spent so many fun-filled hours working with my uncles Giorgio and Dante, and where I met the cast of motley neighbors who daily visited the bakery to buy bread, pepperoni rolls, hoagie buns or to just to shoot the shit with my crazy uncles. Dante and Giorgio were experts in just about everything, and always willing to spin a yarn or express an opinion. I smiled thinking about the many strange conversations I've had with these guys that usually left me either scratching my head or doubled over in laughter.

I noticed several friends of the family gathered in the yard too. I was happy to see that so many of them had decided to join in welcoming me back. I was especially glad to see Jimmie Ponza. He was the first person I walked toward when I got to the picnic. Jimmie was quietly speaking with Uncle Sal.

"Hey Jimmie, it's great to see you. Thank you so much for all you've done to make this day possible." Jimmie then opened his arms to me, and we hugged as I wiped more tears from my eyes.

"Augie, I'm so happy to see you again. Alive and well! I was waiting till you got here. I need to tell you and your uncle something important." He looked over at Uncle Sal.

My uncle motioned for Jimmie and me to follow him. He led us around the side of my grandparents' home to a cellar door. My uncle unlocked the door and moved into the darkened room. He reached to his left and flipped a switch that illuminated the basement with flickering fluorescent light. Then he walked for another ten feet and, with effort, pulled open a heavy wooden door. We followed my uncle onto the earthen floor inside Grandpa's ancient wine cellar. I watched Uncle Sal reach up and pull the string attached to a single bulb that dimly lit the room. I had been in this cellar many times, and the familiar smell – a combination of wine, earth, wood and vinegar – brought me back to a time decades ago when I was called upon to come down here and fetch the wine for dinner. It was always a quick trip for me, though, because the cellar always seemed dark, mysterious and spooky.

Uncle Sal then turned and looked at the septuagenarian owner of the Ruff Avenue Poolroom. "Okay Jimmy. What's up? You seemed pretty anxious to tell me something. But you asked me to wait until Augie got here." There was a nervous lilt to his words. "It's not bad news I hope."

Jimmie looked at me, and then my uncle. "Sal, when you gave me those pictures a few weeks back, you told me to take them to Vito. Up at The Twin Coaches. Well, I didn't do that."

"What do you mean, Jimmie? What did you do? And why didn't you take 'em up there?"

"Yeah. I was going to. But I did something else. I took a chance. It was just a gut feeling I had. Sal, you and Augie heard me talk before about my mob contact, Frankie Silver. He's always treated me fair. Anyway, instead of taking those pictures up and giving them directly to Vito, I gave them to Frankie and..."

"Jimmy, are you crazy?" Uncle Sal was apoplectic. "I'm surprised those guys from up north haven't already been down here shooting up the place..."

"Sal. Listen to me. I wasn't going to give him the pictures at all. I just wanted to give Frankie the whole story about how this situation between your family and Black Hand went sideways. Remember, I go back a long way with Frankie. He used to hang out at the Ruff when he was young. I must have bailed him out of jail ten times over the years. So, I told him how this all began when one of their guys was about to kill Giorgio, and Augie hit the guy with a wooden bread paddle. To keep him from killing Giorgio. And how, when their guy died a week later, Carmine sent a crew down here to find Augie and make him pay with his life. I told Frankie that Augie went on the run, and how the mob guys grabbed two of Augie's friends. That they tortured and killed them both because they wouldn't say where Augie was hiding. I told Frankie about how the mob kidnapped and brutalized Augie's girlfriend. And then I told him how Vito used the trouble with the Costanza's as an excuse to get approval from the mob to assassinate the old boss, Carmine."

All of a sudden, Jimmie stopped his story. He didn't say anything for a moment, and then he looked at Sal and me.

"You know, I had gone this far, and I wasn't sure I had said anything to really help our cause. So, I decided to take a chance. I gave Frankie the pictures of Vito and his buddy all dolled up and dancing with each other. I told him the truth too. Well, mostly the truth. I said that the family used those pictures to keep Vito from telling the mob how the family was going to fake Augie's death. To save him. I told Frankie the pictures were like an insurance policy. And that was the only way the family had to stop the violence between La Famiglia and them. And as long as Vito and his buddy went along with the plan, the pictures would never be shown to anyone. But Sal, I didn't tell Frankie anything about where or how you got those pictures of Vito and the other guy doing weird stuff." Jimmie stopped talking and then he used a handkerchief to wipe sweat from his forehead.

"What did he say, Jimmie? What was Frankie's reaction after you told him all this?"

"He just told me he would be in touch. That's it, Sal. He didn't say anything more. I was terrified that I had made a terrible mistake. After all, Frankie is just a collector for the mob, and I didn't know how much influence he had with the bosses in Pittsburgh. Anyway, that was more than three weeks ago. So yesterday, when I found out Augie was coming home today, I called Frankie. I asked him if he had showed anyone in the crew up there the pictures that I gave him. He simply said "yes." Then I asked him what his guys were going to do with the information and the pictures. If it was bad news, I was going to warn you to keep Augie from coming here today."

"Jimmie, so what did he tell you? Are we in more trouble?" Uncle Sal asked.

Jimmie suddenly walked over to my uncle and hugged him. He was trying to control his emotions, but his voice was breaking. "No Sal. Nothing bad is gonna happen. In fact, Frankie told me to tell you that it's over. Augie can come home for good, and the family doesn't have to worry anymore."

I couldn't believe what I was hearing. That this long nightmare is truly over. I walked over to the two men who had sacrificed and done so much for me, and I put my arms around them both. Then I wept.

Epilogue

Our joyous celebration that day two months ago in Riverview lasted well into the night. It was a truly momentous occasion for both Lou and me. We were finally free from hiding, and the constant fear of being captured and murdered by the mob. Most importantly, we would be able to plan a future together. We would soon be married, and we shared the happy news that day with the whole family. I'm still not sure why things turned out the way they had with La Famiglia Vagabonda, but I am ecstatic and relieved. However, I've had a lingering fear that Vito The Scar might still be a problem for us in the future. I hoped I was just being paranoid.

A few weeks after the homecoming celebration, Uncle Sal called me at Lou's apartment in Washington to ask if we had decided on a date for the wedding. I told him that Lou and I had chosen the first Saturday in April. We had selected that date because it was a time before things got busy at Rattlesnake Vineyard.

Just as we were about to conclude our conversation, I asked Uncle Sal if Jimmie Ponza had heard anything more from Frankie Silver about the status of Vito. I told my uncle about the concern I had that the Scar might still be a problem for us.

"Hey Uncle, aren't you worried about Vito, too?"

"Yes. I had that same fear, too. So much so, that I went to see Jimmie at the Ruff Avenue Poolroom a couple of weeks after you and Lou were here. I told him of my concern about Vito, and I asked him if he had heard anything more from Frankie. Jimmy said the next time Frankie came down to the poolroom on business, he asked the guy if we needed to be worried about Vito? Frankie simply told Jimmie, 'Everything is fine.' And then he added, 'The Scar will never be a bother to anyone – ever again.'"

My uncle stopped talking, and I heard a muffled sound on the phone like he was clearing his throat, or maybe struggling to compose himself.

Then Uncle Sal said, "You know Augie, after Jimmie told me that, he just smiled and looked up. Then Jimmie said, 'We're finally even, Salvatore.'"

Thank you so much for reading *Augie's Wine*.

"Augie's War is a brilliant and
moving story that juxtaposes
Augie's memories of his home life
with his service in Vietnam. Brown
deftly paints his characters and the
settings they find themselves in so
seamlessly that I felt both
rocked and comforted. Augie's war
is most highly recommended."
– Jack Mangus,
Readers' Favorite Book Reviews

"*Augie's World*... details the ex-ser-
viceman's experiences when he
returns home from Vietnam physically unscathed, but emotionally
and psychologically traumatized.
Then something happens that pres-
ents a new and perilous problem
for he and his family. The mafia has
been demanding protection money
from his two uncles who run the
(family) bakery. How Augie's family
goes about outwitting the bad guys,
would make a great Hollywood
movie and provides an ingenious ...
end to an entertaining novel."
– WV Book Team,
Charleston Gazette-Mail

ABOUT THE AUTHOR

John Brown served a year in Vietnam (1969-70) as an Army enlisted man in the Americal Division. After he retired from a career in public relations, he began writing *Augie's War*. John Brown has also written about wine and food as a columnist for The Charleston (WV) Gazette-Mail since the early 1980's. He is a graduate of West Virginia University (BS and MA), and he lives in Charleston, West Virginia, and in Canaan Valley near Davis, WV.